THE MIDNIGHT HOUR

THE
MIDNIGHT HOUR

A Brighton Mystery

Elly Griffiths

MARINER BOOKS
An Imprint of HarperCollinsPublishers
Boston   New York

marinerbooks.com

First published in Great Britain in 2021 by Quercus

Library of Congress Cataloging-in-Publication Data has been applied for.
ISBN 978-0-358-41863-4 (paperback)
ISBN 978-0-358-41919-8 (e-book)
ISBN 978-0-358-57844-4 (audiobook)
ISBN 978-0-358-42416-1 (hardcover)

Printed in the United States of America

1 2021
4500841020

For Corinne

PROLOGUE

Sunday, 19 September 1965

Sunday afternoon, thought Verity Malone, was a blameless time of day. It was a time for snoozing after roast beef, for going on long walks with a dog, for making duty visits to grandparents. Well, Verity was a grandmother herself now, but she was resolutely unvisited. She didn't have a dog and it was years since she'd cooked anything more adventurous than cheese on toast. There was church, of course. St Margaret's was next door and, on Sunday mornings, the bells were both deafening and enticing. Once or twice Verity had got as far as putting her hat on, preparatory to attending a service, but, somehow, she never got further than the front porch. People would stare and, although being stared at used to be part of her job, nowadays she found it rather tiring.

When Verity was a young dancer in variety, Sunday was changeover day. All over the country, the performers would be on the move, from one weekly show to the next: Glasgow to Manchester, Eastbourne to Liverpool, Scarborough to Yarmouth. Hours on provincial trains enlivened only when, at key junctions like Crewe, you saw other pros, huddled on the platform with their trunks containing costumes, props and ventriloquists' dummies. You would chat about last week's run ('The audiences sat on their hands, my dear'), exchange horror stories about bed bugs and lecherous ASMs, then your train would arrive and you wouldn't see your colleagues again for years, unless you were on the bill with them. Then, when you reached your destination, you would haul your luggage through the grey Sunday streets until you found your digs. The landlady would meet you at the door, cigarette on her lower lip, and spell out the house rules. 'Lights out at midnight, no smoking, drinking or followers.' Happy days.

Marriage to Bert Billington had put an end to all that. He was one of the biggest impresarios in the business and was, in Verity's mother's words, 'a good provider'. Detached house in Lytham St Anne's, then Surrey, and now this house in Rottingdean, part of what had once been a hotel beloved of Hollywood stars. It was mock Tudor, all twisted beams and diamond panes. Very picturesque but sometimes, when Verity looked out over the graveyard at St Margaret's, she felt that Tudor Close itself was like a giant tombstone, rising out of the ground, covered in lichen and frost, nothing more than a remembrance of past glories.

A ring on the doorbell. A voice from the present. Verity adjusted her wig before going to answer it. 'Always think of your public,' that's what Madame Fou Fou, the celebrated pantomime dame, used to say. Verity tightened the belt of her kimono and went to the door.

'Hallo, Mum.'

Wonder of wonders, it was one of her sons. At first, with the low afternoon sun in her eyes, she couldn't quite tell which one. Then she saw a motorbike helmet, sinister and black. Aaron then.

'I said I might pop over,' he said, pushing past her. Quite rudely, in Verity's opinion. 'To show Dad the new bike.'

'He's in the sitting room,' said Verity. And she waited until Aaron's casual 'Dad?' turned into something sharper and more urgent.

ONE

Monday, 27 September 1965

'Bert Billington, the theatrical impresario. Poisoned in his own armchair.'

The DI clearly expected this to make an impression, so WDC Meg Connolly arranged her face into lines of wonderment.

'Bert Billington! Amazing.'

DI Willis sighed. 'You've no idea who he is, have you?'

'No,' said Meg. 'Sorry.' She didn't remind her boss that she was born in 1945 and so didn't share his happy memories of the war years and whenever it was that this Bert Billington was famous. What was an impresario anyway?

'He owned theatres,' said DI Willis, in a patronising voice that made Meg think that he wasn't sure either. 'And he produced shows. He was married to Verity Malone.' This name was definitely said as if it should mean something. And it did stir a faint memory in Meg's brain. Something to do with feathers and shiny satin.

'The singer?'

'Yes. The one and only Miss Malone.' The DI sounded like he was quoting now. 'She started out as a dancer but she was really famous as a singer in the 1920s. My mum and dad went to see her once. At the Croydon Empire.'

'I think my dad had a picture of her.' The memory was coming into focus: brilliant smile, costume that was little more than a corset, plus feather boa. 'My mum used to say it was indecent.' Strangely, though the picture had been black and white, Meg's memory of it was in technicolour, yellow hair and red lips, the boa a brilliant, clashing pink.

'Well, we're going to see her now,' said the DI. 'They live in Tudor Close in Rottingdean. Get your stuff together.'

Meg jumped up with alacrity. What 'stuff' did the DI think she needed? Women police officers were meant to carry handbags but Meg never bothered. She was in uniform and she stuffed her purse into her jacket pocket. It was a rare treat to get out of the station on a job that wasn't traffic duty or pounding the beat. From across the room, her colleague, DC Danny Black, pulled a gorilla face at her.

'I thought it would be good,' said the DI ponderously, as they drove along the coast road towards Rottingdean, 'to have a woman officer with me, seeing as how Verity Malone is . . .'

'A woman?' suggested Meg.

'Sensitive,' said DI Willis, frowning slightly. Behind his head the late September sun shone on a blue sea. Meg couldn't rid herself of a 'day out' feeling, which she knew was inappropriate in the circumstances.

'You said Bert Billington was poisoned,' she said, adding 'Sir' because she often forgot. 'How do we know?'

'Post-mortem,' said DI Willis. 'At first the son, who found the body, thought it was a heart attack. Bert suffered from high blood pressure and angina. But Solomon Carter confirmed today that Bert Billington had quantities of rat poison in his blood.'

Solomon Carter was the pathologist, a sinister individual given to bow ties and suggestive comments.

'Rat poison,' said Meg. 'He can hardly have taken it by accident then. Sir.'

'No,' said the DI. After a pause, he said, 'They had the funeral yesterday, as soon as the body was released. The son, Aaron, was on the phone to me today.'

'Saying that his mother did it?'

'He said his mother was becoming confused and may have done it by accident. But he also said that she was resentful towards her husband.'

'Resentful? That's an odd word to choose.' Or was it? wondered Meg. Her own mother's attitude – towards everything really – was one of barely concealed anger. Anger at her parents for leaving Ireland at the turn of the century, anger at her husband for giving her seven children and a council house in Whitehawk, anger at the children for keeping her trapped in the house, taking in ironing for her richer neighbours. Despite this, she wasn't a bad mum really.

'Is this Aaron an only child?' she asked. She had once longed for this status. Fourth child of seven was definitely the short straw. Neither of her parents ever got her name right first time. 'Pass me the milk, Marie, Aisling, Collette . . .' They'd once had a dog called Mollie and even she got a mention before Meg.

'No, there are three sons,' said the DI, stopping at the Rottingdean traffic lights. 'The eldest, David, runs the family business and lives in London. He has two children. The middle son, Seth, is an actor, I believe.' He said the word with a slight distaste, despite being married to a former actress (one who once wore even fewer clothes than the young Verity).

'Seth Billington?' The words came out as a sort of controlled shriek. 'Seth Billington's her son?'

'Have you heard of him then?'

'Heard of him? I've seen all his films. *Black Hawk. The Highwayman. Darkest Before Dawn . . .*'

Meg lapsed into silence. They were driving along the High Street and she remembered a previous case when she had discovered that beneath these neat terraced cottages lay a network of tunnels, once used by smugglers. The whole community had been involved in the trade, even the vicar. It certainly gave another perspective on the picture-perfect village. They passed the pond and the solid mansion once owned by Rudyard Kipling, then they turned left by the church, where once the Reverend Hooker had preached about honesty whilst storing stolen brandy in his cellar.

The DI drew up in front of a timbered building that formed three sides of a square surrounding a smooth, green lawn. The beams were so twisted and gnarled that they looked almost soft. Meg thought of the gingerbread house in *Hansel and Gretel*. She felt as if she could break off one of the door frames and eat it. The windows were the old-fashioned diamond-paned sort and they glittered in the autumn sunshine.

'Do the Billingtons own this whole house?' said Meg.

'No, it's been divided into several houses. Quite some place, isn't it? Used to be a hotel.'

'Is it really Tudor?' Meg was vague about history but Tudor meant Henry VIII, didn't it? A ribald song about his six wives came into her head.

'No,' said the DI with scorn. 'It's all pretend. Nineteen twenties or thereabouts.'

This meant he didn't know either.

There was no sound at all as they walked across the lawn, only the faint buzzing of bees in the hollyhocks. The High Street could have been miles away and Brighton another country. But, even so, there was something about Tudor Close that Meg didn't quite like. The house seemed to close in around them, so many windows, so many doors, yet no sign of life. It's all pretend, the DI had said, and suddenly Meg thought of a film set. She had the strange thought that if she knocked on one of the twisted beams the whole building would collapse like a pack of cards.

The DI didn't seem to notice anything. Meg couldn't

imagine him ever having fanciful thoughts of that kind. He marched up to one of the doors and knocked. After a long wait, it opened and Meg was face to face with the one and only Miss Malone. The former variety star was tall and slim, wearing what looked like a Japanese robe in red and gold. Her hair, still improbably golden, was piled on top of her head, and she wore an array of jewellery, including chandelier earrings and, Meg noticed, rings on every finger.

'Good,' said the apparition. 'You've brought a woman officer. I said I wouldn't talk to you without a woman present.'

So *that* was why Meg had been invited.

'I'm DI Bob Willis and this is WDC Meg Connolly.'

'Glad to meet you, Bob and Meg. Come in.'

Meg could tell by the look of the DI's back how he felt about the use of his first name.

Verity led them into a long, low sitting room, made longer and lower by the presence of ceiling beams and mullioned windows. She offered them tea and coffee which were declined by the DI.

'Meg?' Verity smiled at her. She was old, in Meg's eyes – seventy at least – but the smile was as brilliant as in Dad's indecent photo. 'Would you like a cup of tea?'

Meg longed to say yes, just to see what the DI would do, but decided it wasn't worth it.

'No thank you, Miss Malone.'

'Call me Verity. Miss Malone is long gone and I never answer to Mrs Billington.'

Interesting, thought Meg.

Verity sat on one of the velvet sofas and waited. The DI cleared his throat.

'Mrs Billington. Ah . . . Miss . . . er . . . Verity. We have recently received the post-mortem report on your late husband and I'm sorry to tell you that—'

'He was poisoned. Yes, Aaron informed me. He suspects me. Did he tell you that?'

The DI's ears went red. 'We are investigating the case,' was all that he could manage.

'Perhaps you could tell us what happened on the day your husband died,' said Meg. 'To help us build up a picture of events.'

'I can see why you brought this one along,' said Verity. 'Beauty and brains. Nice and tall too. I can't bear short people.'

It was Meg's turn to blush. At nearly six foot, it was her experience that everyone preferred short people, short girls in particular. And no one had ever – ever! – called her beautiful before.

'It was Sunday,' said Verity. 'We'd had lunch. Just an egg on toast. Neither of us are big eaters these days. Bert can't taste anything much, what with his condition.'

'What condition was that?' asked the DI.

'Bert had a stroke a couple of years back,' said Verity. 'Just a small one,' she added. Although Meg betted that it hadn't seemed small to the sufferer. The DI nodded at Verity to continue.

'We had our lunch in the conservatory and, afterwards, Bert came in here to watch television. I can't bear TV. It's killed entertainment, in my opinion. So I sat in the kitchen listening to the wireless. Then Aaron came round to show us his new motorbike. He went into the sitting room and found Bert sitting in his chair. Dead.'

She gave the word a theatrical flourish but there was no other sign of emotion.

'And did Mr Billington eat anything else besides the egg on toast?' asked Meg.

'Yes, he had a big snifter of rat poison. Don't get excited, Bob. Aaron told me what had killed him.'

'I'm afraid we will need to search your kitchen,' said DI Willis stiffly. 'Are you the only person who prepares food in there?'

'No, we have a daily, Mrs Saunders. She usually makes us breakfast and leaves something cold for lunch. She doesn't come in on a Sunday though.'

'Can you think of anyone who might have had a grudge against your husband?' asked DI Willis.

'Only everyone who ever knew him,' said Verity. Then she laughed. 'I'm afraid you'll have a long list of suspects, Bob. But don't worry. I've got you some help. I've engaged a private detective. A lovely young woman she is too.'

Meg and the DI exchanged glances. There was only one person this could be.

The one and only Emma Holmes.

TWO

'It's a bit embarrassing,' said Edgar Stephens. 'You being the superintendent's wife and everything.'

'You knew this might happen,' said Emma, annoyed with herself for feeling slightly guilty. 'We discussed it.'

Yet, when she set up the Holmes and Collins Detective Agency with her friend, Samantha Collins – known as Sam – she hadn't really expected them to get involved in a big case so soon. So far, their only work had been one missing wife and two missing dogs. The wife had moved to Seaford with her lover and one dog was found locked in a neighbour's garage. The other dog, a St Bernard called Tiny, was still missing though.

'It looks like a fairly open-and-shut case,' said Edgar. 'Bob's pretty sure the wife did it. He and Meg went to see her this afternoon.'

'I saw her in the morning,' said Emma. 'And I think she's innocent.'

Edgar had taken the car so Emma had caught the bus

to Rottingdean that morning. The girls were at school but she had to take Jonathan with her because Mavis, her babysitter, was in hospital having her varicose veins done. As Emma manoeuvred the pushchair off the bus – watched interestedly by the conductor, who did not offer to help – she had reflected that, in books, you rarely read about a private investigator who was hampered by a baby and its accoutrements. Alcoholism, yes. Vindictive ex-wife, yes. Murdered girlfriend, yes. Childcare problems, no. But fictional detectives, private and otherwise, were almost always men. Their children, if they had them, were strictly background material.

Verity Malone had not seemed to mind the presence of Jonathan. She'd even found a wooden box for him to play with as he sat on a rug on the parquet floor of her sitting room. Emma would have quite liked to play with the box herself, a gorgeous ebony object with ivory inlay and secret drawers.

'I used to keep it for my make-up,' said Verity. 'It was a present from an admirer. A stage-door Johnny, as we used to call them.' She grinned at Emma and the effect, despite the wig and the false eyelashes, was dazzling enough to make Emma blink.

'I'm sorry about your husband,' said Emma, getting out her notebook.

'Do you know,' said Verity, settling back in her chair, 'I don't know that I am. I'm sorry that he suffered, of course.

But I'm not really sorry that he's dead. He hated getting old, you know. And that wasn't a situation that was going to change.'

'How old was Mr Billington?' asked Emma. She wondered if she should warn Verity not to make comments like this in front of Bob, who would have been reaching for a set of handcuffs.

'Nearly ninety,' said Verity. 'I'm fifteen years younger.' She patted her startling hair.

'You look younger than that,' said Emma. This was obviously the expected response and it was true in a way. Verity didn't look seventy-five. But she didn't look fifty either. She was oddly ageless in her red robe and gold earrings, like a painting come to life.

'Tell me about Bert,' said Emma. 'He died on Sunday, is that right?'

'Yes,' said Verity. She gave Emma a very straight look, pale eyes framed by thick black eyelashes. 'And my son thinks I did it. That's why I called you in.'

'Your son thinks you did it? Why?'

'He thinks I'm going doolally,' said Verity, with another of her direct looks. 'But I'm not.'

'Why does he think that?' said Emma. 'And which son was it? You've got three, haven't you?' She liked to do her research and in this case it wasn't difficult because Bert Billington was in *Who's Who*.

'Well done,' said Verity. 'I see I've done the right thing

in engaging you. It's my youngest. Aaron. He was always close to his father. Poor soul.'

It wasn't at all clear who was the poor soul in this sentence.

'Does Aaron really think that you killed Bert?'

'I'm not sure if he really believes it but he believes it enough to ring the police. He spoke to a DI Willis.'

'Bob Willis,' said Emma. 'I know him. Did Aaron tell you he'd rung the police?'

'Yes,' said Verity. 'He said he just wanted to know what the police were doing about it, but I know he'll have dropped in some poison about how senile I am and how much I hated Bert.'

'Dropped in poison' seemed a singularly inappropriate phrase in the circumstances.

'Did you hate Bert?' asked Emma, keeping her voice casual. At her feet Jonathan was drumming a lively tattoo on the box lid.

'Sometimes,' said Verity. 'Don't all wives hate their husbands sometimes?'

Emma thought about her husband. She didn't hate Edgar. He was the love of her life; she'd known that the first time she saw him. But she couldn't deny that sometimes, especially when he was being Superintendent Stephens, she found him very annoying.

'Your husband is the police chief, isn't he?' said Verity. 'I read about you in the paper. That's where I got the name of your agency.'

It had been a good article, mostly because it was written by Sam, Emma's fellow private eye and partner in the company. Sam was now a freelance reporter, but she still did a lot of work for the local paper, the *Evening Argus*.

'He's the superintendent,' said Emma. 'But the agency is completely independent of the police. I'm my own boss.'

'That's why I employed you,' said Verity.

'If two people eat a meal,' said Edgar, 'and only one is poisoned, you've got to suspect the other person.'

Edgar and Emma were sitting amongst the remains of their own evening meal. The children had had their supper earlier and were all now in bed. Emma waited to eat with Edgar, feeling, as she put their food in the oven to keep warm, like a dutiful housewife. Well, that's what she is, she supposes. Despite the fact that she now has a job and an office and a set of business cards saying 'Holmes and Collins, Private Detectives', she's still the one who cooks and cleans and looks after the children. She knows that, for some of Edgar's friends and former colleagues, her job is just a joke. A rich woman's whim, like Marie-Antoinette having a cottage where she could pretend to be a shepherdess. Well, she'd show them. Emma had been DS Holmes once, the first woman detective in Sussex. Then she married the boss and, by extension, his house. But detection was still her first love.

'Did anyone analyse Bert's last meal?' she asked.

'No,' said Edgar, sounding slightly defensive. 'By the time we realised that there was anything suspicious about the death, there were no traces of the food in the house.'

'There you are then,' said Emma. 'It might not have been the egg on toast, after all. And, if Verity wanted to kill off her husband, there were plenty of easier ways than poison. Tampering with his medication, for one. He was on all sorts of pills. I've made a list.'

Edgar smiled. 'The famous DS Holmes' lists.' Emma didn't smile back.

'The obvious solution is usually the right one,' said Edgar, putting the kettle on for coffee. They were in the basement kitchen of their Brighton home. Although it was still September, there was a cosy autumnal feel to the evening, lamps lit and curtains drawn. Emma flicked through the pages of her notebook.

'There are three sons. David, Seth and Aaron. Seth is Seth Billington.'

She waited until the penny dropped, as slowly as it did in the slot machines on the pier, rattling to and fro through its metal maze. Unlike his wife, Edgar did not read film magazines.

'The actor?' The penny had reached its target and the light went on.

'Yes. And guess who's making a film with him?'

This time Edgar was quicker. 'Max?'

'That's right. He and Seth are filming *The Prince of Darkness* in Whitby. Seth plays Dracula and Max is his father.'

'Good grief. I never thought I'd see Max play Dracula's dad.'

Max Mephisto was Edgar's old friend from their days in a shadowy army unit called the Magic Men, whose job was to use stage magic in espionage to create illusion and mislead the enemy. In those days Max was a famous magician. Now he was better known as an actor and, in his spare time, Lord Massingham.

'I wonder what Lydia thinks about that.' Max's wife, the Hollywood actress Lydia Lamont, was not known to love spending time in England. Emma wondered if she was with Max in Whitby.

'Are you going to interview Seth?' asked Edgar.

'Yes,' said Emma, meeting his eyes with a hint of challenge. 'I'm going to interview all the sons.'

'Even if Bob arrests Verity?'

'Especially then. Bob's not always right. I know. I used to work with him.'

Bob Willis wasn't a bad officer, Emma remembered, but he was sadly lacking in imagination. Perhaps WDC Connolly would provide the spark. Emma liked Meg but she couldn't help feeling slightly jealous of her sometimes. She, Emma, used to be the intrepid woman officer who solved the case before the men. But Meg was twenty and unmarried; that meant she was allowed to have a police career.

'Do you really think Verity Malone is innocent?' said Edgar, putting the coffee cups on the table. 'Rat poison was found in the kitchen.'

'Exactly. Rat poison. That's not how you kill a husband.'

'Glad you've made a study of it.'

Emma ignored this. 'If you kill someone that way, you're making a point.' She pushed a newspaper clipping across the table. Emma's partner Sam, who as a journalist knew her way around newspaper archives, had found it. It was an advertisement for a pantomime. The Adelphi, Liverpool, 1949. *Dick Whittington* starring Denton McGrew and Annette Anthony. And Bert Billington as King Rat.

THREE

Max watched sourly as the sun set behind Whitby Abbey, the shadows turning the arches into portals to another world. Did Whitby have to go around looking so atmospheric all the time? It was like being trapped in a French art film. The ruins, the cliffs, the houses huddled by the shore, the fishing boats in the bay. The whole town felt like a backdrop. And now, as the cameramen exclaimed about the light, Seth came striding through one of the archways, his black cloak billowing out behind him. The Prince of Darkness, brought to you by Savile Row tailoring.

'Poor lambkin,' said Irene, the wardrobe mistress.

Max liked Irene. He remembered her from the old days on the variety circuit, where she'd been part of a double act with her husband, disconcertingly called the Dodds Boys. He thought she'd had a strong-woman act once, which was useful when hauling laundry baskets around. Irene and Max had gravitated together on the set because there was no one else old enough to remember the war, rationing, or the days of two shows nightly with a charity matinee on Wednesday. Also, Irene was seventy, which meant that even Lydia couldn't get jealous when Max talked to her.

Max turned in his chair, which had 'Max Mephisto' emblazoned on the back.

'Why poor?'

'Get on with you.' Irene aimed a mock slap at him. 'His dad's just died.'

'And a bigger bastard never lived.'

'Still his dad though.'

They watched as Seth did the take again, striding through the archway and pausing, chin lifted, to take in the view. He was actually a pretty good actor, thought Max. It wasn't Seth's fault that he was too good-looking to be taken seriously.

'Mr Mephisto.' One of the runners appeared in front of him. 'They're ready for you now.'

All Max had to do in this scene was to welcome Dracula Junior to Whitby, a sort of vampire family reunion. It was a frightfully silly film and Max knew that he, unlike Seth, wasn't a brilliant actor. He'd once been a brilliant magician and now had an extremely lucrative career playing versions of his stage self; anything involving a top hat and supernatural powers. Marriage to Lydia Lamont, who had recently won an Oscar for playing a woman who thought she was the Virgin Mary, hadn't exactly lowered his stock either.

Max stood on his mark, the sea behind him. A camera swooped in for a close-up and then dollied back to rest lovingly on Seth's face.

'Welcome home, my son,' said Max, putting a hand on Seth's shoulder.

'Cut,' shouted Wilbur Wallace, the director. 'Good work, everyone.'

Five minutes in total, thought Max, including the walk from his chair, and he was done for the day. In the twice-nightly years, he would work six days a week conjuring doves from women's evening bags and sawing his assistants in two. He should be enjoying this easy life – and he was fifty-five now, after all, too old for the slog of weekly rep – but he couldn't help feeling discontented and rather fraudulent. This was no job for a grown man.

'Another day in the salt mines,' said Seth with a grin. This was so much what Max was thinking that he was surprised. He'd always thought Seth a pleasant, though rather vacuous, presence on the set. It was a shock to hear him talking in this ironical, comradely way.

'This must be hard for you though,' said Max. Despite the less-than-taxing day, filming was expensive and their time in Whitby was limited. Bert Billington had died during a weekend break but Seth had been in London and was back in Yorkshire before he'd been told that his father had died.

'It's rough not seeing Ma,' said Seth, detaching his fangs. 'I'm hoping to go to Rottingdean at the weekend.'

Max stopped in his tracks. The sky was dark blue now and a flock of birds swirled above the ruined abbey, adding another layer of atmosphere.

'Rottingdean?'

'Yes, it's a little village outside Brighton. Do you know it?'

'Very well indeed.'

'Max,' said Seth. And his voice seemed different somehow, more urgent, shorn of any movie-star pretension. 'Can I talk to you? It's about Pa. His death, I mean. I know that you've helped the police before.'

'I wouldn't say helped, exactly,' said Max. He wondered why Seth was talking about the police in connection with his father's death.

'I'd just like your advice about something,' said Seth. 'Can you meet me in the hotel bar at seven?'

Advice, thought Max, was often another word for help. Nevertheless, he agreed to meet his co-star for an early evening drink.

'I take it I'm not invited,' said Lydia. She was in her negligee, applying make-up with great concentration, mouth slightly open. Max could see only her reflection, but he wasn't fooled by the casual tone.

'I think Seth wants to ask my advice about something. Possibly to do with his father's death.'

'Is he confusing you with Ruby? She's the detective, after all.'

Max's daughter, Ruby, was not a detective although she

did play the eponymous heroine in a highly successful TV series called *Iris Investigates*. Mentioning Ruby was never a good sign with Lydia.

'I'll just have half an hour alone with him,' said Max. 'Then I'll come back up to fetch you.' He knew there was no way that Lydia would come down to the restaurant on her own.

Lydia turned to face him. Sometimes her beauty, well known to him and to millions of others, could still strike him to the heart. This was one of those times: the curve of her neck, the gleam of her hair, the line of her eyelids.

'I don't mind if you want to talk to Seth,' she said. 'I'll ring home. I might be able to talk to Rocco and Elena before Nanny puts them to bed.'

Max knew that he was being punished. He liked to speak to his children every day, to make them laugh with his array of funny voices. But Lydia was obviously excluding him from this evening's performance.

'Give them my love,' he said lightly. He kissed Lydia on her perfumed head and made for the door.

Seth was already at the bar, halfway down what looked like a stiff whisky. Max asked for white wine. It was a little early in the evening for spirits and he didn't even have bereavement as an excuse. He'd once had the traumatic experience of asking for wine in a Yorkshire pub but the hotel barman took his order without blenching. A tolerable Chablis too.

They moved to a table by the window. The hotel was full

of film people so they were safe from autograph hunters but, even so, the few occupants of the bar looked at them curiously. Max and Seth were not known to be drinking companions.

'My brother Aaron rang me today,' said Seth, looking into his second whisky. 'Apparently they've done a . . . what do you call it . . . post-mortem on Pa. Turns out it wasn't a heart attack at all. He was poisoned.'

'Good God,' said Max.

'And what's more, Aaron thinks Ma did it. He even told the police that.'

'Really?' Max was imagining the scene at Brighton police station. Would the bumbling Bob Willis be in charge or would Edgar think it was time for the superintendent to intervene? He surprised himself by wishing that he was sitting with his old friend in a seedy Brighton pub discussing the case.

'Why would your brother say such a thing?' he asked.

'I don't know. He sees most of the old dears because he lives nearest. He runs a garage in Hove. He's a bit of a rough diamond.'

Rough diamond, thought Max, was a strange oxymoron of a phrase. It usually implied that the uncut jewel was of a lower social class than the speaker. But Aaron was Seth's brother. He thought he'd ask the question again.

'Why would your brother think your mother murdered your father?' It sounded very bald, put like that, almost biblical. Seth winced.

'Ma's been very odd recently. She's been reading all these books from America, saying that women shouldn't do housework. Now she just sits around smoking and talking about the revolution.'

Mrs Billington sounded rather fun, thought Max. He asked if Max's mother was on good terms with his father.

'They seemed to get on all right. Pa's a lot older than her and he needed a bit of looking after. Up till now, Ma's been happy to do it. With the help of Alma, the daily. But now he's been killed and Aaron thinks Ma did it, to get rid of him.'

'What do the police think?'

'That's why I wanted to talk to you. You know the super-intendent, Edgar Stephens, don't you?'

'We served together in the war.'

'Yes, I heard that somewhere. I wondered if you could have a word with him. I mean, there's no way on earth that Ma could have killed Pa.'

'If there's no proof, the police won't convict. They'll be fair. Superintendent Stephens will see to that.'

Seth was silent for a few seconds. His face, often described by critics as 'brooding', now looked almost anguished.

'The thing is, Ma ... she won't cooperate with the police. She says she'll only talk to women. She's even employed these ridiculous girl detectives.'

'Holmes and Collins. They're not ridiculous.'

Now the film star was positively gaping. 'How on earth do you know that?'

'Because I know Emma Holmes and Sam Collins. You won't find two cleverer women anywhere.'

It was Sam who had told him about the detective agency. They'd had a rather furtive meeting last year, after the two of them had got caught up in a kidnapping case. There had been an odd intimacy between them, Max remembered, although Sam wasn't at all the sort of woman to whom he was usually attracted. He hadn't mentioned the agency, or Sam, to Lydia.

'That's even worse, then. If they're clever, they'll find out . . .'

'Find out what?'

'My father wasn't . . . he wasn't always faithful to my mother.'

Max said nothing. Bert Billington was known to be the biggest lech in show business.

'A few years ago, this woman turned up. She claimed to have had his baby.'

'A few years ago? How old was your father when this happened?'

'Eighty-seven I think. The woman claimed the child had been conceived when he was in his late sixties. I don't know what happened to her. I think Ma paid her off. But what if this woman, or someone else with a grudge against Pa, turns up out of the woodwork?'

Was Seth worried about his reputation? wondered Max. He didn't think that having a philandering father would necessarily reflect badly on a film star. But Seth's next words showed that he had something rather darker in mind.

'What if one of these women decided to kill him?'

'It's a bit of a stretch,' said Max, 'from claiming paternity to killing someone.'

'I know,' said Seth. There was another pause, then, 'My dad could be a bit of a bastard.'

'Mine could too,' said Max.

'But I bet your mum made up for it.'

'I'm sure she would have but she died when I was six.'

'I'm sorry,' said Seth. 'But my mum did make up for my dad. She was always so . . . so much fun, you know. I can't bear to think of her going to prison.'

'She won't go to prison if she didn't do it.'

'Are you sure?' said Seth. 'What about Rillington Place? They got the wrong man there, didn't they? Hanged him too.'

'That's true.' Max remembered the case, which happened fifteen years ago. Timothy Evans, wrongly convicted for a murder committed by his landlord, serial killer John Christie. 'This is why I don't believe in the death penalty,' Edgar had said at the time. Well, they were talking about scrapping it now.

'Max.' Seth leant forward. 'Will you at least talk to your friend? Find out what the police are thinking. Tell him that Ma would never do anything like that. She's tough – she's had to be – but she's got a kind heart. She feeds stray cats and wouldn't even kill a spider.'

Lydia was kind to animals too, but Max wasn't sure that this always extended to humans.

'I can't promise anything,' he said. 'But I'll talk to Edgar.'

He'd been looking for an excuse anyway.

FOUR

'So, our main suspect is obviously Aaron,' said Emma.

Emma and Sam were sitting in their office above a jeweller's called Midas and Sons. It was in the Lanes, the maze of narrow streets in the centre of Brighton, full of antique shops and newly opened coffee bars where long-haired students spent all day dreaming over a cappuccino. Their office consisted of one room and a tiny windowless kitchen and was so close to the house on the other side of the road that they often waved at the occupants, two elderly men who owned the hairdresser's below. Holmes and Collins Detective Agency was only about two hundred yards from Bartholomew Square, where the police station squatted below the town hall. There were rumours that the police were soon to vacate the dark, damp rooms for a spacious new location in Hove but, given that the basement had been condemned in the 1930s and yet the station and the cells were still there, Edgar and his team weren't holding their breath. Emma often missed being in the force but, when she thought of the women's chang-ing room where mice ran over your feet, she was glad of the relative luxury of Midas and Sons. At least here, if they leaned out of the top window and craned their necks, they could see the sky.

'Aaron?' said Sam, her feet on the desk. 'Not Verity? She's the obvious suspect. I mean, she prepared his last meal. And didn't get sick herself. Plus, she knew his taste-buds had gone and he wouldn't taste the poison.'

'But she called us in,' said Emma. 'I know murderers are always engaging private detectives in crime novels but it's a bit unlikely in real life.'

'Misdirection?' suggested Sam. She'd been eating nuts and tried to lob a piece of shell into the bin. It missed and joined the others on the linoleum floor. Sam was a great partner, but her untidiness made even Emma – who could live quite happily in the mess generated by three children – feel twitchy. Emma and Sam had met when Emma was a police officer and Sam was a reporter on the local paper. They had become friends when, a few years later, they had run into each other at a village fete; Emma riding the swing boats with toddler Marianne and Sam moodily reporting on the 'guess the weight of the pig' competition. They stayed in contact through two more children and countless local news articles. When tragedy ended Sam's career at the *Evening Argus*, it was she who had suggested the agency, even offering to change her name to Watson.

'You sound like Max,' said Emma. She'd often suspected that Sam had a crush on Max.

Sure enough, Sam blushed before replying, 'It's a good way to appear innocent, hiring a private detective. Maybe she thinks that we'll point the finger at the wrong person.'

'I don't think so,' said Emma. She hated the thought that they might have been hired in the hope that they'd get it wrong. 'Verity read about us in the paper. She knows we're good.'

'Only because I wrote the article,' said Sam.

'I've made a list,' said Emma, ignoring this. She pushed it across the desk, an impressive piece of furniture, rescued from a solicitor's office who were about to throw it out, and pleasingly called a partner desk. It was vast, a wide expanse of mahogany with brass-handled drawers on either side. You could imagine Scrooge and Bob Cratchit sitting facing each other, arguing about the advisability of finishing early on Christmas Eve.

To interview
Verity Malone — Bert's wife
David Billington — eldest son. Runs Bert Billington Productions. Lives in Hampstead, London.
Sheena Billington — David's wife. Helps run the business.
Seth Billington — middle son, actor
Aaron Billington — youngest son. Runs a garage in Hove.

Alma Saunders – daily woman. Lives in Rottingdean.
Ted Grange – gardener. Lives in Woodingdean.
Pamela Curtis – used to be Bert's assistant. Lives in
Hove.

'David, Seth and Aaron,' said Emma. 'Biblical names. I wonder if either of the parents is religious.'

'Jewish?' said Sam. 'They sound Old Testament to me.'

Emma thought back to the house in Tudor Close. She couldn't recall any menorahs or crucifixes or any signs of religious affiliation at all.

'Bags I interview Seth,' said Sam.

'"Bags I",' repeated Emma. 'Are you still at school?' Sam attended a grammar school in Southend, Emma went to Roedean, the famous public school outside Brighton, although she spent a lot of time trying to hide the fact. But, despite the social gulf between these two establishments, they had a lot of vocabulary in common.

'Seth is making a film with Max,' said Sam. *The Prince of Darkness.* One of those Dracula things.'

'I can imagine Seth as Dracula,' said Emma. 'He's got a rather villainous face.'

'Gorgeous, you mean,' said Sam. 'I think they're filming up north. In Whitby.'

Emma was looking at the list. 'The police will start with the family. And they'll go door-to-door in Rottingdean. We should interview someone else. Get ahead of them.'

'It's not a competition,' said Sam. Although she knew it was, really.

'Pamela Curtis lives quite nearby,' said Emma. 'And Verity said that she hadn't given her name to the police. Let's walk into Hove and talk to her. I haven't got long.' Her parents were looking after Jonathan, but they were getting frail now and she couldn't leave him with them for too long.

'OK.' Sam took her feet off the desk. A true reporter, her preference was always for action.

Emma was right. Meg was interviewing the neighbours at Tudor Close. It was slow work. Although the main entrance to the building was rather grand, with a stained-glass shield above a pointed portico, around the sides the sloping roofs almost touched the ground and the low doorways were almost hidden behind ivy and twisted brickwork. Meg would knock and then wait until the resident, inevitably aged and well-spoken, emerged to tell her that they'd seen and heard nothing unusual on the fateful Sunday. They would then shut the trompe-l'œil door very firmly indeed.

It wasn't until Meg had almost finished her circuit that she struck gold. She found a door on the very edge of the west wing. It was actually fitted onto two sides of a right angle, like a window in an advent calendar. Meg knocked and, after a lot of pattering and scuffling, one side of the aperture opened and a large, lean dog appeared, attached to a small not-lean man. Instinctively, Meg bent her knees slightly.

'Good morning,' she said. 'I'm WDC Meg Connolly from the Brighton police. I'm calling about an incident that occurred just over a week ago, on Sunday, nineteenth of September.'

'Was that when Bert Billington was killed?' said the man. 'You'd better come in. Lola will never leave you alone otherwise.'

Lola, a grey, hound-like animal, was trying to get her paws on Meg's shoulders. Meg was very happy to sidestep the dog's embrace and follow the man into the house. For one thing he had said 'killed' and not 'died'.

The house was as twisty inside as outside. Meg followed Lola and her owner along a narrow corridor that took several turns before ending up in a sitting room dominated by a grand piano. There was only room for a small sofa where all three of them sat in a line.

'I'm Eric Prentice,' said the man, extending a hand over Lola's bony back. 'Eric "Piano Man" Prentice.'

Meg was definitely meant to recognise the name. She made an admiring noise.

'I had a comic piano-playing act,' said Eric. 'It's much harder than you think to play the piano badly. I was a serious musician before the war. Then I joined ENSA and started with the comedy stuff.'

Meg's father had told her about ENSA, the Entertainment National Service Association (or Every Night

Something Awful), an organisation formed to entertain the troops during the war. Her dad had seen several ENSA shows when stationed in Egypt. He sometimes said it was the most terrifying experience he'd had while on active service.

'Did you know Bert Billington from your . . . theatrical days?' asked Meg. She wasn't quite sure how to put it.

Eric Prentice gave a bark of laughter, accompanied by an actual bark from Lola.

'Everyone knew Bert. He had the circuit sewn up, especially after the war. But I knew him from before, when he was actually on the boards. He was quite a serious actor once, you know.'

'I didn't know.' Meg was also wondering how old Eric was. His hair was white and it was almost conceivable that he was Bert's contemporary. But he moved and sounded like a much younger man.

'I first met Bert when he was playing Laertes in *Hamlet*,' said Eric. 'That was in Leeds in 1910. I was twenty and had a job with the symphony orchestra. There were a whole group of us actors and musicians and we became quite friendly. Bert was a lot of fun in those days, always ready for anything. Then the war – the first war – came. I got called up and, afterwards, nothing seemed so much fun.'

'Was Bert in the First World War?' asked Meg.

'No,' said Eric, with another short laugh. 'He was too old by then, he must have been nearly forty. The war was when Bert made his money. He started buying up houses, great blocks, tenements, you know. He'd smarten them up a bit and then sell them for a profit. When everyone else was dying – all the lads in my first troop were dead by 1915 – Bert was getting rich. After the war, he started his theatrical agency and he took me on. I was very grateful.'

Meg wasn't quite sure what Eric sounded but it wasn't grateful.

'Bert had married Verity by then,' said Eric. 'He was always one for the ladies.'

'So you knew Bert and Verity well before you moved here?'

'I was here first,' said Eric. 'I'd stayed at Tudor Close when it was a hotel. It was a grand place once, you know. The loveliest hotel on the south coast, people called it. You could rent out a whole house and there was an annex with a swimming pool and billiards room. Bette Davis stayed here. And Cary Grant. Julie Andrews is meant to have visited as a young girl. I heard that it was the first place she sang publicly. I love Julie Andrews, don't you? Have you seen *Mary Poppins*?'

'Yes. I went with my sister last year. We loved it.' They had been blown away by the film, she remembered, as if on one of Mary's magical winds. They had sung 'Super-califragilisticexpialidocious' all the way home on the bus.

Eric was still talking about Rottingdean. 'You know that there were Canadian troops billeted here in the war? There was a village on the Downs, Balsdean, that they used for target practice. Bombed it to smithereens. You can still see the ruins.'

People were always telling Meg stories like this. She'd never seen Balsdean, she'd never even walked across the Downs. She always felt that the countryside belonged to people like Emma Holmes, not girls from Whitehawk.

'When did you move to Tudor Close?' she asked.

'In 1953, just after the hotel closed and they sold off the houses. Verity and Bert moved here about five years ago. Around 1960. You could have knocked me down with a feather when I saw Verity in the gardens one day. They're communal gardens. Very nicely kept. At first, the sun was in my eyes, and I thought I was seeing a vision. She didn't seem to have changed at all since 1949.'

Meg thought of the figure in the Chinese robe with the gold curls balanced on top of her head. The sun must have been very strong, she thought.

'It must have been good to see an old friend,' she said.

'It was good,' said Eric. 'But I don't know if we were friends exactly. Not after all these years. Verity never came here. She's not a fan of Lola – I think she's scared of dogs – but sometimes I go round to her place and we have coffee or a snifter together. Bert kept himself to himself.'

'Did you see or hear anything on Sunday the nineteenth?' said Meg, getting down to business.

'Ted, the gardener, came in the morning,' said Eric. 'We always have a nice chat. Then I took Lola for a walk. Just round the pond and up to the windmill. I saw Verity in the garden at midday. She was cutting some roses which, strictly speaking, isn't allowed. I waved at her but didn't speak. The next thing I knew, the ambulance was outside. I knew it was Bert. I mean, he was ninety and not in the best of health.'

'At the door you said, "when Bert was killed",' said Meg. 'Why did you say that?'

'I assumed that's why a policewoman was knocking at my door,' said Eric. 'Because there was something suspicious about his death.'

Meg still didn't think that this was the first thing that would spring to mind. At any rate, it hadn't sprung to the minds of any other Tudor Close residents.

'You must have had some other reason for saying that?' she said.

In answer, Eric got up and walked to the piano. He played a few dreamy chords before replying. 'Bert was a difficult man,' he said, hands resting on the keys. 'And a successful one. He had enemies. I wasn't surprised to learn that he'd been murdered, put it that way.'

'Can you think of anyone who could have killed him?' asked Meg.

Another arpeggio. 'There was a girl,' he said. 'A girl who died. I'd start there if I were you.'

Pamela Curtis lived on First Avenue, one of the wide boulevards leading up from the sea. It was a sought-after address but Emma always found these streets rather depressing, something about the uniformity of the buildings and their solid, uncompromising façades. We're not here for you, they seemed to say, we're here to present an impressive aspect. When Emma and Edgar were first married they had lived in Hove but their flat in Brunswick Square was very different, dark and slightly damp, full of awkward corners and uneven floorboards. Emma had loved it.

Pamela also lived in a flat, a semi basement that nevertheless seemed light and airy. This was partly because all the walls were painted white, punctuated by the occasional, rather startling, piece of modern art. It was a young person's apartment, thought Emma, but Pamela must have been in her sixties, at least.

'I painted them myself,' she said, when Sam admired a green woman with three breasts. 'I used to be an art student.'

'How did you come to work for Bert Billington?' asked Emma. She had expected someone with a background in the theatre but Pamela, solid and grey-haired, looked far too respectable.

'I answered an advert,' said Pamela. 'I had an interview at his office in Soho and got the job. Bert seemed impressed that I had secretarial experience. He said he was pleased that I wasn't a dolly bird.'

'Charming,' said Sam.

'I didn't mind,' said Pamela. 'It was rather refreshing, to be honest. He said he didn't think I was the type to run off with a chorus boy. I said he was safe there because I preferred women.'

She gave them a rather challenging look. Emma hoped that she wasn't blushing. Although she knew that there were homosexual people in Brighton – the hairdressers opposite, for example – she'd never heard anyone declare their sexuality so openly. Especially a woman.

'Good for you,' said Sam. 'Men are overrated.'

Emma was rather shocked but Sam had obviously hit the right note because Pamela laughed. 'Quite right. Now, what did you want to know about Bert? He could be a real sod but I was sorry to hear that he'd died. He was one of a kind. Thank God for that, really.'

'How long did you work for him?' asked Emma.

'Fifteen years. From 1945 to 1960. I booked all his tours, looked after the actors' contracts, managed his properties, stopped people killing him.'

'That sounds like a lot of work,' said Sam.

'It was,' said Pamela, 'but I loved it.'

'What do you mean,' said Emma, ' "stopped people killing him"?'

'Oh, there was always someone wanting Bert's blood. Some agent or artiste. Some wronged woman.'

'We've heard that he had extra-marital affairs,' said Emma. She'd had this from Verity herself.

'Extra-marital affairs,' said Pamela. 'I suppose you could call it that. He was a randy bastard. I felt sorry for his wife. She was a nice woman, Verity. That's why I agreed to talk to you. Because you're working for her.'

'Verity seemed to know about the affairs,' said Emma.

'She knew,' said Pamela. 'And I don't think she cared much. She had her life, her security, her boys. Seth was such a sweet kid. No, it wasn't the womanising that upset her. It was the other thing.'

'What other thing?' said Sam.

'The dead child,' said Pamela. 'In Liverpool.'

'Was that when Bert played King Rat?' said Emma.

'Yes.' Pamela looked surprised. 'So you do know about Angela.'

'Why don't you tell us about her,' said Emma.

'Bert didn't normally appear in his shows,' said Pamela. 'But the actor playing King Rat broke his leg in rehearsals so Bert went on. He'd been an actor once, by all accounts, but you don't have to do much as a pantomime villain, just appear in a puff of green smoke and be hissed at.'

Emma remembered seeing Max as Abanazar years ago. He too had materialised in green smoke, with firecrackers exploding from his voluminous sleeves. Denton McGrew and Annette Anthony had been in that production too. It was one of the first things that had struck her when Sam showed her the poster for *Dick Whittington* in Liverpool.

'One of the chorus girls was called Glenda,' said Pamela. 'Pretty little thing, she was. She'd been in a few of Bert's shows and there were rumours that they were lovers. She had a child, a little girl called Angela, who was about three. People said she was Bert's. Denton McGrew, he was the Dame, used to say that she was the spitting image of

Bert. I could never see it myself. Well, during the show, Bert started to sniff around one of the other chorus girls. Can't remember her name. Brenda or possibly Barbara. Anyway, Glenda was so upset that she killed herself. Killed the child too. They were found lying in the bed together. Gassed.'

'Oh my God,' said Emma. She felt very shaken by the story, told in Pamela's no-nonsense voice. She could understand killing yourself while in the depths of despair, but to murder your own child . . .

'Everyone was devastated, of course,' said Pamela. 'But the show went on. We were only halfway through the run. Lots of people blamed Bert. Verity was in pieces. Brenda or Barbara left the show and I heard that she fell on very hard times. But, you know how it is. People forget, even something like this. And Bert was a powerful man. You couldn't afford to get on the wrong side of him.'

But, in Emma's experience, people didn't forget. Memories gather strength with age. She thought that someone out there remembered King Rat very well indeed.

FIVE

'A girl who died,' said the DI. 'That's not much to go on.'

They were driving up to London to interview David, Bert's oldest son, and his wife Sheena. Meg was torn between the excitement of a day out and the potential awkwardness of being in close proximity with her boss. She was sure to do or say something unfortunate. Sure enough, before they reached the Brighton gates, she had asked if the car had a radio – it hadn't – and revealed a too-encyclopaedic knowledge of the Beatles' private lives (in answer to a question from the DI about their music). She thought that they were both relieved to be talking about the case.

'Bert had an affair with a girl and she killed herself,' said Meg. 'That's all Eric would tell me.'

'Do you think he knew more?'

'Maybe. I got the impression that he didn't like talking about those times. He said that he'd been friendly with Bert once but he didn't seem very keen on him now. They rarely saw each other, despite living so close. Eric did say that he occasionally had coffee or a drink with Verity. I think he might have been a bit sweet on her. I worked out that they were exactly the same age.'

'Verity Malone was a very good-looking woman once,' said the DI solemnly.

'Eric also said that Bert was one for the ladies,' said Meg. 'That might be worth pursuing.'

'It's hardly a question we can ask his son,' said DI Willis.

But it was David's wife who first introduced the subject. They'd hardly sat down in the elegant Hampstead sitting room when Sheena said, 'Of course Bert wasn't a good husband. He had countless affairs.'

Meg and the DI looked at each other. The DI started clearing his throat but Meg thought that it would be some time before words came out. She said, 'How long ago were these affairs?' After all, Bert was ninety when he died. Surely he couldn't still be staggering after women?

It was David who answered. He was a tall man with greying dark hair. Even dressed in casual clothes – slacks and a golfing jumper – he looked like a businessman. Sheena, in a tweed skirt and twinset, seemed like the sort of woman who described herself as 'just a housewife' but turned out to have the organising abilities of a four-star general.

'We weren't aware of the er . . . extra-marital affairs as children but, later on, especially when I took over the business, they rather came to light.'

'Women would contact David saying they'd had Bert's

children,' said Sheena, lighting a cigarette. 'David had to pay them off.'

'How often did this happen?' asked Meg.

'There were three that I can remember,' said Sheena. 'I work with David. I'm the secretary and general dogsbody.' She smiled. This sounded like something she'd said before. It also sounded completely untrue. Meg was willing to bet that Sheena ran the show.

'Could you give us their names?' The DI had found his voice at last.

'I'm sure I can,' said Sheena.

'I'm sorry if this is distressing for you,' said Meg, addressing herself to David. 'But I heard that a woman connected to your father killed herself.'

David and Sheena exchanged a glance. Meg tried to read the emotions that went into it. Fear, certainly. Embarrassment. Maybe also anger. There was a silence, broken only by the ticking of an ornate clock on the mantelpiece. The room was full of objects that looked both expensive and useless. Meg assumed that the younger Billingtons were very well off.

When David spoke he sounded as if he was reading from an official statement. 'In 1949 a woman called Glenda Gillespie killed herself. It transpired that she had had an affair with my father and was distressed when his affections . . . went elsewhere.'

'She killed their child too,' said Sheena, in such a matter-of-fact voice that Meg didn't at first take in her meaning.

It was the DI who said, 'This woman, this Glenda, killed herself and her child?'

'Yes,' said David. 'It was a great tragedy. My mother was heartbroken.'

'And your father?' Meg couldn't help asking.

'He was shaken,' said David. 'Of course he was. I was too. I was working in the firm then. We tried to help Glenda's family but they didn't want anything to do with us. I can't say I blamed them.'

'Do you have an address for Glenda's family?' asked the DI.

'It'll be in the files,' said Sheena.

But David was starting to realise the implications of the question. 'You can't think there's a link with . . . with my father's death?'

'We're investigating anyone who might have had a grudge against Mr Billington,' said the DI. Meg was starting to think that it would be a long list.

'Can you think of anyone who might have had a grudge against your father?' asked Meg. *Only everyone who ever knew him* had been Verity's answer to this question. But Verity had also said that Aaron, the youngest son, suspected her of the murder.

'I can't think . . .' David ruffled his hair so that it stood up in a crest. For a moment, he looked like his film star brother. 'I mean . . . Dad had enemies but I can't think of anyone who would kill him.'

'What about Alma?' said Sheena.

'Alma Saunders?' said Meg. 'The cleaning lady?'

'She was more than that,' said Sheena. 'Alma used to be Verity's dresser. She knew everyone's secrets.'

'Oh come on, Sheena.' David sounded positively angry with his wife, something Meg was sure didn't happen often. 'Alma would never hurt Dad. She was like a second mother to us.' He turned to Meg and the DI. 'Alma helped bring us up. She was our housekeeper when we lived in Lytham.'

'And then she followed Verity and Bert to Rottingdean?' It sounded rather far-fetched to Meg.

'Well, actually Ma and Pa followed Alma,' said David. 'She moved to Sussex first. I think she had family there.'

'We're interviewing Mrs Saunders tomorrow,' said the DI.

Meg was looking forward to it.

Emma and Sam were in a vegetable patch. Or, rather, they were standing on wooden planks bordering the growing area. Jonathan, strapped into his pushchair, strained to get out and play with the lovely mud. Ted Grange was digging up potatoes and not about to stop because two young girls (his words) were asking him questions.

Ted's allotment was in Woodingdean, behind the racecourse, not far from the flat Sam shared with two other women (her words). The Billingtons' gardener had agreed to talk to them, but it was proving difficult because it was a windy day and Ted was slightly deaf. He'd given his age as seventy-five but moved with an agility that Emma found herself envying. Just thinking about gardening made her back ache. Thank goodness their house only possessed a paved back yard.

'Can you think back to the day Bert died?' said Emma, raising her voice slightly. 'It was Sunday the nineteenth of September.'

'I know when it was,' said Ted. 'I always do Tudor Close on a Sunday.'

'Are they communal gardens?' asked Emma.

'Eh?'

Emma didn't know if Ted's incomprehension was due to deafness or her word choice. Sam said, 'Do you just work for the Billingtons or for everyone who lives in the houses?'

'I work for them all,' said Ted, lobbing a potato into a nearby trug. 'A collective, they call themselves. There are no divides between the gardens, you see. But some of the folks I know better than others.'

'Do you know the Billingtons well?'

'Her, I do,' said Ted. 'Nice lady. She always gives me tea and biscuits. Chocolate ones. I never really talk to him.'

'What happened that Sunday?' said Emma. 'Did you see Verity and Bert?'

'I saw her when I went round to do the back,' said Ted. 'She brought me out a mug of tea and two biscuits.'

'What about Bert? Did you see him?'

'No. I think he was watching telly. I could hear it in the background. He always had it on loud. Think he was getting a bit mutton. Mutt and Jeff. Deaf.' He grinned at them, showing several gaps in his teeth.

'Did you see anyone else going into the house?' asked Emma, more for form's sake than anything.

But Ted straightened up and leant on his shovel. 'I did see someone, yes.'

Emma looked at Sam. 'You did?'

'Yes. When I was doing the front lawn I saw a woman going into the Billingtons' place. She let herself in. She must have had a key or maybe the door wasn't locked. She walked in as if she owned the place.'

'What time was this?' asked Emma.

'Must have been about eleven-thirty. I started at eleven.'

Bert had been found dead at three p.m., Emma knew, but who was to say when he actually died? Annoyingly, she hadn't been able to see the pathologist's report.

'Can you describe this woman?' Emma turned to a new page in her notebook.

'She was wearing a brown coat,' said Ted.

'What sort of brown?' asked Emma. 'Camel hair?'

Ted looked blank and Sam prompted, 'Light or dark brown?'

'Dark.'

'Anything else?' said Sam. 'Was she old or young? Big or small?'

'Biggish,' said Ted. 'Bulky, you know.' He grinned again. Almost a leer, thought Emma. 'I prefer my women like that. Girls today are too skinny.'

'Was she wearing a hat?' asked Sam briskly.

'No,' said Ted. 'She had light-coloured hair, I think.'

'Blonde?' asked Sam, gesturing towards Emma. 'Like hers?'

'No,' said Ted. 'Though I like a blonde. This was more grey.'

'Did you tell the police about this woman?' asked Emma.

'Nah,' said Ted. 'They sent round this bloke who trampled all over my bedding wallflowers. I didn't tell him nothing.'

Emma was willing to bet that was Sergeant Brendan O'Neill. From Edgar's description, he wasn't the sort to look where he was walking. How remiss of Bob. He should have sent Meg to interview the gardener.

'What about Verity?' she asked. 'Did you mention the woman to her?'

'No. I thought she knew about her. Thought she must be a friend of the family. Like I say, she let herself in. I need to get on now.'

He turned back to his digging. Jonathan, straining at his bonds, yelled, 'Out! Out! Out!' like a junior trade unionist. Sam and Emma thanked Ted and made their way out through the maze of greenhouses and sheds. Emma was thinking hard. The woman might have been a friend of the family, but she might also have been the killer. At any rate, she was their first real lead.

And a lead not shared by the police.

SIX

Alma Saunders was a surprise to Meg. She'd expected a grey-haired old lady, the sort described by rich people as 'a treasure', a cuddly nurse who'd been a second mother to David and his brothers. Instead, the yellow front door of the former fisherman's cottage in Rottingdean was opened by a slim figure in green slacks with a bright red ponytail. The hair was definitely dyed – it was the colour of a fire engine – but the effect was one of youth and vigour. The DI actually blinked.

'I was expecting you,' said Alma. The door opened directly into the sitting room, a small space that seemed full of knick-knacks and shiny objects. Meg's mother would have loved it. She always complained that all her ornaments, even her holy water stoup from Lourdes, became chipped or broken the moment they entered the house. Alma offered tea and, when it arrived, the tray was groaning under the weight of matching china, apostle spoons and sugar tongs.

Meg's cup was so thin that it looked translucent. She held it carefully with both hands.

'We're talking to everyone who knew Bert Billington,' she said. 'You must have known the family really well. David said you were with them for years.'

Was it Meg's imagination, or did the mention of the eldest Billington son make Alma slightly nervous?

'You could say that,' said Alma. 'I've worked for Verity for nearly fifty years. Since I was sixteen. I was her dresser, you see. When she was in variety.'

'What is a dresser exactly?' asked Meg. This had been bothering her ever since Sheena used the word.

'A dresser looks after an artiste's clothes,' said Alma, 'but I was more than that. I was Verity's right-hand woman. I made sure that her dressing room was as it should be. I booked train tickets and hotels. We travelled all over the place together, a different show every week. I could tell you a few stories. Then Verity married Bert and became respectable. A few years later I married Dave and I couldn't really keep dashing round the country, especially when I got pregnant with Fred. I lost touch with Verity for a bit but, a few years later, she wrote to say she needed my help.'

'What sort of help did she need?'

'Help with the kids and with the house. Verity and Bert were living in Lytham, near Blackpool. A beautiful place they had there. Bert's from Blackpool, you know. It was home to him but it felt very strange to Verity. She's a

London girl. Born within the sound of Bow Bells, though you wouldn't know it now. Verity felt out of place in the north. She had a nanny and a housekeeper, but she wanted someone who was on her side, as she put it. Well, Dave was a jobbing carpenter. He could get work anywhere. So we moved to Lytham.'

That was devotion, thought Meg. It was all very well for Alma to say that Dave could find work anywhere, but she'd said earlier that they were both Londoners 'born and bred'. Lytham must have felt as alien to them as it did to Verity. She asked how long they had stayed in Lancashire.

'Almost thirty years. Then Verity and Bert moved to Weybridge. It was what Verity wanted, she said it was too cold in the north. Well, we didn't like Surrey – Dave couldn't stand all those rhododendrons everywhere – so we came down here, to Rottingdean. Dave's parents had retired to Peacehaven, you see, and we fancied being near the sea. Dave loved it here. It was sad that he didn't have long to enjoy it. He died five years after we moved here. Heart attack.'

'I'm sorry,' said Meg.

'It was a shock,' said Alma. 'He seemed so healthy, then, one day, he dropped down dead on East Brighton Golf Course.'

'How awful,' said the DI. Meg knew that he was a keen golfer, probably a member of that same club.

'Yes, it was,' said Alma. 'I felt very lost for a while. Then Verity and Bert moved here.'

'Was that a surprise?' asked Meg.

'Yes. I thought they were settled in Surrey. But I was pleased. It meant I could work for them.'

Meg noticed that Alma had immediately assumed the role of helper and employee. Why had Verity and Bert moved to Sussex? Maybe Verity wanted to be near her right-hand woman again. She wondered how Verity had taken Alma's defection from Surrey. Not liking the local flowers seemed a rather weak excuse, especially when Dave and Alma had previously been prepared to travel the length of the country for the Billingtons.

'Did Verity and Bert like it in Rottingdean?' she asked.

'It was a bit quiet for them, I think,' said Alma. 'Dave and I were part of the community. Dave used to drink in the Black Horse, I was quite a one for amateur dramatics. Verity wasn't interested in any of that, even though she'd been in the business. Neither of them went to church or got involved in village life. I think they felt a bit lonely, to tell you the truth. It didn't help that Bert's health was failing. For years he'd never shown any signs of aging, then it seemed to catch up with him. Verity ended up looking after him, which wasn't her thing at all.'

'Were they friends with any of the neighbours? I spoke to Eric Prentice on Tuesday. He said that he knew Verity and Bert from way back.'

Alma made a noise that could almost be described as a snort. 'Eric wasn't a friend. Oh, he was always hanging round Verity with his tongue hanging out, just like that stupid dog of his, but she couldn't stand him.'

This was interesting. Eric had definitely given the impression that he was on friendly terms with Verity, although he had said that she didn't like his dog. Suddenly Meg remembered Verity saying, 'I can't stand short people.' Had she been thinking of Eric Prentice?

'We're trying to build up a picture of what happened on Sunday the nineteenth,' said the DI. 'The day Bert died. Did you see the Billingtons that day?'

'No,' said Alma. 'I don't go in on a Sunday. The first I heard was when Verity rang me that evening. She said that Bert had been "taken". It seemed a funny word to choose. But then Verity had had a very religious upbringing.'

'What did you do?' said Meg. 'Did you go round to the house?'

'Of course,' said Alma. 'By the time I got there, David and Sheena had arrived. Aaron was there too. He was the one who actually found his father's body. That must have been terrible for him. They were very close.'

Meg remembered this afterwards. It was the first time she had heard of anyone being fond of Bert Billington.

'What about Seth?' Meg couldn't help asking.

'He's away. Filming up north somewhere. He's meant to be coming home this weekend. That'll please Verity.'

'Is Seth her favourite?' asked the DI. It seemed an unusually human question, coming from him.

'Verity tries to be fair,' said Alma, 'but Seth is the apple of her eye. Although that's understandable. He was always such a sunny, lovable boy.'

Seth is your favourite too, thought Meg.

'As you may know,' said the DI, reverting to his normal 'policeman on duty' voice, 'we are treating Mr Billington's death as suspicious. Do you know anyone who might have wished him ill?'

Wished him ill. Where did the DI find that one? It sounded like a curse.

'No, I can't think of anyone,' said Alma. Meg thought of Sheena saying that Alma knew everyone's secrets. Well, if she did, she wasn't revealing them.

'David mentioned a woman who took her own life,' said the DI. 'Were you aware of the tragedy?'

'Glenda Gillespie?' said Alma. 'Of course I remember. It almost broke Verity's heart. That poor, silly girl.'

Was she referring to Glenda or Verity? wondered Meg.

'Verity almost had a breakdown when Glenda and Angela died,' said Alma. 'It was a difficult time for her. Her marriage was under strain. The older boys were growing up, David was married. That was when she decided to leave Lytham. She wanted to come back down south.'

And you moved to Rottingdean, thought Meg. She wondered whether this, too, was due to the shock waves from Glenda's death.

'Do you know if the Billingtons ever heard from

Glenda's family?' asked the DI. 'David said that he'd offered compensation, which was refused.'

'David was very cut up about Glenda,' said Alma. 'I almost think he was in love with her too. Of course, he was married to Sheena by then. They might even have had Anton.'

David and Sheena had two children, Meg knew. Anton and Deborah. Anton, now aged seventeen, would have been a baby when Glenda died.

'Do you know if Glenda's family stayed in contact?' the DI asked again.

'No, they didn't,' said Alma. 'As for Bert, he never mentioned her name again.'

But you remembered it, thought Meg. And you remembered her daughter too.

They left Rottingdean and drove over the racecourse hill to Hove, where they were interviewing Aaron Billington in the garage he owned. Although Meg had lived in Brighton all her life there were still parts of Hove that were a mystery to her: mansion blocks with names like Montpelier and Sackville, builders' yards and railway arches and strange little shops where you couldn't imagine anyone ever making a purchase. Billington Motors was in one of these places, a secret courtyard surrounded by high-rise flats.

'It's a mews,' said the DI. 'These used to be stables once. There would have been a grand house nearby. Look at that gateway.'

There were no gates now, just an archway guarded by two stone lions. The DI sounded wistful. Meg thought the DI was just the sort of person to think everything was better in the past. She preferred the future herself.

Aaron was under a car when they arrived. He wheeled himself out using one of those planks on wheels. Meg's brother Declan had one. He sometimes brought it home to let the younger ones play on it.

The DI made the introductions. Aaron stood up. He was tall, like his brothers, and very similar to look at, although his hair was longer and slightly lighter than David's. In his blue boiler suit Aaron didn't look much like the son of a famous impresario and Meg thought that he'd modified his accent to suit his surroundings. Verity might have been born within the sound of Bow Bells but now she was drawlingly posh, 'daahling'. David had the clipped voice of a businessman, but Aaron swallowed the ends of his words in the way that Meg did. She'd already noticed that her sister Aisling, after five years at grammar school, sounded subtly different from her siblings.

Aaron led them into a small office that smelt strongly of petrol, an aroma that Meg liked. The DI wrinkled his nose though and seemed reluctant to sit on the stool that was offered to him.

'As you know,' he said stiffly, 'we're now treating your father's death as suspicious.'

'I knew,' said Aaron. 'I knew as soon as I saw him.' He rubbed his eyes with an oily hand.

'Can you take us back to that day?' said the DI. 'I think you arrived at your parents' house at about three p.m. on that Sunday?'

'Yes,' said Aaron. 'I often pop in on a Sunday afternoon. Mum met me at the door. She seemed a bit vague but that's usual these days. She was fussing about some roses she'd picked. I went into the sitting room and Dad was sitting in his armchair, his glass of whisky next to him, just like he always did.' Aaron's voice shook. He, at least, had been genuinely fond of his father, thought Meg.

'I went up to him,' said Aaron, 'and as soon as I saw his face, I knew. It was all wrong. As if it had been frozen. Almost sneering. I took his hand to find a pulse. Nothing. I told Mum to call an ambulance. Which she did. Eventually.'

'What do you mean, "eventually"?' asked Meg.

Aaron looked at her as if registering her presence for the first time. At least he was slightly taller than her which made the scrutiny less embarrassing.

'She just stood there for ages,' said Aaron. 'I had to shout at her.'

It would be normal to be shocked, thought Meg. But was Aaron implying that there was more to Verity's inertia than shock?

'Did you notice anything odd in the room?' asked Meg. 'Anything that looked out of place?'

'Not really,' said Aaron. 'I wasn't really thinking. Everything was just like it always was. Dad's empty lunch plate was on the table next to him and his whisky glass.'

'Was that empty too?'

'No. Half full, I think.'

Meg thought that the DI was thinking the same as her. If foul play had been suspected immediately, they could have examined the glass and its contents. As it was, all evidence of Bert Billington's last meal had been cleared away.

'What happened next?' asked DI Willis.

'The ambulance came and they did all that mouth-to-mouth stuff but I could see it was useless. They took him to the hospital though and I followed on my motorbike.'

'What about your mum?' said Meg. 'Did she go in the ambulance?'

'No,' said Aaron, 'she stayed at home. I told her to telephone Alma to come and sit with her but she didn't call her until later. I telephoned David and Sheena from the hospital. They came down immediately. They were at Tudor Close by the time I got back.'

'Mr Billington,' said the DI, 'when we first spoke on the telephone, you expressed a concern that your mother might have accidentally caused your father's death. Is that still something that you think?'

Aaron rubbed his face again, leaving black marks on either side of his nose. 'Mum was tired of looking after Dad,' he said. 'She read all these books by Americans. You know, the ones protesting about the war in Vietnam.'

Meg felt as though the war in Vietnam had been going on all her life. She thought of photographs she'd seen of protestors carrying banners saying, 'Bring our GIs home' and 'Ho Chi Minh is going to win'. The people in the photographs, men and women, all had long hair and grim expressions.

'Mum read a book by some American woman,' said Aaron. 'It was called *The Feminine Mystery*. Something like that. After that Mum started to say that women shouldn't have to stay home and be housewives and look after men. She said they should have jobs.'

'Imagine that,' said Meg.

To her surprise, Aaron laughed. 'She'd approve of you, all right. Doing a man's job better than a man, that's what she'd say. I'm all for women being equal. It's just . . . it was tough on Dad.'

'Your father didn't agree with it?' said the DI.

'Well, he was getting older,' said Aaron. 'He had a right to expect Mum to look after him. I mean, he'd supported her all his life. Supported all of us. We never wanted for anything.'

Meg tried and failed to imagine herself making a similar statement. She felt that she had wanted for almost everything when she was growing up. Despite this, her father often referred to himself as 'the breadwinner'.

'Did your mother say she didn't want to look after your father?' she asked.

'She didn't say it outright,' said Aaron, 'but I knew it was what she was thinking.'

'Did your mother ever say that she wanted to harm your father?' asked Meg.

'Not as such, no,' said Aaron. 'But she used to say that she felt trapped. Sometimes she looked at Dad like she hated him.'

'Mr Billington,' said DI Willis. 'Your brother David mentioned a woman called Glenda Gillespie to us. Does that name mean anything to you?'

'Why was he talking about that?' said Aaron. 'Glenda's got nothing to do with Dad. She died years ago.'

'Do you remember her death?' asked Meg.

'I remember people talking about it,' said Aaron. 'I was living at home then, just about to start National Service. I remember Mum crying and Dad trying to comfort her.'

Meg had written all the dates in the front of her notebook because she was bad at mental arithmetic. Aaron was born in 1931, which would have made him eighteen when Glenda committed suicide. Old enough to have known exactly what was happening. David, born in 1923, would have been twenty-six, married with a young child. Seth would have been twenty.

'Are you close to your brothers?' she asked. 'I've got a little brother of eight and I sometimes feel that I'm like a second mum to him.'

This wasn't true although Meg's mother had worked hard to foster this illusion.

Aaron had looked defensive at first but seemed to soften slightly at the mention of Meg's brother, a common reaction with people who hadn't met Connor.

'I was close to Seth when we were growing up,' he said. 'But then he was away at drama school and acting. David always seemed a lot older. He was in the war and then working in London.'

'Can you think of anyone who might have had a grudge against your father?' The DI asked his favourite question.

'No,' said Aaron. 'Everyone loved Dad.'

Meg almost thought that he believed it.

Meg and the DI drove back to the police station in silence. The DI seemed deep in thought, probably dreaming of the days when garages were stables and apartment blocks were grand houses. Meg was thinking about Aaron saying, 'Sometimes she looked at Dad like she hated him.' Had Verity hated Bert enough to kill him? She was still the most likely suspect.

'What did you think of Aaron?' the DI asked at last, as he parked behind Bartholomew Square.

'He seemed OK,' said Meg. Then remembering that DI Willis had once condemned 'OK' as an 'Americanism', she said hastily, 'He seemed genuinely fond of his father, unlike David or Sheena.'

'Have you heard of the book he mentioned?' asked the DI. '*The Feminine Mystery*?'

Meg was quite flattered to think that the DI saw her as a reader. She wasn't a great one for books, although she liked reading the stories in Aisling's magazines.

'No,' she said. 'But I could find out about it.'

'You do that,' said the DI. 'It sounds like it might be up your street.'

They were almost at the entrance of the imposing building that housed the unimposing CID offices. Meg stood aside to let two higher-ranking officers go past and, by the time she reached the double doors, the DI had disappeared.

What did he mean by saying the American book sounded up her street? Meg wasn't sure that it was a compliment.

Emma was reading to Marianne and Sophie. They were on *The Hobbit* at the moment, which they were all enjoying although Emma couldn't help noticing the total lack of female characters. It seemed that hobbits, elves and dwarves lived in all-male communities, like monks. Or Oxford dons.

While Bilbo was outwitting the trolls, Emma heard the phone ringing downstairs. As she finished the chapter, she heard the receiver go down. When she got down to the sitting room, Edgar was sitting on the sofa, looking slightly dazed.

'Who was that on the phone?' asked Emma.

'Max,' said Edgar. 'He wants us to have lunch with him and Lydia on Sunday. At the Grand.'

'Gosh,' said Emma. In her mind she was sorting through her wardrobe. Did she even possess a garment suitable for lunch with Lydia Lamont at the Grand? There was her blue silk, which was safe but a bit dull. There was the green shift that she'd bought last time she'd had a meal with Max but that seemed a bit hippy-ish for Lydia. Maybe she should buy something new? But she didn't have time to go shopping and, besides, it was a waste of money. She realised that Edgar was speaking.

'Max said that there's no filming this weekend. Seth Billington's coming down to see his mother. I'll send WDC Connolly to interview him.'

Emma and Sam would have to find a way to interview Seth too. Surely Verity would invite them over? She was the one who had engaged them, after all. Emma had telephoned Verity to ask if she'd seen the woman in the brown coat but Verity had only said something vague about everyone wearing brown these days and what a shame it was. Emma needed to talk to her again. She hadn't told Edgar about the mysterious caller described by Ted Grange. It's because I need to investigate further, she told herself. But she was honest enough to know that she also wanted to get ahead of the police, to present them with the solution to the case with all the loose ends tied up in a bow.

'Max said that Seth was worried about his mother,' said Edgar. 'He said that the younger brother, Aaron, suspects her of killing his father.'

'She said as much to me,' said Emma.

'She mentioned it to Bob too. He and WDC Connolly went to see Aaron today. They said that he seemed genuinely cut up about his dad but he didn't have any proof against his mum apart from her believing in women's equality.'

At least Edgar said this with the regulation amount of irony. Emma answered in kind. 'If she believes in women's rights then she's definitely a murderer.'

She wouldn't tell Edgar about the woman in the brown coat yet.

SEVEN

'I can't ask Seth Billington for his autograph,' said Meg. 'Not in the middle of an interview.'

Three pairs of eyes stared accusingly at Meg across the breakfast table. They belonged to Aisling, seventeen, Collette, ten, and – amazingly – Meg's mother, Mary, forty-eight years old and, Meg would have thought, far too old to care about film stars.

'What about a signed photo?' said Aisling. She was studying for her A-levels and the acknowledged brains of the family. You wouldn't think it now though.

'Great idea, Ash,' said Meg. 'I've got a few questions to ask you about your father's murder, Mr Billington, but first will you sign a photo for my little sister?'

'And for me,' said Collette.

'For God's sake.'

'Margaret,' called Mary, from where she was leaning against the gas stove because she wouldn't smoke at the table. 'No blasphemy in this house, please.'

At the sound of her raised voice, Padre Pio, the budgerigar, start to chirp loudly. He was christened by Patrick, Meg's older brother, after the Italian priest who was the only other creature to enjoy Mary's uncritical adoration. Mary, a devout Catholic, often bemoaned the fact that, out of seven children, not one was in holy orders. The eldest, Marie, was married with a child of her own. Patrick and Declan had recently moved out to share a flat in Portslade. Patrick was an electrician and Declan an apprentice car mechanic. Nobody, not even Father Costello, had ever considered them potential priests.

'Was his father really murdered?' said Aisling, letting milk drip from her spoon.

'That's what we're investigating,' said Meg. She shouldn't have said the word aloud but the desire to put her siblings in their place was too strong.

'It was the wife,' said Mary. 'That's what I think. She's no better than she should be, that one.' Meg had noticed before that her mother was always on the side of the patriarchy, however little it had done for her. But maybe she was still resentful about the picture of the one and only Verity Malone in her husband's wallet.

Meg got up, washed her cup and plate and put them on the drying rack. She wasn't going to do her sisters' washing up too.

'I'm off, Mum,' she said. 'DI Willis is picking me up at the end of the road.'

'You shouldn't have to work on a Saturday,' said Mary.

'I'll get a day off in lieu.'

'I'd better get going too,' said Aisling. She worked at the local greengrocer on a Saturday. 'Time and cauliflowers wait for no man.'

She winked at Meg. Her sisters weren't that bad really. She would see what she could do about an autograph.

It was still a shock to see Seth Billington in the cluttered sitting room at Tudor Close. He looked too *shiny* to exist in real life, his hair too dark, his teeth and shirt front too white. He stood up when Meg and the DI entered and his head brushed the chandelier.

'Watch out, Seth,' said Verity. 'You clumsy clot.'

Clumsy clot. Meg could hardly believe her ears. This was the man described by *Film Frolics* as 'the handsomest actor alive today'.

'Thanks, Mum,' said Seth, smiling. Again, 'Mum' sounded wrong. It was what Meg called Mary. Surely Seth should say 'Mother' or 'Mama'?

They sat down and Verity offered tea or coffee. Again, the DI refused. Was this because he suspected Verity of being a poisoner? Meg thought that Verity seemed to want to stay in the room but after a few minutes she drifted away. Meg was sure that she was still in listening distance, though.

'We're very sorry about your father,' said DI Willis stiffly. 'Please accept our condolences.'

Seth inclined his head but said nothing.

'You may know,' said the DI, after a pause, 'that there are some irregularities surrounding your father's death.'

'You mean he was poisoned?'

'It looks that way, yes. We're speaking to all of the family and we're asking everyone, can you think of anyone who would have wanted to hurt your father?'

Seth looked at them steadily, his dark eyes serious. He looked both sad and straightforward, thought Meg. But then, he was a very good actor.

'This is rather a sensitive subject,' he said. He looked at Meg as he said this, as if she would understand. She could feel herself reddening.

'In what way?' asked the DI.

'Dad wasn't . . . He wasn't always faithful to Mum. It was an open secret. We all knew. Mum knew. I remember a woman coming up to me after a show once, thrusting a child in front of me and saying, "This is your half-sister." And, a few years ago, a woman turned up here. I remember it because Dad was in hospital – it was when he had his mini-stroke – and I was here, keeping an eye on Mum. Anyway, this woman turned up and said that she'd had an affair with Dad and had a child by him who was now eighteen. She wanted some money to set him up in an apprenticeship.'

'What did your mother do?'

'She gave her the money, I think.'

'Did you see this woman yourself?'

'Briefly. Mum took her away and spoke to her in the study. I couldn't give a very good description, I'm afraid.'

'Do you remember the child's name? Or the woman's?'

'No. I think the son had one of those modern names. Kit or Kim maybe.'

Meg remembered Sheena saying, 'Of course Bert wasn't a good husband.' This was beginning to sound like an understatement. She glanced at the DI and addressed Seth: 'Sheena, your sister-in-law, said that at least three women contacted David saying they'd had Bert's children. Do you think this woman was one of them?'

'I don't know,' said Seth, running a hand through his hair in a way that mysteriously made it look more styled than ever. 'It sounds like the sort of thing Sheena would say.'

What did that mean? Meg wondered. She sensed the DI was going to ask his grudge question and sure enough . . .

'Can you think of anyone who might have harboured a grudge against your father?'

'I can think of a good many people,' said Seth.

'But did any of them have access to your father's food that day?' said DI Willis.

'I don't know,' said Seth, his smooth brow creasing.

'As far as we can make out, the only people with access were your mother and the daily woman, Mrs Saunders.'

'Now look here.' Seth's face changed as suddenly as if a director had said 'action'. He stood up and Meg was suddenly aware of his height and strength. 'There's no way my mother or Alma would have killed my father. They both loved him. It's impossible.'

'We've spoken to Alma,' said Meg, trying for a soothing tone. 'She's been with the family for a long time.'

'Yes,' said Seth. 'She helped bring us up. She'd never harm any of us.'

Seth seemed to be back in control. He sat down and smiled at them but now the smile looked mechanical. It didn't reach his eyes.

'I'm sorry,' he said. 'It's an emotional time for all of us.'

'We understand,' said the DI.

'It must be very hard,' said Meg. 'When did you last see your father?'

'In early August,' said Seth. 'I've been busy shooting a film in Whitby.'

'*The Prince of Darkness*,' said Meg.

'Yes,' said Seth. 'Are you a film fan?'

Meg said that she was. Seth chatted about the film for a while and was so friendly that, when they took their leave, she was emboldened to ask for autographs for Aisling and Collette, carefully spelling out the tricky Irish names. She could feel waves of disapproval emanating from the DI as Seth wrote in her notebook. When they got outside, she saw that he'd signed 'To Aisling' and 'To Collette' but also 'To Policewoman Meg'. She put the book carefully in her bag.

She expected some comment from the DI but, as they drove around the village pond where children were feeding the ducks in the sunshine, he said only, 'You know who didn't love Bert Billington? His son, Seth.'

And, despite the generosity of the autographs, Meg had to agree with him.

EIGHT

'The Triumph Tiger Cub,' said Aaron Billington. 'That's a gutsy little bike.'

Sam Collins gave herself a mental pat on the back for thinking of visiting Aaron Billington on two wheels. He hadn't been exactly keen to speak to a private detective. 'I can't see the point,' he said on the phone. 'The police are dealing with it.' Sam had persuaded him to give her ten minutes but, when she roared into the mews on her blue and silver steed, Aaron's attitude had changed immediately. He welcomed both Sam and her bike into his workshop and made them instant coffee from a lime-encrusted kettle. Aaron walked around the Tiger Cub, examining it with an expert eye. He was a tall man, physically not unlike the handsome Seth, but nervier, less comfortable in his skin.

'I love it,' said Sam. 'It's perfect for getting around Brighton.'

'I used to have a Triumph Tiger,' said Aaron. 'I've got a Royal Enfield now.'

'Is that the bike you brought over to show your parents that Sunday?' said Sam.

'To show my father,' said Aaron. 'Mum wasn't interested.'

He sounded like a sulky teenager, but Aaron Billington was, by Emma's calculations, thirty-four years old, two years younger than Seth and eight years younger than David.

'Was your dad interested in bikes?' asked Sam. Ask different questions, Emma had said. The police will have asked Aaron about finding his father's body. He won't want to go over it again. Find a different path. It looked as if Sam's path was the open highway.

'Yes, he was,' said Aaron. 'Dad was interested in anything mechanical. He always had the best cars. I remember him picking us up from school in the Lagonda. Everyone stared. Seth said it was embarrassing but I loved it.'

Interesting, thought Sam. There was genuine emotion in Aaron's voice. However much of a bastard Bert Billington had been, his youngest son had obviously loved him.

'Dad gave me the money to buy this garage,' said Aaron, loquacious now. 'I was never any good at school, not like David and Seth. Mum didn't like me working with bikes. "Nasty, dirty things", was what she said. Last year, when the Mods and Rockers were fighting in Brighton, she supported the Mods because "they had nicer clothes".' He put on an affected voice when imitating his mother.

'Sounds as if your mother and father were very different,' said Sam.

'You could say that,' said Aaron. 'Dad was much older, of course. He was over fifty when I was born. But, I don't know, he seemed younger. Even recently – I know his health wasn't good – but he didn't have a hearing aid or carry a stick. He had all his own teeth. And he was always interested in new things. Mum was stuck in the past, with her wigs and false eyelashes and calling everyone "darling". It was as if she was still on stage. Seth's the same, always smiling and being charming, but he doesn't really care about anyone but himself.'

'It sounds as if you were the one who saw your parents most often,' said Sam. 'It's the same with mine. I live nearer so I do all the visiting.' This was actually completely untrue. Sam's parents – fit and healthy in their late fifties – lived in Southend, a few streets away from her brother and his family.

'Yeah,' said Aaron. 'Seth's too busy swanning about being a film star. He's at home at the moment though. Mum waiting on him hand and foot. Dave's in London. That's fair enough, he runs the company and he's got kids. But it's me that has to take the oldies to the doctors and pick up their prescriptions and all that. Dad gave up driving after the last stroke. Mum never learnt. Typical. There's a Rolls in perfect condition in their garage. It's a tragedy.'

He really did mean the car, thought Sam.

'What do you think happened to your dad?' she asked, trying to keep the same light tone. But Aaron's face darkened immediately. When he was angry, he looked even more like Seth.

'I think Mum killed him,' he said. 'She was fed up with looking after him. She kept going on about being a liberated woman. Well, she liberated herself, didn't she?'

Emma was having a frustrating day. Normally she liked Saturdays. She took Marianne and Sophie horse-riding in the morning and loved watching them trotting round the ring, so serious and so happy. She even loved the smell of horse manure and the constant battle to stop Jonathan playing with it. Sometimes her friend Vera, who owned the stables, let Jonathan sit on a pony for a few minutes. Watching his face, wreathed in smiles as he clung to the bristly mane, never failed to make Emma's heart contract.

But this morning she kept thinking about the case. She envied Sam who was interviewing Aaron and then, possibly, Seth. It should be me, she thought. I'm the one who used to be a detective. Why wasn't Edgar supervising the riding lessons? Because he had to work, of course, and his work always trumped everything. The previous superintendent had spent most of his time on the golf course but Edgar was more conscientious. It was one of the things Emma had loved when he was her boss. It seemed far less lovable now, though.

At least she had the car. For years they had managed without, borrowing a police vehicle when they needed to, but last year Edgar had surprised Emma with a five-year-old Morris Minor. It rattled when you drove over thirty and let in water when it rained but Emma loved it. So did the girls, who called it Betsy. They were in a raucous mood driving home, singing Beatles' songs and arguing about who was best at the rising trot. All you need is love, thought Emma, as they drove past Roedean, looking as bleak as a prison even in the autumn sunshine. If only that were true.

She parked in the underground garage and they walked back to the house. Well, Emma walked. Marianne and Sophie trotted, cantered and galloped, occasionally neighing loudly. Jonathan refused to move at all and had to be carried. Emma wished that she had brought his pushchair but it was such a pain getting it into the little car. As they approached their front door, the human ponies shied and stopped. Emma, her arms full of Jonathan (as heavy as lead at nearly two), caught up with them. 'What is it?'

'It's a lady . . .' said Sophie uncertainly.

It was, in fact, a vision of loveliness: pink shift dress, white tights, white shoes, shiny black hair pulled back with a brilliantly clashing red scarf.

'Ruby?' said Emma.

'Oh hi,' said Ruby. 'I thought I'd just drop in. Hallo, kids. Goodness, is that the baby? He looks bigger than you.'

'You'd better come in,' said Emma.

*

Ruby French was probably the most famous woman on British television. She had once been a stage magician and had even briefly appeared in a double act with her father, Max Mephisto. For years Ruby had played a fictional version of herself in a highly successful TV show called *Ruby Magic*. Now she was fearless private detective Iris Green in *Iris Investigates*. Emma had helped her research the series, which Ruby also directed. They were – cautiously – friends, only slightly complicated by the fact that Ruby used to be engaged to Edgar.

Emma invited Ruby to stay for lunch and the girls were so awed that they changed out of their jodhpurs without a protest and even helped lay the table. Ruby sat smoking and asking them a series of quickfire questions.

'Who's your favourite Beatle?'

'If you could be any animal, what would you be?'

'Dogs or cats, choose now.'

The girls soon lost their shyness and started shrieking the answers. Jonathan joined in from his highchair, shouting his favourite word, 'Dad, Dad, Dad.'

'Where is Dad?' said Ruby, when Emma put the gala pie and salad on the table.

'Working,' said Emma.

'My dad's a policeman,' said Sophie.

'Really?' said Ruby. 'Mine's a magician. He can make people disappear.'

Emma was struck by the way that Ruby seemed eternally youthful. She and Emma were almost exactly the same age but Ruby seemed almost like one of the children whereas Emma felt like such a *grown-up*. But Emma was a mother and, whilst that made her ageless in a way, it didn't make her young.

'Edgar makes himself disappear,' said Emma. Then, aware that she was sounding sour, she asked Ruby what she was doing in Brighton.

'Visiting my mum,' said Ruby. 'And meeting a friend. Max is in town too.'

'I know,' said Emma. 'Edgar and I are having lunch with him and Lydia tomorrow.' She wondered if she should ask Ruby's advice about clothes.

'So tell me,' Ruby leant forward, 'are you really investigating the Bert Billington murder?'

'*Pas devant les enfants*,' said Emma.

'That's French,' Marianne told Sophie. 'It means not in front of us.'

'*Sacre bleu*,' said Ruby. 'Don't be so stuffy. I'm sure they like a good murder.'

'They're only nine and seven,' said Emma.

'Really?' said Ruby. 'I'm no good at children's ages. Tell me, Marianne, have you ever heard of Seth Billington?'

'Yes,' said Marianne immediately. 'My friend Sally's got his picture in her bedroom.'

So that was Ruby's mysterious 'friend', thought Emma.

NINE

Max still wasn't sure why he had agreed to come to Brighton for the weekend. Filming had stopped to allow Seth to visit his mother and Max had assumed that he and Lydia would go home to Somerset to see the children. But Lydia had wanted a 'break', she wanted to see Brighton and she wanted to stay at the Grand. Max couldn't exactly see why Lydia, who had been relaxing at the Royal Whitby for weeks, would need a break and why she'd want to stay at another hotel. But he had acquiesced. Perhaps he'd agreed they could come because of Ruby, who was in Brighton on mysterious business of her own. Or maybe it was because he wanted to see Edgar and talk murder again?

Lydia had been delighted with Brighton so far and Max had to admit that it was looking its best in the early October sunshine. They had visited the pier and the Lanes and walked past the Theatre Royal, where Max had spent many happy nights sawing women in half. 'What a darling little theatre,' Lydia had said. But she hadn't seen the stage door, in a noisy side street, or the subterranean dressing rooms with their prevailing smell of gas and damp clothing. Thinking of those backstage corridors gave Max a stab of nostalgia so acute that it almost made him gasp.

Lydia was in such a good mood that she hadn't minded too much about Ruby joining them for a drink.

'Is she coming to supper too?' Lydia had asked.

'No, she's got plans of her own.'

He wasn't sure what those plans entailed but the sound of them certainly seemed to placate Lydia. She went as far as to say that she'd be pleased to see her stepdaughter.

Her smile didn't even falter too much when, in the cocktail bar at the Grand, Ruby greeted her with, 'Hallo, Mum.'

'Hallo, Ruby.' Lydia stood up to kiss her on the cheek. The two women couldn't look more different, thought Max. Lydia, blonde and ethereal, wearing black lace with ropes of pearls, Ruby, dark-haired and vibrant, in a pink dress so short that sitting down presented a real challenge. They were both beautiful enough to send heads spinning though and Max suddenly felt very proud of them.

'Have you seen your mother?' he asked Ruby, to remind them all that Ruby possessed her own maternal parent. Max wasn't exactly on close terms with Emerald, an ex-snake charmer, but he had to admit she'd been a very good mother to Ruby.

'I'm seeing her tomorrow,' said Ruby. 'Sunday lunch and all that.'

Max had invited Emma and Edgar to join him at the Grand for Sunday lunch. He hoped that Emma and Lydia would hit it off and allow him time to chat to Edgar.

Ruby asked for a champagne cocktail which was brought by a waiter who professed himself 'your greatest fan'. Max and Lydia drank martinis. Lydia started to tap her fingernails on the table.

'How's the TV show?' Max asked Ruby.

'We're just about to start filming a new season,' said Ruby. 'It's tough trying to think of new things for Iris to investigate. The scriptwriter wants to give her more love interest but I put my foot down. Romance is so boring.'

'Are you still dating Dex?' asked Lydia. For the last year Ruby had been seeing a jazz trumpeter called Dex Dexter. Max liked Dex although he wasn't a big fan of his music. The trouble with jazz, he thought, was that you never knew when it was going to end.

'Yes,' said Ruby, sounding less than enthusiastic herself. 'It's not a big thing though. We're just friends really.'

'I think you're very brave,' said Lydia. 'In America there would be a scandal if an actress went out with a black man.'

Ruby's eyes flashed. 'Then thank God we don't live in America. All my fans have been lovely about Dex.' This wasn't entirely true. Max knew that Ruby and Dex had faced some unpleasant reactions when seen in public together. Ruby would never admit this to Lydia though. And there was a definite emphasis on '*all* my fans'. Lydia was a genuine Hollywood star but Ruby was more famous in England.

'I saw Emma this lunchtime,' Ruby said to Max. 'She's investigating the Bert Billington case.'

'I know,' said Max. 'Seth told me.'

'Oh yes,' said Ruby. 'I keep forgetting you know Seth. Do you think Bert was murdered?'

'I haven't the faintest idea,' said Max. He didn't know why but he was reluctant to discuss the case in front of Lydia.

But Lydia leant forward with more enthusiasm than she'd shown all evening, 'Tell me about the murder,' she said.

'Here you are,' said Aisling. 'I got it out of the library on my way home.'

She put an orange book on the table. The title was written in that trendy type that looked as if it was reflected in water. The words swam in front of Meg's eyes. *The Feminine Mystique* by Betty Friedan.

'I can't believe they had it in Whitehawk library,' she said.

'They didn't,' said Aisling. 'I walked to the Dome.'

The main Brighton library was in the palatial surroundings of the Pavilion. The Dome had apparently once been the Prince Regent's stables but it was a grand building by anyone's reckoning, with ornate ceilings and a vast curving staircase. Meg had always been too intimidated to enter the library although, as Aisling always told her, 'it's free for everyone'.

Meg opened the book and read, 'part of the strange newness of the problem is that it cannot be understood in terms of the age-old material problems . . .' She looked at Aisling who was still in her greengrocer's apron. 'Have you read any of it?' she asked.

'I read a bit on the way home,' said Aisling. Aisling was famous in the family for being able to read while she walked. She'd once finished *Jane Eyre* while walking to the bus stop.

'What's it about?' asked Meg.

'It's about women wanting more than husbands and children,' said Aisling. She was now opening the cake tin in a search that Meg could have told her would be useless. 'Betty Friedan says that magazines are full of pictures of women happily doing housework but the magazines are all written by men. I suppose that's the "mystique" bit. I couldn't read any more because I nearly walked into a phone box.'

The Feminine Mystery, Aaron had called it and it was still a mystery to Meg. Had this book convinced Verity to kill her husband?

'Can you read some more?' she asked. 'And tell me what it says?'

'OK,' said Aisling, absent-mindedly hoovering crumbs from the empty tin with a moistened finger. Meg knew that reading was never a chore to her sister, but it was very kind of her to track down the book after a day's work. And, luckily, Meg had something to give her in return.

She got out her notebook and opened it at Seth's autograph, waiting for Aisling to register the magic words.

Although Emma could still not quite believe it, she and Sam were enjoying early evening drinks with Seth Billington and Verity Malone. Sam had rung just after lunch: 'Verity suggested that I go round at six. Could you get away for an hour? It would be good to meet Seth together.' So, when Edgar got in at five, Emma had thrust Jonathan at him and dashed upstairs to change. Now, wearing a summer dress that was just slightly too thin for the cooler evening air, she was sitting on the patio at Tudor Close, watching the starlings swirl over the church tower.

And there was Seth opposite her, wearing a blue fisherman's jumper and drinking beer. He was even better-looking in real life. Verity and Emma were drinking gin and tonic. Sam had opted for orange juice, 'otherwise I'm a danger on the bike'.

'We had the police here earlier,' said Verity. 'Bob Willis and Meg Connolly. I like her but I think he's an awful stick.'

'Emma used to work with Bob Willis,' said Sam.

'Did you?' Verity batted her sooty-lashed eyes at Emma.

'Yes,' said Emma. 'He's not a bad detective. Just a bit plodding.' She felt a slight twinge of disloyalty to Bob, who had, in truth, always been a good colleague to her.

'He's married to an ex-chorus girl,' said Sam. 'In fact, she used to be one of those living statues, standing around naked on stage pretending to be Cleopatra and what have you. I wrote them a terrible review when they appeared at the Hippodrome.'

'Oh, that makes me feel more kindly towards Mr Willis,' said Verity. 'Mind you, I bet his wife's gone ultra respectable. They always do.'

Did *you*? wondered Emma. Verity was right about Betty though. Bob's wife was the mainstay of the local WI, never seen without twinset and pearls.

'We went to see Pamela Curtis,' said Emma. 'She was very helpful.'

'I always liked Pamela,' said Verity. 'She's one of those, you know.'

'Mum,' said Seth. 'You can't say things like that. It's 1965.'

'I like queer people,' said Verity. 'I always have. I had lots of lovely pansy friends when I was on stage.'

'Mum!' Seth almost groaned, sounding very much like Marianne when Emma did something excruciatingly embarrassing. Like breathing.

'Pamela told us about Glenda and Angela,' said Emma, conscious of introducing a new chill to the evening. 'That must have been an awful shock for you all.'

'It was terrible,' said Verity, shutting her eyes so that the lashes seemed to fuse together. 'You were at drama school then, Seth.'

'I remember it though,' said Seth. 'I remember you

ringing and telling me about ... about the child.' His voice sounded hoarse, as if remembering were an effort.

'I just wondered if you knew anything about Glenda's family,' said Emma. 'Did she have parents? Brothers and sisters?'

'I think her family were from Liverpool,' said Verity. Her eyelashes had unglued themselves and she fixed Emma with a shrewd gaze, her pale eyes wide. 'Is that what you're thinking? That one of Glenda's family killed Bert? In revenge?'

'It's just a line of enquiry,' said Emma. 'I haven't seen the official report but I spoke to the pathologist and he said that Mr Billington didn't ... er ... vomit when he died. That suggests to me that he'd been ingesting the poison for some time. So, the killer might not necessarily have been in the house when he ... passed away. I think the choice of rat poison is significant too. Bert was playing King Rat when Glenda committed suicide.'

Now both Seth and Verity were staring at her.

'Max was right,' said Seth. 'You are good.'

Emma felt herself colouring. Had Max really said that?

'I don't like to ask,' she said, 'but can you think of anyone else who might have had a grudge against Bert?'

'Do you want me to make a list of Bert's mistresses and illegits?' said Verity. 'I'm quite happy to.'

'That would be great,' said Emma, glancing at Sam.

'I spoke to Aaron today,' said Sam. 'He said that Bert hadn't an enemy in the world.'

Seth gave a bark of laughter that sent the starlings spiralling upwards. Verity said, 'Aaron hero-worshipped his father. It's very sad.' She didn't say if it was the hero worship that was sad, or her husband's death.

'Have you spoken to David yet?' said Seth.

'Not yet,' said Emma.

'Well, you'll get a very different story from him,' said Seth. 'He told the whole sob story to the police. How he's the one that gets the letters from the penniless women claiming to have had a child with Bert Billington.'

'David runs the family company, doesn't he?' said Emma.

'Yes,' said Seth. 'It wasn't what he'd planned to do. He wanted to go to university after the war but it was getting too much for Dad and someone had to do it. And he's done well, streamlined the company, made it more efficient. Sheena helps him a lot. She's helped him cut out the dead wood.'

'Sam is seeing David and Sheena on Monday,' said Emma. She noted that while 'someone had to do it', that someone was not going to be Seth, who'd been able to escape to drama school.

'Well, don't have a meal with them,' said Verity. 'She's the worst cook in North London. Rat poison is cordon bleu by comparison.'

TEN

Rather to everyone's surprise, Emma and Lydia took to each other immediately. Max watched Lydia's face when Emma entered the restaurant, saw her registering the fair hair, the good fur coat, the well-cut but unexceptional blue dress and noticed her relaxing visibly. Lydia had been afraid of another Ruby, a dashing sixties girl (at thirty-five Ruby was still a girl to Max) with a sports car and a feisty attitude. Emma was obviously a relief.

Lydia was gracious when Emma talked about her children, and got out pictures of Rocco and Elena to be admired. Max felt a pang when he saw the photos emerging from their Kodak wallet. He should be home in Somerset with his children, not eating overdone roast beef in a hotel restaurant. But it was good to see Edgar and Emma again. He thought Emma looked happier than when he'd last seen her. Being a private eye obviously suited her. What surprised Max was how interested Lydia was in Emma's work. As soon as the children had been tucked back into handbags, Lydia was questioning Emma about surveillance, fingerprints and whether criminals always made a fatal mistake. Was Lydia hoping to star in a detective drama? Max couldn't see it somehow but wouldn't put it past Lydia to want to outdo Ruby as a screen sleuth. The main thing was that Lydia was happy and Max was free to talk to his old friend. When, after coffee and petits fours, Emma and Lydia announced their intention of taking a walk along the promenade, Max and Edgar took their brandies onto the glassed-over terrace. They watched as the two blonde women walked towards the Palace Pier, heads close together.

'I never saw that coming,' said Edgar. 'Our wives becoming best friends.'

Edgar hadn't changed much over the years, thought Max. He still had that lean, athletic frame and the self-deprecating grin that would have made him a fortune in sidekick roles. His sandy hair was now greying at the temples but that wasn't a bad look on him. Max's hair was still black apart from a rather dramatic streak in the centre. Lydia kept nagging him to dye it, but Max rather liked the grey. It was very Dracula's dad, he thought.

'I still can't get used to having a wife,' said Max. 'I never thought I'd get married.'

Edgar gave him a rather sharp look. 'Lydia seems very nice.'

'She's not that nice,' said Max. 'But she suits me.'

'I'd like to meet your children one day.'

'They're great,' said Max. 'Rocco's very sweet-natured, reminds me of my mother. Elena's a firecracker.'

'It's funny the resemblances you see,' said Edgar. 'Johnny's named after my brother but I keep seeing my dad in him, especially when he was a baby. Perhaps because they were both bald.'

'How's life as a superintendent?' said Max.

'OK,' said Edgar, looking into his glass. 'Busy. It's not like the old days.'

'Nothing is,' said Max. 'Are you investigating this Bert Billington case?'

'Yes,' said Edgar. 'Did you know him?'

'Everyone in the business knew him,' said Max. 'He was a prize creep, always sniffing around the showgirls even when he was in his seventies. He had real power, though, because he owned so many venues and produced so many shows. You couldn't afford to get on the wrong side of him. He was the sort of person who prided himself on being rude. "I can't stand you myself," he once said to me, "but the women seem to like you." I had to laugh as though he meant it as a joke but he wasn't much of a one for jokes, Bert.'

'Did you know his wife, Verity?'

'The one and only Verity Malone. I appeared on the bill with her a few times. She wasn't a great singer – she started as a chorus girl – but she was really gorgeous. She used to have this gold sequinned dress that was . . . well, mesmerising. Verity mesmerised men. She even mesmerised Bert.'

'Why did she marry him, if he was such a creep?'

'I've always assumed it was for the money. Verity told me once that she came from a very poor family, brought up in an East End slum. Bert was a lot older than her but he was rich. Plenty of women would have made the same decision.'

'What's the son like?'

'Seth? He's a pretty good actor even in this ridiculous Dracula film. I'd say that Seth has all Verity's charm. I told you he actually asked me to speak to you about the case. To tell you that his mother couldn't have done it. He suspects one of Bert's spurned mistresses.'

Edgar looked uncomfortable. 'I can't really discuss . . .'

'Don't worry. I know you can't. But if you start looking for Bert's enemies, it'll be a long list.'

'Emma's the one for lists. It's a bit awkward, her investigating the case too.'

'Are you worried she'll solve it before Bob?'

No,' said Edgar. Too quickly, Max thought. He waited and Edgar said, with a slightly self-conscious laugh, 'Bob's very twitchy. He thinks that Emma will find a vital clue before he does but I assume that Emma will tell us if she finds anything really significant.'

Max thought that this might be an assumption too far.

'What about Sam Collins?' he said. 'Where does she fit in?'

'She's great at the research,' said Edgar, 'and she has all sorts of contacts from being a journalist. I think they make a good team.'

'A formidable one,' said Max. He drained his brandy. The windows were open and he could hear the music from the merry-go-round, the screams of thrill-seekers on the big wheel. But he was thinking of winter in Liverpool and a mesmerising woman in a golden dress.

Emma and Edgar walked back to Kemp Town, threading their way through day trippers and people trying to sell them Kiss Me Quick hats. Back at home they found Emma's parents watching a show written, directed by and starring Marianne. Emma's mother, Sybil, was sitting on the sofa wearing a paper crown. Her father, Archie, had a bow in his sparse white hair. Jonathan was running around, completely naked, and Sophie was crying because she didn't have any lines in the play. Downstairs the remains of the lunch prepared by Emma were still on the table.

Emma already had a headache from a gin and tonic and two large glasses of wine. Now her head positively pulsated but she kept smiling while she made tea for her parents, got Johnny dressed, comforted Sophie and told Marianne that her play 'The Girl Who Won the World' was the best thing ever written. Then Edgar drove Sybil and Archie home and Emma turned on the TV. Edgar didn't like to watch anything but the news but Emma was a big fan of the box as a temporary babysitter. Sure enough, although a rather tedious historical drama called *Hereward the Wake* was showing on BBC1, it seemed to transfix all three children. Emma crept downstairs to tidy up and wash down two aspirin with a mug of black coffee. She was just sitting down at the table to read the paper when she saw trim feet in ballet pumps descending the basement steps. Sam.

Emma felt only a small pang for the *Sunday Times*. Sam meant real news. She hurried across the room to let her in.

'Hi,' said Sam, sitting down at the table. 'How was lunch with the beautiful people?'

Emma put on the kettle to make Sam coffee. 'It was fun,' she said. 'I actually liked Lydia. She's quite down-to-earth really. And she's very interested in crime.'

'Aren't we all?' said Sam. 'How was Max?'

'The same as ever. He never changes. He asked after you.'

'Did he?' said Sam, with what sounded like elaborate casualness. 'Anyway, enough of movie stars. I've got a real clue.'

Emma put a mug of coffee in front of Sam.

'Tell me.'

'I went into the *Argus* this morning to file some copy. I was on my way back, on the bike, and I saw Ted Grange in his allotment. I thought I'd stop to say hallo. Turns out he likes motorbikes so we chatted a bit.'

Sam's Triumph Tiger Cub was turning out to be quite an asset, Emma reflected. At the thought of Sam zipping through Woodingdean on her motorbike, she felt a twinge of envy, even though she'd spent the day having a meal with film stars at a luxury hotel.

'Anyway,' said Sam. 'I asked Ted about the woman in the brown coat, just to see if he remembered anything else. People do remember things, odd things, a long time past the actual event. And he said something interesting.' She paused, eking out the moment.

'Spit it out,' said Emma, although she'd recently told Marianne off for using this exact phrase.

'He said that Alma Saunders had been in the house that day. Sunday the nineteenth.'

'Really? I thought she didn't work on a Sunday.'

'She doesn't but Ted said she popped in with some shopping for Verity.'

'When was this?'

'Ted wasn't sure, but he thought it was about midday.'

'And the woman in the brown coat arrived at eleven-thirty?'

'That's right. It's possible that she was still in the house.'

'Good point,' said Emma. 'Are you still interviewing David Billington tomorrow?'

'Yes. I'll get the nine-thirty to Victoria.'

'I'll have Johnny with me, but I'll try to call on Alma Saunders. I can ask her about the mystery caller.'

'What mystery caller?' Edgar stood in the doorway.

'Just a lead we're following up,' said Emma. 'Want a cup of coffee?'

'Thanks,' said Edgar. 'I think I'm hungover.'

'Me too,' said Emma.

'How the other half lives,' said Sam.

But Emma thought that she didn't sound envious.

ELEVEN

Max was not in the sunniest of moods as he waited for his train on Monday morning. He hated public transport at the best of times – the queuing, the grubbiness, the risk of sharing a seat with a garrulous stranger – but his beloved S-Type Jaguar, a new purchase that had almost supplanted his beloved pre-war Bentley in his affections, had developed some kind of engine trouble and was languishing in a Whitby garage. He couldn't delay their weekend because it was the only break in the schedule so he and Lydia had been forced to undertake the long train journey via York to St Pancras and then on to the south coast. Seth, Lydia informed Max, was driving to Brighton in his Aston Martin but they could hardly ask him for a lift. Besides, it was a two-seater.

Lydia had quite enjoyed the journey down. She'd remarked on the cuteness of the trains and the dinkiness of the buffet car, where they'd been served brown Windsor soup in thick china bowls. But, last night, Lydia had informed Max that she wanted to stay in Brighton for a few days. 'The sea air will do me good,' she said vaguely. 'I've been feeling a bit under the weather lately.' Max knew that Lydia's health was her hobby, she took the curation of Lydia Lamont very seriously indeed, so he didn't query this. He thought that Lydia enjoyed staying in the Grand and liked the bohemian chic of the town. Lydia said she'd stay in Brighton for two days and then motor to Somerset to see the children. Max found himself promising to hire a car for her.

So now, Max was left to take a long, tedious journey on his own. At least the train was the Brighton Belle, the legendary all-electric luxury Pullman, and he had *The Times* and *Punch* to keep him company. He thought of Edgar, who loved to do *The Times* cryptic crossword, racing through it with flourishes of his pen and, it seemed to Max, barely time to think. Edgar had once told him that it was a crossword that had led to his recruitment to the Magic Men. Edgar had been filling in the clues when he'd been spotted by Colonel Cartwright, on the lookout for a bright officer to lead the group. Well, Cartwright was dead now and Edgar was the superintendent of Brighton Police. He seemed happy enough in his job, and in his marriage, but then Edgar had always hankered after domestic bliss. Unlike Max.

He was so deep in thought that he didn't notice the woman approaching him until she said 'Hi' very loudly by his ear. Max jumped ('Never show surprise on stage,' the Great Diablo used to say) and saw that it was Sam Collins, intrepid journalist and private investigator.

'Hallo, Max. Did I give you a shock?'

'Not at all.' Max felt at a slight disadvantage. 'I was just thinking.'

'My mum used to say, "Don't think, it makes your head stink." I think that was mainly aimed at me though. Thinking is bad for women.'

She grinned up at him in a rather challenging way. As usual she was dressed in an eclectic mix of unflattering clothes: duffel coat, check trousers, tennis shoes. Max could imagine Lydia's look of horror but he rather liked Sam's style, or lack of it. He also liked the way she dived straight into a conversation without the usual niceties. He asked if she was going to London.

'Yes. So lucky to get the Belle. I always think of that film, *London to Brighton in Four Minutes*.'

The speeded-up film was made in the 1950s. Max remembered it well. The train was no longer the last word in modernity but it was still a symbol of pre-war luxury. He said as much.

'Yes,' said Sam. 'Even second class is a treat.'

Max proffered his tickets. 'I've got a spare first class seat if you'd care to join me.'

Emma took the girls to school in the car (a great treat) and then drove to Rottingdean to interview Alma Saunders. Jonathan was in the back seat, occupied by two

Dinky cars, a rag doll and a disintegrating bread roll. Alma lived in a fisherman's cottage just off the High Street. Emma parked by the village hall, heaved Jonathan out of the car and walked the few hundred yards to the house, hampered by Jonathan dropping his cars and wanting to stop every few minutes to pat seagulls.

'Sorry about bringing my little boy,' said Emma. Jonathan was looking speculatively around the small sitting room. Emma held his hand tightly; there was an alarming number of ornaments around.

'That's OK, dear,' said Alma. 'I know what it's like when you have to work. I used to bring my boys with me when I cleaned. Barry used to stand on the hoover.'

'How old are your children?' asked Emma.

'Freddie's forty now, Barry's thirty-six. Both married with kids of their own.'

How old was Alma? wondered Emma. She'd looked remarkably youthful when she opened the door, with bright red hair and a slim, almost girlish, figure. Now, under the electric light, she'd aged a bit and Emma could see where the lipstick had bled into the fine lines around her mouth. If Freddie was forty, she thought, Alma must be at least sixty. And Barry was exactly the same age as Seth. Had the two boys played together as well as riding the hoover? Alma fetched Barry's old train set for Jonathan and he sat down happily to orchestrate terrible railway disasters. Alma also provided tea and biscuits. Emma was tempted to stay all day.

'You know that Verity has asked me to investigate Bert's death,' she said. 'I run a detective agency.' It sounded very grand put like that, and very far removed from the rooms above Midas and Sons.

'She told me,' said Alma. 'I'm glad. Verity needs all the support she can get.'

'You must know the Billington family very well,' said Emma.

'I know Verity very well,' said Alma. ' I've worked for her on and off for nearly fifty years. I started out as her dresser.'

This was interesting. Whilst Verity had described Alma as her 'daily' and 'a treasure', she hadn't hinted at such a long and intimate relationship. Interesting, too, that Alma said she knew Verity well, not the wider family.

'Verity was twenty-six when I first met her,' said Alma. 'I thought that she was the most beautiful creature I'd ever seen. She was just becoming famous but she was really simple and unspoilt. She'd had a rather religious upbringing and was still quite naive about some things.'

That explained the children's names, thought Emma. Alma told her about life on the road with Verity ('I could tell you a few stories') and about working for the Billington family in Lytham.

'We were surprised when they came to Rottingdean but it meant I could work for Verity again, be part of the family. My Dave had gone by then.'

Emma noted that Alma still considered herself to be

working exclusively for Verity. Also that she considered herself part of the family. She asked how Alma had got on with Bert.

Alma was silent for a minute, watching a horrific train crash unfolding on her carpet. Then she said, 'I got on well with Bert. He wasn't such a bad person really.'

It was hardly a ringing endorsement, thought Emma. She waited.

'He'd fought in the Boer War,' said Alma. 'I think it affected him, like the First War affected all the chaps of my generation. Dave never forgot the trenches. He had awful nightmares sometimes, couldn't bear anywhere dark or enclosed. Bert seemed so tough, but I think that was because he saw such terrible atrocities, most of them done by the British. "I'm finished with patriotism," he used to say. "I'm going to make my money in this war." That was the Second World War but he'd made enough in the First. Verity met him in 1920 and he was rich by then.'

'I imagine you have to be quite ruthless in his line of work,' said Emma. She knew that this was the excuse offered by every successful businessman, including her father, to absolve any kind of sharp practice.

'Yes,' said Alma. 'And Bert was ruthless. But he always provided for his family. And he did love Verity, in his way.'

'Verity told me that Bert had extra-marital affairs,' said Emma. 'She's offered to make me a list.'

Alma laughed. 'That sounds like Verity. She's very practical. In lots of ways, she and Bert were a good match. Bert did have affairs – we all knew that – but I don't think he ever thought of leaving Verity. Like I say, he loved her.'

'What about Glenda Gillespie?' asked Emma. 'Did Bert love her?'

'Glenda was a lovely girl,' said Alma, rather sharply. 'I think you should let her rest in peace.'

Once again, Emma waited. She saw, with misgiving, that Jonathan was getting bored with the train and looking speculatively at the china ornaments.

'Verity was very upset about Glenda,' said Alma at last. 'It was a terrible tragedy.'

'Tell me about Verity and Bert,' said Emma. 'How did they get on in later life? After they'd moved to Rottingdean?'

'They got on fairly well,' said Alma. 'But it was hard for Verity. Bert had looked after her all her life and suddenly she had to look after him.'

'What about their sons? Did they help?'

'Aaron visited quite a bit. He only lives in Hove so he'd ride over most weekends on one of his motorbikes. But Aaron's not one to make you feel better about a situation. Seth, he brings the sunshine. David's comforting too, in his way. I think Aaron just caused more problems.'

'In what way?'

Alma sighed. 'Aaron was always a bit of a lost boy. David was clever. After the army he went into the family business and was running it in a few years. Seth was always destined to be a star. Aaron was never good at school and didn't seem to know what to do with himself when he left. I think Bert and Verity spent a fair bit of money on his various schemes.'

'Aaron runs a garage now, doesn't he? My partner Sam visited him there at the weekend.'

'He runs it,' said Alma, with slight asperity. 'But he never seems to do anything but tinker with his own bikes. Bert paid for it all, of course.'

'What about the day Bert died,' said Emma, trying for a casual note. 'Were you around that day at all?'

Was it her imagination or did Alma pause slightly too long before replying? Jonathan was trying to pull two mangled trains apart.

'I don't usually work on a Sunday,' said Alma, 'but I popped in with some groceries at about eleven fifty.'

'Did you see anyone there?'

'Ted, the gardener. He was mowing the lawn.'

'Anyone else?'

Alma bent down to help Jonathan with the trains. When she straightened up, she said, 'I saw Verity. She was in the kitchen listening to the wireless. She helped me put things away. Not that she ever knew where anything was.'

'You didn't see a woman in a dark brown coat?'

'No,' said Alma. 'A woman in a brown coat? Who could that have been? Verity would never wear brown. It's all bright colours with her. That or fur.'

'I was hoping you'd tell me. Ted said that he saw a woman entering the house at about eleven-thirty that day.'

'I didn't see anyone,' said Alma. 'And Verity didn't

really have any local friends, not anyone who would just drop in.'

She folded her arms as if to put an end to the matter. Emma thought it was probably time to go. Jonathan was looking wistfully at a herd of china horses grazing on the mantelpiece.

As Emma stood up, Alma said, 'Thank you for helping Verity. I do worry about her, you know.'

'Horse!' said Jonathan, pointing.

'Yes, lovie,' said Alma. 'Do you want one? Have a present from me.' And she put the delicate, china animal in Jonathan's outstretched hand.

There was an illicit feeling about the journey to London, thought Sam. This was almost entirely due to the Brighton Belle and the presence of Max Mephisto. There was something about the gold and green upholstery, the draped curtains and the fringed lamps on the tables. It gave their meeting an intimacy that it wouldn't otherwise have had.

Max said that he was on his way back to Whitby.

'Is it exciting?' asked Sam. 'Making a film?' The waiter had brought coffee and, at Sam's request, toast and jam. Max said that he never ate breakfast.

'It's very boring,' said Max. 'Hours of hanging about before you say your one line of the day. And it's not filmed in sequence, so it's hard to remember where you are and what you're meant to be feeling. Not that my character feels very much. They're an unemotional lot, vampires.'

'What's Seth Billington like to work with?'

'I'm disappointed in you, Sam,' said Max, pouring more coffee. 'That's what everyone asks.'

'I met Seth on Saturday night,' said Sam. 'I thought he seemed rather sad.'

'Sad?'

'Not about his dad dying. Just a bit melancholy generally. His face looked sad when he wasn't smiling.'

'Actors are generally a melancholy bunch. Especially comedians.'

'I've heard that,' said Sam, buttering toast. 'What about magicians?'

'I'm not a magician any more.'

'Well, that certainly sounded melancholy,' said Sam. 'But it's not such a bad thing to be a movie star. I'm sure it beats being a jobbing reporter.'

'I thought you were a private detective now?'

'I am,' said Sam. 'And I'm on my way to interview a suspect.'

She knew that she probably shouldn't say anything about the case to Max but the train worked its magic and soon she was telling him that she was on her way to see David Billington.

'I've only come across him once or twice,' said Max, 'and he seemed pleasant enough. I got the impression that he had to do all the dirty work at the agency.'

'The dirty work?'

'Dealing with disgruntled actors and melancholy comedians. That sort of thing.'

'Seth said that David was always having to pay off women who claimed to have had Bert's children.'

'Well, that too.'

'Did you know Bert? What was he like?'

'An utter bastard,' said Max. 'More toast?'

Sam felt quite disappointed when the Brighton Belle pulled into Victoria Station. Max was on his way to St Pancras and offered to share a taxi with her.

'I'll get the tube,' said Sam. 'It's only a few stops to Leicester Square, change at Green Park.'

'You know your way around London.'

'I was at university here,' said Sam. 'UCL. It's my happy hunting ground. It's an easy journey to St Pancras too.'

'All the same,' said Max, 'I'd rather get a taxi.'

'Bye then,' said Sam. She had a sudden feeling that he was going to kiss her goodbye. She could almost feel his lips on her cheek, smell his lemon-scented aftershave. But Max simply lifted his hat.

'Goodbye, Sam. Hope we meet again soon.'

Instead of joining the queue, he raised his hand and a taxi stopped in front of him. Sam watched the black cab join the traffic and then she descended into the Underground.

Sam enjoyed the journey, tube train and all. Growing

up in Southend, the capital had been her Mecca. Studying English at UCL had been a dream come true, living in shabby digs off Holborn, spending hours in Lyons' Corner Houses discussing animal metaphors in *Wuthering Heights*. After university she got a job on a Croydon newspaper and then made the move to Brighton, travelling further and further south. Now she enjoyed making her way through the streets of Soho, watching the errand boys delivering parcels and, at the corner of Sherwood Street, an actual dray piled high with beer barrels and pulled by magnificent bay horses. She liked the seediness of the signs saying 'Private Club' and the occasional blast of jazz music from upstairs rooms. Were there stripteases going on at eleven in the morning? She'd always thought that the sex industry, like newspapers, was primarily a night-time business.

The headquarters of Bert Billington Productions was in Golden Square, where tall classical buildings looked down on a dusty square of green. This was definitely the respectable face of Soho. Sam rang the bell and was buzzed up to the third-floor offices. The receptionist was extremely polite, offering coffee with a welcoming smile. When she got up to make the drink, Sam saw that she was wearing an orange minidress held together by large gold hoops. It made Sam feel suddenly dowdy and provincial.

David Billington, though, was not an intimidating figure. He was tall and dark like his brothers but had a slight stoop and his hair was receding fast. He looked older than his forty-three years but then David had served in the war and that aged people. Sam often noticed the difference between men in their forties and those in their thirties. The men who had been old enough to fight had a haunted look – even Edgar had it – while their younger brothers often looked callow and slightly guilty. By Sam's reckoning, Seth had just missed the call-up though he would still have had to do National Service.

'I fought in North Africa and Italy,' said David, in answer to her question. 'I was only twenty-three when it was over but I felt like an old man. I could have gone to university – there was a scheme to encourage officers to apply – but I decided to go straight into the family business. And, well, I've been here ever since.' He gestured at the well-proportioned room with its view over the tops of the plane trees. It wasn't exactly a prison cell, thought Sam, but there was something of that in David's tone.

'Was it hard working alongside your father?' she asked.

'Dad wasn't easy to work with,' said David with a smile. 'But we found a way. I dealt with the property side. Bert negotiated with the artistes. His assistant was a great help. Have you met Pamela?'

'Yes.'

'She's a wonderful woman. I can't tell you the number of times she smoothed things over. Then I met Sheena, my wife, and she came to work on the financial side. She's a trained bookkeeper.'

'Is Sheena here today?' Sam had wanted to meet both

Billingtons. Always talk to the wife, any journo knows that.

'She's joining us in a minute. She's just tied up with a phone call.'

'I'm so sorry about your father,' said Sam, realising that she should have said this earlier. 'It must have been a terrible shock for you.'

'It was,' said David, fiddling with his tie. 'I mean, Dad was ninety and not in great health but . . . It was still a shock. And then to find out that he died in that way . . .'

'You know your mother has asked us to investigate his death?'

'Yes,' said David, with a more genuine smile this time. 'Mum said that she needed some women on the case.'

'Do you have any idea who could have killed your father?'

'No,' said David. 'I mean, Dad had enemies. Any successful man does . . .'

What about successful women? thought Sam. She said, 'Your brother Seth said that you had letters from women claiming to have had Bert's children.'

'Typical Seth,' said David. 'Always dramatising everything. We've had a couple of approaches over the years, that's all.'

Sheena joined them at that moment. Sam was worried that her presence might stop David talking about his father's mistresses but Sheena, an elegant brunette in a slim black dress, took over the subject without embarrassment.

'There was one woman who was clearly chancing it but two of them seemed to have valid cases. Bert made provision for the children.'

'Could I have the names?' said Sam. It would be interesting to see if they appeared on Verity's list of 'by-blows'.

'If you like,' said Sheena.

'Have either of you heard of a woman called Glenda who had a daughter called Angela?'

The Billingtons exchanged glances.

'She was the woman who . . . who killed herself,' said David. 'That was a terrible tragedy. I remember it well. It was during *Dick Whittington* in Liverpool.'

'The show went on,' said Sheena, repeating Pamela's words in a flat monotone.

'We offered the family money,' said David. 'Just to help with . . . with funeral expenses and suchlike. But they refused.'

'Can you blame them?' said Sheena.

'We're interested in contacting Glenda's family,' said Sam. 'Would you know how to reach them?'

'Their names will be in the files,' said Sheena. 'I told that to the police. Do you honestly think they could be involved?'

'It's a line of enquiry.'

'If you ask me,' said Sheena, 'it's Alma you need to talk to. Verity would never do anything without Alma's say-so. The woman's a Svengali. And all that creepy mystic stuff. She had a real hold on Verity and Bert.'

'Alma would never hurt Dad,' said David. 'She adored him. All of us. She was a second mother to me.'

'Exactly,' said Sheena.

Emma was lucky enough to find a parking space near the Lanes. Then she and Jonathan enjoyed a Welsh rarebit in a café before walking to the offices of Holmes and Collins, Johnny still clutching the china horse. In the upstairs room they sat at opposite ends of the partner desk, Jonathan scrawling random shapes on blotting paper and Emma thinking about Alma Saunders. She clearly adored Verity and saw herself as her protector. She'd been surprisingly perceptive about Bert too. Alma was the first person to mention Bert's experiences in the Boer War and to offer them as an excuse for his ruthlessness in business. But Alma hadn't wanted to talk about Glenda Gillespie and she'd been distinctly cagy about her visit to Tudor Close on the day of Bert's death. Why?

A knock at the door surprised both mother and son. Leaning out of the window Emma could see the edge of a blonde fur coat. Who would wear fur on a warm Monday afternoon? For a moment she thought of Verity Malone who, according to Alma, only wore bright colours or fur. Leaving Jonathan at the desk, she ran downstairs to admit the visitor.

'Hallo, Emma.' Lydia Lamont swept past her, the voluminous mink taking up almost all of the passage. 'Surprised to see me?'

'Very,' croaked Emma.

She led Lydia upstairs where Johnny was now approaching a wall clutching his crayon.

'Adorable,' said Lydia, moving herself and her coat away from him.

Emma put Jonathan on the floor with the horse and one of his toy cars. Lydia sat at the desk and lit a cigarette, first slotting it into an elegant amber holder. Emma had an old music hall poster on the wall, a present from Max. It said, 'Nosmo King' in large red letters. Nosmo King, No Smoking. Emma didn't think it was worth explaining the implied message to Lydia.

'I thought you were going back to Whitby today,' said Emma, sitting opposite Lydia and trying not to cough.

'I decided to stay in Brighton for a few days,' said Lydia. 'I want to help you with the case.'

'With what case?'

'With the Bert Billington murder, of course. Believe me, I know where all the bodies are buried.'

It was a cliché, Emma knew, but somehow it didn't sound like one.

'What do you mean?' she asked.

'Everyone knew about Bert Billington. He was a monster. Verity was terrified of him. The children were terrified of him. You heard about the girl who killed herself and her child?'

'Glenda Gillespie.' Perhaps she shouldn't have given the name but she wanted to show that she was up on the case.

'Yes,' said Lydia, drawing her coat around her although the room seemed quite warm to Emma. 'But there are others.'

'How do you know this?' It occurred to Emma that Lydia, a Hollywood star, wouldn't normally come across a British theatre producer and his family. From what Lydia had said yesterday, she had been born and raised 'dirt poor' in the Midwest and had gone to Hollywood 'to seek my fortune' while still a teenager. Emma suspected that there was a world of hardship behind these light phrases but, nevertheless, it wasn't a world that overlapped with the Billingtons.

'How do I know?' said Lydia, blowing a smoke ring. Emma hated cigarettes but she had to admit that Lydia made smoking look very cool. 'Because of Max, of course.'

'Because Max is making a film with Seth?'

Lydia narrowed her eyes but that could just be because the room was now full of smoke.

'No,' she said. 'Because Max had an affair with Verity.'

'What!?' Emma thought of Verity with her blonde wig and false eyelashes. Could she conceivably have had an affair with Max? It was possible, she supposed. Verity was seventy-five, twenty years older than Max. He'd once had an affair with his landlady, a woman whose age had been a closely guarded secret but who had been considerably older than him. Emma had wondered at the time if Max was attracted to older women because his mother had died when he was young. But, looking at the vision opposite her, Emma doubted her own theory. Lydia could only be in her mid-thirties. Her own age, in fact. And then there had been Florence . . .

'It was when he was a kid,' said Lydia, her American accent suddenly very pronounced. 'Only about eighteen. Verity must have been one of those predatory older women. I've seen a lot of them in my time. And Max was probably vulnerable. Hard to believe, I know,' she added drily.

'How do you know?' asked Emma. 'About the affair, I mean?'

'I found a picture in one of his old wallets,' said Lydia. 'There was Verity, all dolled up like a vaudeville tart. And written across it was: "To the one and only Max Mephisto." Then a row of kisses. Very tacky.'

This had been Verity's line, Emma knew. *The one and only Verity Malone.*

'That doesn't necessarily mean they were having an affair,' said Emma.

'Of course they were!' said Lydia. 'And Max seems to know a hell of a lot about the family. The oldest son runs the business now. I met him once. He's very creepy. He could be in league with Verity.'

'In league to kill Bert?'

'Yes. Then David would be free to take over the company.'

'I thought he'd already taken it over.'

'Easier with the old man out of the way.'

'My colleague is interviewing David today,' said Emma. 'I'll see what she reports back.'

'Or else . . .' Lydia seemed to be relaxing. She'd even shrugged off her coat to reveal a black sweater dress. 'Or else it was someone else entirely. A hit man.'

'A hit man?' Emma had the strangest feeling that she had strayed onto the set of an American gangster film. Lydia Lamont was the star, of course. Emma was just a bit part, a stooge to ask the right questions. Or the wrong ones.

'Bert was rich,' said Lydia. 'And rich people always have secrets. Trust me, I've been in Hollywood long enough to know that. And I heard Wilbur, the director of *Prince of Darkness*, talking about Bert. He said that he owed money to some very dangerous people.'

'He didn't say who these people were?'

'No, but I thought that's where I could be useful to you. I could keep an eye out. Ask a few questions. Seth Billington is the star of the film, you know.'

'I know.' Emma couldn't resist adding, 'I interviewed him on Saturday.'

Lydia shot her a look that didn't seem entirely friendly. 'Did he say anything interesting?'

'Only that his father had affairs, which seems to be common knowledge.'

Lydia was starting to shrug on her coat again. 'How

about it, Emma? I'm in Whitby all the time, hanging around while Max does his stuff. Shall I be your eyes and ears? A sleeping partner.'

And Emma heard herself agreeing to go into partnership with Lydia Lamont.

TWELVE

'Lydia Lamont actually sat here?' said Sam. She looked around the room as if expecting to see fairy dust sprinkled on the floor.

'Right in that chair. Wearing a mink coat that must have cost a thousand pounds.'

'And a few hundred animals their lives.'

Emma felt guilty about her own fur coat, which had been a wedding present from her mother. She said, hastily, 'Lydia said that she knew where the bodies were buried. I asked her what she meant and she said that Max had had an affair with Verity.'

'But she's years older than him!'

'She's twenty years older. Lydia found a picture of Verity in one of Max's old wallets signed to "The one and only Max Mephisto". Verity was always described as "the one and only".'

'Lydia goes through Max's old wallets?'

'Apparently so.'

'And why is it relevant that Max once had an affair with Verity?'

'Lydia thinks it's given her an insight into the family.'

'I met Max on the train to London,' said Sam. Emma thought that she was trying very hard to sound casual about it.

'I can't imagine Max on a train,' said Emma.

'His car was in the garage,' said Sam. 'Of course, he was travelling first class. Come to think of it, he must have been expecting Lydia to go with him because he had an extra ticket.'

'Which he gave to you?'

'That's right. First class on the Brighton Belle. Best morning I've had for years.'

Once again, Emma felt a slight twinge of envy. It had been ages since she'd been on a train and she'd never been on the Belle.

'To get back to work,' she said briskly. 'Lydia said that Verity was terrified of Bert. One of her theories was that Verity killed him, probably helped by David.'

'By David?'

'Apparently he's very creepy.'

'I quite liked him,' said Sam.

'Another theory was that Bert was killed by a mafia hit man.'

'What?' Sam, who had been rocking to and fro in her chair in a rather alarming way, now almost toppled over.

'Not necessarily mafia but I think that was the

implication. Apparently, the director of the Dracula film said that Bert owed money to some dangerous people.'

'Who's this director?'

'Wilbur Wallace. He directed that other film of Max's. The one about a grown-up Little Lord Fauntleroy.'

'*Golden*. Starring Bobby Hamro. It was actually quite a good film.'

'Well, Lydia thinks that Bert might have been killed by someone he owed money to. She offered to find out more. To be our eyes and ears in Whitby.'

'Gosh,' said Sam. 'I never thought I'd be sharing the billing with Lydia Lamont.'

'My thoughts entirely. I was quite dazzled at the time. I would have agreed to anything. But afterwards I thought, why would Lydia want to help us? What's in it for her?'

'Maybe she wants to play a detective in a film. Like Ruby.'

'Ruby was in Brighton at the weekend too. She came to lunch on Saturday.'

'You did have a starry weekend. What was Ruby doing in Brighton?'

'Visiting her mum, she said. I know she lives in Hove. But something she said made me wonder if she was also seeing Seth.'

'Ruby French and Seth Billington,' said Sam. 'I'm almost tempted to leak it to the gossip columns.'

'Please don't.'

'I'm joking. Shall I tell you about David and Sheena?'

'Yes,' said Emma. 'Please.' She got out her notebook.

'Well, like I said, I quite liked David. He seemed to be the son who was left clearing up after his dad's mistakes.'

'Seth said something similar, didn't he?'

'Yes, but I didn't get the sense that David hated his father. He seemed quite shaken by his death.'

'Did you ask about Glenda and Angela?'

'Yes. They both obviously remembered it well. David said that the Billingtons had offered Glenda's family money but they'd refused. Sheena said something like, "who can blame them?"'

'Interesting.'

'She said something else interesting. She said that Verity was controlled by Alma Saunders. She described her as a Svengali.'

'I went to see Alma yesterday,' said Emma. 'She used to be Verity's dresser and she worked for the family when they lived in Lytham.'

'And is she sinister and controlling?'

'No, she seemed very nice. She gave that to Johnny.' Emma pointed at the china horse, which was on the desk, grazing at the blotting paper. Jonathan had had a major tantrum when he realised that it had been left behind.

'Who's looking after the havoc-maker today?' asked Sam.

'Astarte,' said Emma with a grin. 'She offered.'

Sam gave a bark of laughter. 'That's perfect. Do you know what Sheena said about Alma? That she was into all this weird mysticism, tarot cards and crystal balls and all that. Well, if you live near Brighton and you're interested in the supernatural, where do you go?'

'To Madame Astarte,' said Emma.

Astarte and Jonathan had clearly been having a riotous morning. They were both wearing red lipstick, and on the floor was a wild collage of seaweed, shells and red and blue handprints.

'We went to the beach,' said Astarte. 'I found a hag stone. It's meant to protect you against witches.'

She looked at them through the hole in the stone.

'I thought you were a witch,' said Sam.

'A white witch. That's different.'

Astarte might be a witch, thought Emma, but she was a pretty good babysitter. There was newspaper on the floor and Jonathan's hands had been thoroughly cleaned. He was sitting at the table eating an apple cut into the shape of a crown.

Emma had met Astarte twelve years ago, when she was investigating the death of her grandmother, a fortune-teller with a caravan on the Palace Pier. The case had been complicated and dangerous, but it had brought a friend-ship with Astarte and with her father Tol, short for Ptolemy. Tol had subsequently made a fortune opening the first coffee bars in Brighton, married a rich widow and emigrated to the south of France. But Astarte, still single despite her otherworldly beauty, carried on the spiritualist business.

Emma made coffee and the three women sat at the kitchen table. They were old friends. Jonathan banged his plastic mug in an amiable, percussive way.

'Astarte,' said Emma, 'do you know a woman called Alma Saunders?'

'I can't divulge names of my clients.' Astarte gave her a prim look.

'So she is a client, then?' said Sam.

'Do you really think I'd fall into that trap?'

'What about Verity Malone?' said Emma.

'Why are you asking?' Astarte fixed her with her extraordinary blue-green gaze. Emma had never met anyone with eyes like Astarte. 'Is it to do with Bert Billington? I heard that he'd died.'

'Did you ever meet Bert?' said Emma.

'Once,' said Astarte with a slight shudder. 'He wanted to be my manager. He thought I had a future as a stage medium. But it wasn't my path.'

Another way of saying that Astarte would rather be burnt at the stake than appear on stage under the aegis of Bert Billington.

'What about Verity?'

'I've met her a few times. A nice lady.'

'And Alma?'

'I don't remember the name.'

'Verity is employing us,' said Sam. 'She thinks that the police will frame her for Bert's murder.'

Astarte gave them a rather unfocused look. 'Verity is capable of violence,' she said.

'I thought you said she was lovely,' said Emma.

'She is lovely. And passionate. Love and hate are often confused.'

There was a brief silence then Jonathan knocked his juice on the floor, Astarte's eyes came back into focus and Emma hurried to get a cloth.

Emma thought about the Billingtons all day. Even when she had collected the girls and was giving them their tea, her thoughts were with the timbered house where King Rat had died in his armchair. Was Alma Saunders an evil Svengali or a devoted retainer? Was Verity, so vulnerable in her faded glory, really capable of violence? What about David, described as very creepy by Lydia? Or Seth, who 'brought the sunshine'? Sam had liked Aaron, but that was because they had bonded over motorbikes. Could the youngest son have nursed a grievance over the years?

When Edgar got in, it was all Emma could do not to ply him with questions about the case. But she managed to wait until the children were all in bed, Jonathan and Sophie asleep, Marianne reading *Ballet Shoes*. Emma and Edgar were in the sitting room, watching the nine o'clock news. The United States were bombing Cambodia. A satellite with the unromantic name of Orbital Vehicle 1 was orbiting the earth.

'How's Bob getting on with the Bert Billington murder?' asked Emma as, on screen, a small white dot tracked across the blackness of space.

'He says the investigation's going well,' said Edgar, rather cautiously, Emma thought. 'They've interviewed all the sons.'

'Well, we've done that too,' said Emma. 'Has he got anything else?'

Edgar turned to look at her. 'Have you found something?'

'Lydia came to see me yesterday,' said Emma, avoiding the question.

'Max's Lydia? I thought they'd gone back to Whitby.'

'Max has gone back. Lydia's staying in Brighton for a bit. She wants to help with the case.'

'With the Billington case? Why?'

'She says she knows about the family. She said that Max once had an affair with Verity.'

'Did he? Well, he had an affair with everyone else, I suppose.'

'Don't you think it's odd that he didn't mention it to you?'

'I suppose so. He's pretty secretive about some things though. I didn't know about Emerald until Ruby turned up.'

And you fell in love with her, Emma added silently. She

could still remember the anguish of the days when she had been in love with her boss and he had, seemingly, been unaware of her existence as a woman, having eyes only for his glamorous fiancée.

Edgar was silent for a few minutes, staring at the TV, now showing the weather forecast. High winds and storms approaching. Then he said, 'I think we should have a meeting. Bob and me, you and Sam. Pool our information.'

'No,' said Emma, before she could stop herself.

'That was very quick,' said Edgar. 'Why not?' The laughter in his voice enraged Emma still further.

'We're pursuing different lines of investigation,' she said.

'All the more reason to put our heads together,' said Edgar. 'You're really good at getting information out of people, Emma. I remember that when you worked for me.'

'I didn't work for you,' said Emma. 'I worked for the police.' She was aware that she was sounding pompous but she didn't like the implication that Edgar was the big boss and she was the underling, useful only for winkling out stray pieces of information.

Edgar didn't answer but nodded as if he understood. This, Emma remembered, was a favourite interrogation technique of his. It worked because, a few seconds later, she said, 'I thought Bob was convinced that Verity killed Bert.'

'He's keeping an open mind,' said Edgar. 'And if you've got any information that might help Verity . . .'

Edgar was clever, Emma had to admit, and, unlike Bob, he really did have an open mind. Emma thought quickly.

There might be some advantages to sharing information with the police. She would be able to get hold of the post-mortem results, for one thing.

'I'll talk to Sam,' she said at last. 'But I suppose we could have a meeting. Will Meg be there?'

'I wouldn't think so,' said Edgar. 'She's only a WDC after all.'

Emma suddenly felt strangely protective of Meg. She thought that Meg was, instinctively, a better detective than Bob. And she would have been working hard on the case, only to be shut out of all the interesting meetings.

'I think she should be there,' she said.

'All right,' said Edgar. 'We'll have a meeting, you, me, Sam, Bob and Meg.'

'Will you show me the post-mortem results?'

'If you tell me all your best clues.'

Again, Emma resented the teasing note, but she agreed, with dignity. She couldn't help thinking she'd been out-witted somehow. They let the subject drop and, after another hour of television, went to bed. Edgar fell asleep immediately, but Emma lay awake for a long time. It was a windy night and she could hear the tiles rattling on the roof. A bin fell over in the street and, out to sea, she thought she heard the foghorn moaning.

In the morning, she still felt on edge, as if she hadn't slept at all. Somehow, she wasn't surprised when Edgar took a call to say that Alma Saunders had been found dead in her Rottingdean home.

THIRTEEN

Meg didn't know who was more shocked when she opened the front door in her dressing gown to find the DI on the doormat.

'I tried to telephone,' said DI Willis. He actually had his hand raised as if frozen in the act of knocking. 'But you aren't in the book.'

'We haven't got a phone,' said Meg. 'I was just getting the milk.' She pulled her tatty towelling robe tighter. Like many of her clothes, it had been made for someone far shorter.

The DI stooped and solemnly handed her the milk bottles.

'We need to go to Rottingdean urgently,' he said. 'Alma Saunders has been found dead.'

'Blimey,' said Meg, before she could help herself. 'Sorry. You'd better come in. Sir.'

She led him into the kitchen where Aisling and Collette, both in their school uniforms, were eating breakfast.

Connor, the youngest in the family, whose angelic blond looks belied his true nature, was still in his pyjamas. Mary, in a pink quilted robe, was making toast and haranguing them about homework, cigarette in hand. In the background Padre Pio was squawking loudly. At the sight of a strange man in a dark suit, they all fell silent, even the budgerigar.

'This is DI Willis,' said Meg. 'I've got to get dressed. I won't be a minute.'

And she fled upstairs. She heard her mother say, 'Will you have a cup of tea, DI Willis?' but she couldn't hear the boss's answer. She pulled on her uniform, fumbling with her tie and all the unnecessary buttons. She couldn't find any tights without a ladder so settled for the pair where the run was least obvious. It was a shame that her skirt was slightly too short, especially when she sat down. She laced up her flat, black shoes and polished them with her sleeve. She had to have her hair tied back but there wasn't time to put it in a bun. Meg settled for a low ponytail that wouldn't get in the way of her hat. Not exactly chic policewoman of the year but it would have to do.

In the kitchen, the DI was actually drinking tea out of the best china cup. Aisling and Collette were still staring at him dumbly. Mary put a slice of buttered toast in front of Meg.

'I haven't got time,' said Meg.

'Sure and you need your breakfast,' said Mary. 'Isn't that right, DI Willis?'

Meg flashed her mother a look but the DI said, 'Yes. You've got time to eat your toast, WDC Connolly.'

The use of her official title made Collette collapse into giggles. Meg crunched her toast and wished she could make her family disappear. The real Padre Pio was apparently able to bilocate. If Meg prayed really hard, perhaps that would happen to her.

She forced the last crumbs down. 'Ready. Thanks, Mum. See you later.'

The DI stood up. 'Thank you for the tea, Mrs Connolly.'

'Any time,' beamed Mary.

Collette was still giggling.

It wasn't until they were past Roedean that Meg found her voice.

'I'm sorry,' she said.

'What for?' The DI was driving at his usual sedate pace. If Meg had been behind the wheel, they would be in Rottingdean by now, but women weren't allowed to drive police cars.

'For not being ready. And . . . everything.' For having a giggling sister, a chatty, chain-smoking mother and a lunatic budgie. For living in a council house. For possessing a dressing gown several sizes too small and tights with holes in.

'You weren't to know that I'd turn up on your doorstep at eight in the morning,' said the DI. After a short silence, he said, 'I liked your mum. She reminded me of my mother.'

'Really?' Meg was amazed. She didn't know anything about the DI's background, but the super had once described him as 'ultra respectable'. Surely, in that case, his family couldn't resemble Meg's?

'Yes,' said the DI. 'No one gets out of my mum's house without a cup of tea. She's always feeding people too. When my brother was in the air force, she used to send him food parcels.'

'Your brother was in the RAF?'

'Yes. He's a hell of a fellow. Got the DFC. Of course, I was too young to serve.'

Meg thought of the DI asking Alma if Seth was Verity's favourite son. It had seemed an unusually human question at the time but now she thought she knew why he had asked it.

'I bet your mum's proud of you being a DI,' she said.

DI Willis's ears went pink and he didn't answer. Meg had gone too far again.

They stopped outside the row of fisherman's cottages. There was a uniformed officer at the yellow front door of number three. As they approached, the super himself emerged.

'Ah, Bob,' he said. 'DI Willis. And you've brought WDC Connolly. Good.'

'I came as soon as I could,' said the DI. He didn't blame Meg for the delay, which was decent of him.

The super beckoned them to come closer. Well, he beckoned the DI and Meg followed.

'Mrs Saunders was found dead by the milkman at seven this morning,' he said. 'He was due to be paid and she normally leaves the money in an empty bottle on the doorstep. When it wasn't there he knocked. Then he tried the door and it was open. He went in and found her on the sofa. He rang the local police and the duty officer contacted me.'

'Cause of death?' said DI Willis.

'Looks like strangulation,' said the super. 'And, from the rigidity of her body, I'd say it happened last night. We're waiting for Solomon Carter now.'

'Have next of kin been informed?' asked the DI.

'Not yet.' The super looked slightly shifty for a minute, running his hands through his hair. 'From what Emma says, she's a widow but there are two sons. Their names are Frederick and Barry.'

'Their details might be in the house,' said Meg. 'An address book or something like that.'

'Good thinking, Connolly,' said the super. 'Can you go in and look? Then I'll need you to interview the neighbours.'

'I'll send for Sergeant O'Neill to coordinate the door-to-door,' said the DI.

That was all Meg needed. Sergeant Brendan O'Neill was a hard-drinking Irishman who frequently said that he had only one use for women, and then went on to say what that was. She was intrigued by the super's mention of Emma. Did that mean that Emma had also visited the dead woman? Meg pushed open the yellow door and, once again, found herself in the pleasant, crowded sitting room. Only this time there was a dead body opposite her.

At the age of sixteen Meg had been taken to see her grandfather's body, lying in the church on the night before his funeral. She remembered the candles and the sacristy light glowing, her mother and her grandmother sobbing, but she didn't remember the look of the corpse. Maybe she had closed her eyes. She did remember pressing her lips to her granddad's cold forehead. He'd always been kind to her and had been the only person to call her by her full name, Margaret Mary.

This figure was very different. It wasn't lying in a coffin, surrounded by candles. It was upright on the sofa, as if turned to stone. Meg wondered if, as an intrepid policewoman, she should examine the corpse, but she decided that was best left for Solomon Carter. Her job was to search for an address book and she did so, trying very hard not to look at the shape that was once Mrs Saunders. The room was full of ornaments – china horses, petticoated figurines, souvenirs from various resorts – but there were no books of any kind. Then she thought of the telephone, still embarrassed by her family's lack of this essential modern device. Maybe telephone numbers would be kept beside the receiver. A door at the back of the room led to a small, spotless kitchen. There was the phone, fixed to the wall, and beside it a calendar showing 'The Beauties of Lancashire'. And – yes – scribbled across

Pendle Hill (January) she found a number for Barry. She wrote it down in her notebook and went back through the sitting room, not looking to the left or the right.

Outside, the super and the DI were in conversation with Solomon Carter, who saw Meg and winked at her. Meg ignored him and, when the men had finished talking, presented the number.

'Well done,' said the super. 'I'll go back to the station and telephone.'

'Shall I do it, sir?' said the DI.

'No, you stay here and keep an eye on things. Solomon, can you go inside and start your examination? The coroner's van is on its way.'

'Right you are, chief.' The pathologist turned away, whistling 'Give Yourself a Pat on the Back'.

Meg was left with the DI.

'Do you think it's the same person who killed Bert Billington?' she asked.

'Different MO,' he said, frowning at the yellow door. 'Modus operandi – way of operating,' he explained, unnecessarily: Meg had seen enough films to know that one. 'Bert was poisoned, this appears to be strangulation. But it does look suspicious. After all, Mrs Saunders was one of the people who knew the family best. Betty says that the dresser always knows the star's secrets.'

The DI must be feeling rattled, thought Meg. He rarely mentioned his wife and he *never* referred to her show-business past.

But there was more to come. The DI raised his eyes to heaven and said, 'Emma, Mrs Stephens, says that Alma was at Tudor Close on the day that Bert Billington was killed.'

'Sounds like we should talk to Emma,' said Meg, greatly daring.

'The super said he was bringing her back with him.'

'Really? Do you think this means that she knows something we don't? Do you think she and Sam Collins have come up with a lead?'

'I doubt it,' said the DI. But Meg thought he sounded nervous.

FOURTEEN

Meg had knocked at all the doors in the little street by the time that the super came back. Out of eight houses, there was no answer at three of them, three had seen and heard nothing, but Mrs Hawkins, at number five, remembered a caller at number three last night.

'What time would that have been?' asked Meg.

'About eleven,' said Mrs Hawkins, a sharp-faced woman in a blue housecoat. 'I just happened to look out of the window.'

Meg thought Mrs Hawkins was the sort of woman who 'just happened' to look out whenever anyone had visitors. Her parents' neighbours had this habit too. All the same, this was very useful.

'Can you remember anything about the caller?' she asked.

'It was a woman,' said Mrs Hawkins. 'Grey-haired, quite large, wearing a brown coat.'

'Light or dark brown?'

'Dark. One of those big cloth coats.'

Meg wrote this description down in her notebook.

'Did you see the woman leave?' she asked.

'Yes,' said Mrs Hawkins. 'She left about half an hour later.'

About. Meg was willing to bet that it was exactly thirty minutes.

'Thank you,' she said. 'That's very helpful. We might have to call on you again to take a statement, if that's OK?'

'Happy to do my duty,' said Mrs Hawkins. 'What happened to Alma? I saw the police outside.'

'I can't tell you any more at the moment,' said Meg. 'But someone from the police will contact you soon.'

'I'll be waiting,' said Mrs Hawkins, making it sound like a threat.

Back at the house, Meg saw the super getting out of a Morris Minor, accompanied by Emma who, to her surprise, was attached to a stout, fair-haired toddler.

'Hallo, Meg,' said Emma. 'This is Jonathan.'

Meg squatted down to the child's level. 'Hallo, mate. I like your car.' The boy had a toy police car in one hand.

Jonathan pointed to the yellow front door. 'Horse!' he said.

'Mrs Saunders gave him a china horse,' said Emma. 'She seemed very kind. This is horrible.'

'It is,' said Meg, glad to have some acknowledgement of this. All morning the police – Meg included – had been determinedly matter-of-fact, but it *was* horrible that a woman had been killed.

'Anything from the door-to-door, WDC Connolly?' asked the super.

'One potentially useful lead,' said Meg. She could see Sergeant O'Neill talking to a group of officers and was determined to hold on to her clue for as long as she could.

'Right,' said the super. 'The local police station is just in the next street. Let's go there and have a conference.'

'WDC Connolly,' said the DI, eying Jonathan warily, 'perhaps you could look after . . . ?'

'No,' said Emma. 'We need Meg. Anyway, you're his god-father. You should look after him.'

She smiled when she said this but Meg didn't think that it was entirely a joke. The DI coloured but made no further objection as the super led the way to a cutting – a twitten they were called round here – between the houses. The two men walked ahead while Meg followed Emma, who was encumbered by the slow-moving child.

'I had to bring him,' Emma explained. 'Our babysitter is recovering from an operation.'

'My sister Collette would babysit for you,' said Meg. 'She's at school but she could do evenings or weekends. She's the queen of babysitters round our way.'

Emma flashed her a brilliant smile. 'That would be super. Thanks so much. I love Johnny to bits but he's a real nuisance if I'm meant to be working.'

Meg had forgotten how posh Emma was. *Super.* But she

was being incredibly nice, almost as if they were friends. And she'd insisted that Meg, a lowly WDC, should attend this meeting while O'Neill and co were left plodding up and down the High Street.

In Rottingdean police station, they crowded into a small room dominated by a large portrait of the Queen. Meg thought that the duty sergeant looked quizzically at a group that included a small child and a uniformed WDC but he was very polite and actually offered to make tea, the first time a male colleague had ever made a hot drink for Meg. It was welcome, too. It had been very cold outside, the remnants of last night's storm blowing in from the sea.

'So,' said the super, when they were all seated around the table, 'let's look at this latest development.' At first there had only been two chairs, which had prompted an embarrassing stand-off. Should Emma and Meg sit because they were women, or the DI and the super because they were the highest-ranking officers? In the end Emma and the super had sat down and Meg and the DI waited until the sergeant staggered in with two more chairs. Jonathan was running his toy police car up and down the window ledge.

'Mrs Saunders knew the Billington family well,' said the super. 'I think we need to entertain the possibility that the two cases are connected.'

'Entertain the possibility', Meg knew, was super-speak for 'this is what I think happened'.

'Emma,' said the super, 'tell us what you found out about Alma Saunders.'

Emma shot a glance at the DI. Was it an apology for stealing his thunder or satisfaction at having stolen the upper hand? Meg couldn't tell.

'Alma was at Tudor Close on the day that Bert died,' said Emma. 'The gardener, Ted Grange, saw her entering the house at around eleven-fifteen a.m. I asked Alma about it and she said that she was delivering groceries. But Ted also saw someone else at the house. He saw a woman in a brown coat entering through the front door at around eleven-thirty. He didn't see her leave.'

Meg uttered a strangled sound. The DI and the super both turned to look at her.

'A woman in a dark brown coat?' she repeated.

'Yes,' said Emma, raising her eyebrows.

Meg got out her notebook and tried to sound as much like Emma Holmes as possible. 'Mrs Hawkins from number five saw a woman in a brown cloth coat knocking on Alma's door at eleven last night. She left about half an hour later.'

'That's our first solid lead,' said the super. 'Well done, WDC Connolly. We haven't got a time of death yet but my guess is that Alma Saunders was killed at about midnight or just before. Is there anything else from the witness description?'

'Quite large,' Meg read from her notes. 'Grey-haired.'

'The gardener described her as "bulky",' said Emma.

'Could it have been Verity Malone?' asked the super.

'She's slim,' said Emma, 'but she could have been wearing lots of clothes underneath the coat. And she wears a wig. Her hair could be grey or even white. She's seventy-five, after all. The gardener said that Verity was in the kitchen when the woman called at the house, but I suppose she could have gone out of the back door, disguised herself, and come in again at the front.'

'People don't do things like that,' objected the DI.

'Like what?' said Emma. 'Disguise themselves? Actors do it all the time.'

'Even Alma enjoyed amateur dramatics,' said Meg. 'She told us so herself. Didn't she, sir?'

'But Alma couldn't have been the woman in the brown coat,' said the DI. 'Unless she knocked on her own door last night.'

'It could have been a man, I suppose,' said Meg. 'I mean, anyone can buy a coat. Or a wig.'

A brief silence greeted this.

'Good point, Meg,' said Emma. 'The gardener said that the woman walked up to the Billingtons' front door as if she owned the place. That sounds like a man to me.'

The super gave her a look that seemed both affectionate and exasperated. He said, 'It could be a man, you're quite right, WDC Connolly. But it could also have been Verity Malone. Someone needs to call on her. To inform her of Alma Saunders' death, if nothing else.'

The DI cleared his throat. 'She seems to prefer to talk to women officers.'

'That settles it,' said Emma. 'Meg and I will go and tell her now. You two don't mind looking after Johnny for half an hour, do you?'

Meg didn't know who looked more discomforted, the super, the DI or Jonathan himself, who emitted a loud squawk and threw his police car onto the floor.

Emma and Meg walked briskly along the High Street, skirted the pond and turned into Dean Court Road. The trees around St Margaret's Church were blowing wildly and, when they reached Tudor Close, the smooth front lawn was littered with leaves.

'It's very pretty,' said Emma, 'but I wouldn't like to live here, would you?'

'No,' said Meg. 'It's like it's pretending to be something else.'

'Nineteen twenties pretending to be Tudor,' said Emma.

But Meg had meant something deeper than that, something to do with disguises and people never being quite what they seemed. But she couldn't put it into words eloquent enough for Emma Holmes.

Verity opened the door, fully made-up and wearing her yellow wig.

'Well, if it isn't my two favourite women. What are you doing together? I thought the police never worked with private detectives.'

'I'm afraid we've got some bad news,' said Emma. 'Can we come in?'

Meg admired the way Emma delivered the news. She said quickly that it wasn't about Verity's sons, then she described what had happened, compassionately but without embellishment. Alma Saunders had been found dead and the police believed that she had been murdered. Alma's son had been informed and was on his way.

Verity put her hand over her mouth. Her face was alarmingly white.

'Can I get you a glass of water?' said Meg.

'Brandy,' said Verity, in a surprisingly strong voice. 'On the side table.'

Meg easily spotted the table because it was groaning with spirits and alcohol of every kind. Underneath was a variety of glasses. Meg poured a generous measure of brandy into one of them.

Verity drank most of it in one gulp. The colour came back into her cheeks and she raised her hand to her hair. Her rings glinted in the light reflected through the diamond panes of the windows.

'Poor Alma,' she said. 'She was always a good friend to me. Seth will be heartbroken.'

No mention of the other sons, thought Meg.

'Verity, I know it's difficult,' said Emma, 'but do you have any idea who might have done this? The first few hours of an investigation are vital. We need to find the killer before they kill again.'

Emma still sounded like a police officer, Meg noticed. The DI would probably have used exactly the same words.

'I can't think . . .' said Verity. 'I mean, it can't be the same person who killed Bert.'

'Why not?' said Emma. She had carefully avoided saying how Alma had been killed.

The heavy eyelashes came down over Verity's eyes. When she opened them again, Meg thought that she looked different, more guarded somehow. 'You thought that Bert had been killed slowly. Small doses of poison, you said. This sounds like someone broke in and killed her.'

This was the first time that Meg had heard this theory. She tried to remember what she had been told about the effects of poison. She hadn't been allowed to see the post-mortem report, either because she was too junior or because the DI thought it would upset her delicate feminine sensibilities.

Emma was regarding Verity steadily. 'It looks like Alma was strangled,' she said.

'Strangled,' said Verity. 'Oh my God.' She drank the rest of the brandy. Meg wondered if she should offer to get more.

'When did you last see Alma?' asked Emma.

'Yesterday,' said Verity. 'She came in and cleaned as usual. We had a nice chat about the boys and the past. That sort of thing.'

The boys must all be in their thirties, or even forties, thought Meg. Funny how mothers never let their sons grow up. It was different with daughters.

'The last thing she said was that she'd see me tomorrow. I said, "See you later, alligator." It was a joke we had. David and Fred used to love Bill Haley and the Comets.'

A clatter at the front door made Emma and Meg jump. But Verity just said, 'It's the post. It always sounds like more than it is.'

'Shall I get it?' said Meg.

No one answered this, so she went to the hall and came back with three letters, two in brown envelopes, one in a white.

Verity put the brown envelopes to one side. 'I never answer bills.' But she opened the white one carefully and unfolded the contents. And then she gasped.

'What is it?' said Meg.

Verity handed over what looked like a flyer for a show. A pantomime. *Dick Whittington* at the Adelphi in Liverpool. The cast list was written in cheerful red and blue capitals but, across it, someone had written in wavery black ink, 'King Rat'.

FIFTEEN

'Don't touch it,' said Emma quickly.

Meg was irritated. She knew this without being told. She was the police officer after all. The envelope and the flyer could have fingerprints on them. The super was dead keen on fingerprints. Turning her back on Emma, Meg looked at the list of names.

Dick Whittington	Annette Anthony
Alice Fitzwarren	Lucy-Anne Montgomery
Dame Fanny Fitzwarren	Denton McGrew
The Cat	Sheila Percival
Fairy Bowbells	Dolores Del Monte
King Rat	Bert Billington
Jack 'Nimble Fingers' Fitzwarren	Eric Prentice

She looked at Emma, who was staring at the envelope

as if she could make incriminating prints appear on it. Verity was still prostrate in her chair.

'There's someone we need to talk to,' said Meg.

On the short walk across the leaf-strewn lawn, Meg filled Emma in on Eric Prentice. 'He was in variety. He had an act playing the piano. And he knew Bert from the old days, when he was a proper actor. He knew Verity too. I think he was sweet on her. It was Eric who first told me about Glenda. "The girl who died," that's how he put it.'

'It was Pamela who told us about Glenda,' said Emma, as they paused by the strange corner door. 'Bert's assistant.'

'We haven't spoken to Pamela,' said Meg. She thought that Emma looked rather pleased to hear this. 'Alma Saunders didn't sound very keen on Eric,' she said. 'It'll be interesting to hear what he says about her.'

Meg raised her hand to knock but a loud baying had already announced their arrival. One side of the folding door opened to reveal Eric and Lola.

'Hi,' said Meg. 'Do you remember me? WDC Meg Connolly. This is Emma Stephens. Holmes. Can we come in?'

Eric looked rather bemused but he stood aside to let them in. Then he edged past to lead the way along the twisting corridor into the room where the piano loomed, very black against the light from the window. The lid was up. Did that mean he had been playing it? thought Meg. If so, they hadn't heard any music.

Emma and Meg sat on the sofa. Eric took the piano stool which was the only other seat in the room. Lola lay at their feet, looking martyred.

'I'm sorry to say that we're investigating another death,' said Meg. 'Alma Saunders. Did you know her?'

'Verity's dresser?' said Eric. 'I knew her a little. She used to come and clean for Verity. How did she die? She wasn't that old, was she?'

Alma had been sixty-six. The police had found her old ration book. Not old in anyone's book.

'I'm afraid I can't say,' said Meg. 'But we're treating her death as suspicious. Can you remember the last time you saw Alma?'

'I think it was yesterday,' said Eric. 'Monday.' His hand shook as he stroked Lola's ears. 'I saw her leaving the house about midday. Lola and I were just coming back from our walk. We just passed the time of day, that sort of thing.'

'Were you friendly with Alma?' asked Meg.

Eric waited a second before answering. His hand pressed down on the dog's head, flattening her ears.

'Alma was very defensive about Verity,' he said. 'Jealous almost. She didn't like anyone talking to her. Especially someone from the old days.'

'Did you remember Alma from the old days?' asked Meg.

'Yes,' said Eric. 'She was always there. Always with Verity. Protecting her.'

'Protecting her from what?' asked Emma.

'Men,' said Eric. 'There were always men hanging around Verity. Most of them harmless but you know what men are.'

He stopped, apparently unwilling to say more.

'How did Mrs Saunders seem yesterday?' asked Emma.

'Fine. The same as usual. I think I asked how Verity was getting on and she said that she was bearing up. Seth had been down at the weekend, which would have cheered her up.'

Meg remembered interviewing Seth on Saturday. It seemed years ago. She asked if Eric had seen Verity at the weekend. 'I saw her in the garden on Saturday evening,' he said. 'She was having drinks with Seth and two women. I think one of them was you,' he added, with a sudden sly look at Emma.

'Maybe,' said Emma coolly. But her face had gone bright red. As a fellow blusher, Meg sympathised.

'When we spoke before,' said Meg, 'you mentioned a girl who died. You said that you didn't know her name. But we've just found out that you were in the pantomime that was showing when she died. *Dick Whittington*.'

Eric smiled, showing an alarming array of false teeth. 'I was in so many shows. They all merge into one after a while.'

'I think you might remember this one,' said Emma. 'Bert Billington played King Rat.'

'Oh yes,' said Eric, re-sheathing the teeth. 'He was delighted to get back on the stage. The old ham.'

'Glenda Gillespie killed herself in December 1949,' said Meg. 'While this pantomime was showing in Liverpool. Killed herself and her daughter.'

'Yes,' said Eric. 'Such a tragedy.' His voice trembled. Lola put her head on his knee.

'Did you know Glenda?' asked Emma.

'Not really. I'd seen her around. She was a pretty girl. But then Bert always did like the pretty girls. He had his eye on one of the dancers in the panto. I think that's what sent Glenda over the edge.'

Meg was putting on her gloves. Seeing this, Lola barked and wagged her tail, clearly interpreting the movement as preparation for a walk. But Meg stayed seated. She drew the white envelope out of her bag. Then she extracted the flyer and held it in front of Eric.

'Have you seen this before?' she asked.

'It looks like a cast list . . .' said Eric.

'It's the cast list for *Dick Whittington*,' said Meg, 'and it was posted to Verity yesterday, postmarked Brighton. As you can see, someone has written "King Rat" across the names. We assume that refers to Bert Billington.'

Eric said nothing.

'Did you send this?' asked Emma, keeping her tone carefully casual.

This seemed to rouse Eric from his reverie. 'No!' he said. 'No. Of course not.'

'Have you got any idea who did?' asked Meg.

'No. Why are you asking me these questions?'

'Because you told me that Bert had been killed because of the girl who died. Why did you say that?'

'It was the first thing I thought of,' said Eric. 'It was, what's the word? Nemesis.'

Meg didn't know what this meant. Emma explained it outside. Nemesis was another word for getting what you deserved.

Back at the police station, they found the super, the DI and the desk sergeant all lying on the floor, playing peek-a-boo with Jonathan. Meg thought that she'd treasure this image for the rest of her life.

The DI was the first to get up and smooth down his hair.

'You took your time, WDC Connolly,' he said. Of course he didn't dare to direct this at Emma. 'Did you find anything useful?'

'Yes,' said Meg. She described the arrival of the King Rat flyer and their interview with Eric Prentice.

'Do you think this Prentice sent the flyer?' asked DI Willis. He had the peevish look he always adopted when cases became unnecessarily complicated.

'He said not,' said Emma. 'But it's clear to me that Glenda's death is integral to Bert's murder. Eric said so. Both Seth and David mentioned their father's affairs. So did Pamela Curtis. Then there's the manner of Bert's death itself. Rat poison. King Rat.'

This had the effect of silencing the DI.

'Glenda died in 1949,' said the super. 'Sixteen years ago. That's a long time to wait before getting your revenge.'

'Revenge is a dish best served cold,' said Meg. It was something her mother had once said. And her food *was* often cold because it took a long time to serve seven children.

'"Ellum she hateth mankind, and waiteth",' said the DI. This was so unexpected that they all stared at him. 'It's a poem,' he added, sounding rather defensive. 'Kipling, I think. It's about elm trees hating people and waiting for their moment to drop branches on their heads. We had to learn it at school.'

'I can't bear Kipling,' said the super.

'Apparently Kipling moved from Rottingdean because people in double-decker buses could see into his garden,' said Emma.

Meg thought of Kipling's house behind its high flint walls. She thought of Tudor Close with its hidden doors and glittering windows.

'Maybe Alma knew who killed Bert,' she said, 'and that's why she was killed.'

'It's possible,' said Emma. 'But Alma was strangled. That requires intimacy and savage violence. It's very different from slow poison.'

Meg admired the way that Emma pronounced the words 'intimacy and savage violence' without a tremor in her cut-glass accent.

'We need to find the woman in the brown coat,' said Superintendent Stephens. 'She's our only real lead and she links the two deaths. Do you think your witness would be able to work with an artist to come up with a likeness, WDC Connolly?'

'I expect so,' said Meg. 'But those likenesses never really look like anyone, do they?'

Emma laughed but Meg thought that the DI and the super both looked irritated. She really had to learn to watch what she said. She realised that Emma was speaking, in her calm 'I know what's best' voice.

'We should also follow the Glenda Gillespie lead,' she was saying. 'I think Meg and I should go to Liverpool.'

SIXTEEN

Meg was still not quite sure how it happened but, three days later, she was sitting opposite Emma on a train from Euston to Liverpool. Somehow, Emma had managed to convince the super that they needed to interview Glenda Gillespie's family. She must have done a good job because apparently the super was actually taking the day off to look after the children.

They had caught the early train from Brighton. Meg had arrived at the station at seven-thirty, feeling nervous about the journey (the furthest north she had ever been in her life was a visit to her Auntie Beryl in Luton) and relieved that she and Emma were wearing similar clothes, slacks, jumpers and short jackets. They were to spend the night at a hotel in Liverpool so Meg was also clutching her mother's overnight case, royal blue with gold fittings. Emma had a Gladstone bag which mysteriously managed to look both shabbier and posher. They had negotiated the Underground from Victoria to Euston.

Emma seemed to know which tube to take. Meg followed anxiously, gripping her bag because of Mum's warnings about pickpockets. Now they were seated on the 10.07 to Liverpool Lime Street.

'When do we get there?' Meg asked Emma. She knew really. She just wanted to remind herself that she was actually on a journey with Emma Holmes, the two of them were working together, two free-spirited, independent women – like Ruby French in *Iris Investigates*.

'One o'clock,' said Emma. 'We can get some lunch and then interview Mr and Mrs Gillespie.'

It had been easy to find Glenda's parents. They still lived at the address given to the police by Sheena Billington. Why would you stay in the place where you had witnessed so much tragedy? wondered Meg. But then again, how could you leave it?

'Do you think we'll see the Beatles?' said Meg.

'I think they all live in London now,' said Emma, who was casually flicking through *Film Frolics* magazine. 'Shall we get some coffee from the buffet car?'

Even the coffee was exciting. It came in thick china mugs with the British Rail logo on the side, accompanied by two rich tea biscuits wrapped in cellophane. Emma read her magazine and occasionally stared out of the window. Meg was surprised that Emma would read anything as frivolous as *Film Frolics*. She'd brought *The Feminine Mystique*, partly to impress Emma, but she was finding it as impenetrable as ever. Eventually she, too, took to watching the scenery, the grey houses giving way to sudden stretches of green countryside, cows grazing oblivious to the locomotive thundering past.

They left their bags at the Station Hotel, where they were staying the night. The hotel was a gloomy, soot-stained building overlooking the railway lines but Liverpool itself was a surprise. Meg hadn't expected so much grand architecture or so many people. It was almost like London except for the fact that, when they rounded a corner, she could see the huge bulk of a ship.

'Is it by the sea?' she asked Emma. She wished she'd thought to look at a map before leaving home.

'It's a port,' said Emma. 'Come on, this café looks OK. Let's have lunch here. Then I think we can walk to the Gillespies' place.'

The café was painted dark red inside but you couldn't see the walls because they were plastered with photographs, mostly of the Fab Four but also Cilla Black, Billy J. Kramer, the Searchers and others Meg did not recognise, although, now that they had a TV, she never missed *Top of the Pops*. One whole wall was dedicated to footballers, also in red. A motherly woman came to take their order. Her smile was friendly, but her accent sounded almost incomprehensible to Meg, a mixture of her most Irish uncles and something harsher and more guttural.

Emma seemed to have no such trouble and ordered an omelette and coffee. Meg asked for the same, just to be safe.

'On your holidays?' said the woman. At least Meg thought that's what she said.

'We're visiting someone,' said Emma. 'They live just off Scotland Road.'

'Scottie Road!' repeated the woman, clearly amazed. 'How do youse know anyone from there?'

'Our auntie and uncle,' said Emma promptly. 'Auntie's been ill so we're visiting.'

'Are you sisters then?' said the woman.

Meg had to stifle a giggle. She and Emma could not look less alike. Meg was tall and dark, Emma small and blonde. Besides, Emma must be at least fifteen years older than Meg. It was true that they were dressed alike and the woman hadn't yet heard Meg's Whitehawk accent, but even so . . .

'Cousins,' said Emma with a smile.

When the woman was out of earshot, Meg whispered, 'Why did you say that?'

'I thought it might be better not to say that we're with the police,' said Emma. 'People are always suspicious of anyone in authority.'

You're not with the police, thought Meg. But she said nothing. 'You're in charge,' the DI had said to her before she left, 'Emma . . . Mrs Stephens is a civilian.' But the DI had worked with Emma, he must have known that she would take charge in any situation.

Meg insisted on paying for the meal because the DI had given her some money for 'expenses'. She asked Emma how much she should leave for a tip and it must have been generous because the waitress bade them an affectionate farewell and told them to come back again soon.

Emma (of course) had brought a map. She'd even marked their route, which looked fairly straightforward. Scotland Road was a busy thoroughfare with tall buildings on either side – cinemas, churches, even a police station – but, as they walked, the houses got smaller and closer together. Several were boarded up and there were gaps in the terraces, maybe left over from bombing in the war. They passed a parade of shops and a group of women queuing outside a fishmonger's. There was much talk and laughter and Meg thought that it seemed a friendly place, but Emma said, 'There's a lot of deprivation round here.'

'There's a lot of it everywhere,' said Meg.

Emma consulted her map and led them down a side street. In front of them was a vast block of flats curving in a half-circle. There were balconies on the first and second floors and women were hanging out clothes and calling to each other in that strange local accent that always seemed to be on the edge of laughter or anger. In a funny way it reminded Meg of Tudor Close, the flats arranged around a central point, all the eyes looking inwards.

A group of boys were playing football on the grass. Meg wondered why they weren't at school. Or were they old enough to have left? It was hard to tell. The game paused as Emma and Meg walked by. There was some laughter and some – mercifully – incomprehensible comments.

'The Gillespies are on the first floor,' said Emma. They climbed iron stairs and made their way along the walkway. Someone shouted, 'It's the bizzies,' which didn't make any sense to Meg. She got the feeling that it wasn't exactly welcoming though.

Emma knocked on a door in a line of identical doors. It was opened so quickly that Meg was sure that the householder somehow knew to expect them.

'Mrs Gillespie?' said Emma.

'What's it to you?' said the woman, who was small and white-haired, with shrewd eyes behind wing-framed glasses.

Emma took a step backwards. Meg thought that it was her turn to speak. 'I'm Meg Connolly,' she said, 'and this is Emma Holmes. We've come from Brighton. We're investigating the death of Bert Billington.'

'Are you from the police?'

'I'm a policewoman,' said Meg. 'Emma isn't. We'd just like a quick chat, if that's all right.'

'You're very tall,' said the woman, but in a more conciliatory tone. Meg knew there was nothing people liked more than informing tall people that they weren't, in fact, short.

'Can we come in?' she said, trying to smile down from her immense height.

'All right.' The woman stood aside and ushered them through a narrow hall and into a sitting room where a man sat reading a newspaper.

'Norman. They're from the police.'

'Can't get up,' said Norman, 'bad leg.' He was a large man with sleepy down-turned eyes. One leg was propped up on the coffee table. An ashtray with a smoking cigarette butt was balanced on the arm of his chair. Despite his size, Norman seemed less hostile than his wife. He motioned to them to sit down.

Meg and Emma sat side by side on the sofa and Meg realised, with a slight surprise, that Emma was, once again, waiting for her to start.

She cleared her throat. 'As you might know, Bert Billington died three weeks ago.'

'Good riddance,' said Mrs Gillespie.

'We understand that you knew Bert,' said Meg. 'Or rather that your daughter, Glenda, knew him.'

Both Gillespies looked towards a photograph on top of the television. It showed a blonde woman holding a large blonde baby.

'He broke our Glenda's heart,' said Mrs Gillespie. 'As good as killed her. I'm glad he's dead.'

'Steady on, Sandra,' said Norman. 'I'm guessing these two young ladies think we had something to do with it.'

'We'd just like a bit more detail about Bert,' said Emma. 'If we find out more about what he was like as a person, it will help us find his killer.'

'He was murdered then?' said Sandra. 'Good.' After a short silence, she said, 'Glenda met Bert in 1946. She'd been in ENSA during the war, entertaining the troops.

Then she got a part in one of his pantos. She was so happy. "I've finally made it," she said. "A Bert Billington show." *Cinderella*, it was. She was one of the dancing fairies. It was so beautiful. Norm and I went five times.' Her voice wobbled slightly and she stared into the distance, perhaps recalling the dancing fairies. Meg felt that she could see them too, all in silver tulle with stars in their hair.

'Is that when they fell in love?' she asked.

Sandra gave a humourless laugh. 'If that's what you call it. Glenda introduced us to Bert after one of the performances, but he just seemed like an old man to us. Then she got a job in another show. And another. Suddenly she was buying a little house in Bootle. Norman confronted her about it and she admitted that she was Bert's mistress. He told her, "We've never had anything like that in our family." '

'But we didn't turn our back on her,' said Norman. 'She was still our daughter. The only one we've got, though we've got three sons. And when she had little Angela, we doted on her. Such a lovely baby, she was. She had the right name because she really was a little angel. Always smiling.' Now it was his turn to falter, covering his eyes with a shaking hand.

'Glenda wasn't well after Angela,' said Sandra. 'The baby blues. You know.'

'I do,' said Emma. 'I got them badly after my third.'

'Your third!' said Sandra. 'You don't look old enough.' But she seemed to soften towards Emma and now addressed her remarks to her as well as Meg.

'We did what we could, but we were both working then. I wish we'd been there when . . .'

'Don't beat yourself up, Sand,' said Norman. 'We did what we could.'

'It started when Bert had a show at the Adelphi,' said Sandra. 'A panto. *Dick Whittington*.'

'Bert played King Rat,' said Norman. 'Good casting.'

'Glenda was upset because Bert was in Liverpool and he didn't go to see her,' said Sandra. 'Eventually she went to the theatre with Angela and she found him there with this other girl, Barbara. One of the dancers. Glenda went mad. She always had a temper. Apparently she threw a typewriter at him. Bert's assistant told me. Then she went home and . . . you know the rest. She got into bed with Angela. There was a gas fire in the bedroom and she turned the gas on.'

There was another silence. Meg could hear the shouts of the children playing outside. She said, 'I'm so sorry.'

'It's a long time ago, love,' said Norman. 'But it's funny how the pain never gets any better. We've got six grand-children now but we'll never forget Angela. Or Glenda.'

'Bert didn't even send flowers to her funeral,' said Sandra. 'His wife did though.'

'Verity Malone?'

'Yes. She was a nice enough woman by all accounts. Of course, she was carrying on too. She was having an affair with that magician. Max Mephisto.'

Meg didn't look at Emma. 'Was he in the show too?'

'No, I think he was performing in Manchester. Some-where like that. He was a big star in those days. People said all sorts of things about him, that he'd been a spy in the war, that he was a traitor, that he'd sold his soul to the devil. Glenda said that she walked in on Verity and Mephisto once. He was a lot younger than her but that didn't seem to put either of them off.'

It seemed to Meg that Glenda had a knack of finding people in compromising positions.

'What about Barbara?' she asked. 'What happened to her?'

'Poor Babs,' said Sandra. 'I never blamed her. I knew her mother. She was in the business too. Barbara was very upset about Glenda. Bert dropped her, of course, and I heard that she'd turned to drink. I think she's dead now.'

'Mrs Gillespie?' said Emma. 'Were you in show business?'

Meg couldn't think why she'd asked the question. There was nothing in Sandra Gillespie, a neat figure in a purple housecoat, that spoke of the bright lights. But Sandra gave a funny little smile and said, 'Yes. For a few years. I was on the stage when I met Norm.'

'A lovely dancer, she was,' said Norman. 'Glenda took after her.'

'Have you had any contact with the Billingtons since . . . since Glenda died?' asked Meg.

'They tried to give us some money,' said Norman, 'but we said no. The son got in contact. But we didn't want anything else to do with them.'

'Did you ever meet Alma Saunders?' said Emma. 'She was Verity Malone's dresser.'

'I don't think so,' said Sandra. 'As I say, we never even met Verity. The only time she got in contact was to send those flowers. We heard that she was very cut up about . . . about Glenda.'

'Who did you hear that from?' asked Emma.

Sandra gave her a rather sharp look. 'Bert's assistant. Miss Curtis. She stayed in touch for a bit. She wanted to help but, as Norm says, we didn't want anything to do with any of them.'

'Would you mind telling us where you were on Sunday the nineteenth of September?' asked Meg. She was almost embarrassed to ask the question.

But Norman gave a short laugh. 'I was in hospital,' he said. 'With my leg. It's gout, you see. Like Henry the Eighth.'

Meg and Emma laughed dutifully but there was something rather Tudor about Norman Gillespie. Maybe it was just his girth.

'And I visited him in the morning and the evening,' said Sandra. 'You can check.'

They would check but Meg believed her. In any case, it was hard to think of the elderly couple – Norm on crutches, perhaps – struggling down to Rottingdean to put rat poison in Bert's food.

'What about your sons?' asked Emma. 'You said you had three sons.'

'And you think one of them nipped down to Brighton and finished Bert off?' said Norman. 'I wouldn't have blamed them if they had. They worshipped Glenda. She was the youngest, you see. But Tom, our oldest, is in Scotland. Roddy emigrated to Australia and Angus lives in Liverpool. He took me to the hospital and back.'

Meg asked for contact details for the Gillespie sons just to be on the safe side. Then she asked the sixty-four-thousand-dollar question, as they said on TV shows.

'Can you think of anyone else who might have had a grudge against Bert Billington?'

She expected the usual 'too many to count' answer but, to her surprise, Sandra had someone specific in mind.

'Try that Mephisto,' she said. 'By all accounts, he tried to kill him once before.'

SEVENTEEN

Edgar started the day with the best of intentions. He took the girls to school and then walked to Queen's Park where he and Jonathan fed the ducks before going to the playground. Edgar loved Jonathan's wholehearted appreciation of everything he saw. 'Ducks! Tree! Poo!' The morning was sunny and it was fun to push his son on the swings, the toddler's sturdy legs kicking the sky. There were two other children there with their mothers. Edgar imagined the women thinking, 'What a kind, involved father. He must be one of those modern men we keep reading about.' He started to think about lunch. Maybe they'd go to a café. He might bake a cake for the girls' tea. Then he looked at his watch. It was only ten o'clock.

How could that be? Edgar felt as if he had been in the park for hours. He wondered whether Emma was on the Liverpool train yet. She'd seemed very happy and confident when she set off that morning. She was longing to have two days of detection work. Edgar thought there was a good chance that she'd find something useful – which was one reason why he had persuaded Bob to allow the trip – but he was also slightly worried that Emma would override Meg Connolly and take charge of the investigation. Meg was a promising officer but she seemed a little in awe of Emma. Well, that was understandable. Edgar was in awe of her as well. But Emma was not in charge of this case.

A sudden gust of wind sent leaves swirling around the playground. Edgar was aware that the sun had gone in and that his back ached. Jonathan started to cry. Edgar extracted him from the swing and found that his bottom was wet. Emma had been trying to potty train Jonathan, without much success, and had put a nappy on him today. It felt sodden. Edgar put Jonathan in his pushchair and wheeled him past the mothers and children. He now thought that they were looking at him accusingly. 'What a terrible, neglectful father. He must be one of those unemployed wastrels we keep reading about.'

Edgar walked quickly through the park and up the hill towards home. Jonathan stopped crying eventually but Edgar could tell by his hunched shoulders that he wasn't happy. In the house, Edgar changed Jonathan's nappy and put him in his highchair. Maybe he'd stay there for a bit while Edgar had a cup of coffee. Perhaps he should give him something to eat. Emma said that apple slices were good for children when they're teething. Edgar cut up an apple and put the slices in front of his son. With a look of disdain, Jonathan threw the pieces across the room. Edgar picked them up and put them in the bin. He proffered a rusk.

'Biscuit!' yelled Jonathan, his face going red.

Edgar gave him a chocolate biscuit. This allowed Edgar enough time to make himself a black coffee. But, by the time he'd turned back to Jonathan, the toddler's face was covered in chocolate. Edgar cleaned his face, which provoked more tears. He took Jonathan out of his highchair and upstairs to the sitting room. There was a playpen in the corner of the room but Edgar had once found a woman's body in a child's playpen. He could never bear to see any of his children behind the bars. He'd never told Emma this and so she thought his objections entirely unreasonable. Edgar put Jonathan on the floor and offered him a toy train. 'Choo-choo,' he said, rather desperately. Jonathan eyed him coldly.

Edgar set out to make a train track. It was rather fun, clicking the wooden pieces together, but Jonathan soon got bored and trotted off towards the stairs. He was halfway up them before Edgar noticed and brought him down again. They sat on the sofa and looked at each other. Edgar offered a picture book. Jonathan bit it. Edgar tried a puppet show, using two socks on which Emma had sewn eyes and tongues. Jonathan was so bored that he screamed. Edgar found himself looking longingly at the television. He had been against buying a set and, at first, had insisted on only turning it on for the news. Now he wished that children's programmes were on all day. Wasn't there something called *Watch with Mother* at lunchtime? He and Jonathan could smash the stereotype and watch it together. Where was the *Radio Times*? By the time he had located it, Jonathan was upstairs again, sorting through Emma's toiletries. Edgar removed a lipstick from his grasp and led him downstairs. It was still only half past eleven.

The phone was ringing in the hallway. After a second's thought, Edgar put Jonathan in the playpen with the toy train and raced downstairs.

It was Bob. 'Hallo, boss. How's the child-minding?'

'Great,' said Edgar. 'I've just been playing trains.'

'All right for some. Thought you'd like to know. We've had the post-mortem report. Alma Saunders was strangled. Death occurred between nine p.m. and midnight.'

'So it could have been the mysterious woman in brown.'

'Yes, but there's more. You remember the King Rat flyer sent to Verity Malone? We dusted the envelope for fingerprints. And there's a match.'

'A match? With whom?'

'Remember we took the family's fingerprints so we could rule them out?'

'You're saying it's one of the family?'

'The son. Seth.'

'Seth Billington. Bloody hell.'

'Exactly.' Edgar heard Bob cough. Even the mildest swearword made Bob uncomfortable.

'You need to talk to him,' said Edgar.

'I'll telephone today. Trouble is, Seth is back in Whitby.'

'Time for a trip to Yorkshire?'

'I've got enough officers gallivanting round the country,' said Bob. Then, remembering who he was talking to, 'Not that WDC Connolly is gallivanting.'

'I know what you mean,' said Edgar. There was a loud cry and a thump from upstairs. 'I'd better go.'

'Why did you ask her if she'd been in show business?' asked Meg, as they left the Gillespies' flat, their feet ringing on the iron walkway. On the floor above Meg could hear two women arguing about a cat. Either that or a car.

Emma gave a funny, crooked smile. 'When she talked about Barbara's mother, she said that she was "in the business too". I thought it was worth a guess.'

'It was a good guess,' said Meg.

The boys were still playing football outside. The game seemed more intense now and the players didn't have time for more than a few half-hearted wolf whistles in their direction. Heads held high, Meg and Emma made their way through the alleyway that led to Scotland Road.

'Do you know what we should do now?' said Emma.

'No,' said Meg. 'What?' Don't let Emma take charge, the DI had said, but how could you help it?

'We should go to Whitby,' said Emma. 'Confront Max before he has a chance to get his story straight.'

'He tried to kill him once before,' that's what Sandra had said about Max and Bert Billington. According to Mrs

Gillespie the affair between Max and Verity had been going on a long time, 'since before the war'. There had been an occasion when a part of a stage set – a 'flat' – had fallen down, narrowly missing Bert. Later it was discovered that the guy ropes had been cut; also that the flat was part of Max's act. 'Ever so good at scenery, he was. They say that, in the war, he painted fake airfields that looked just like the real thing.' Nothing had been proved but Max had, apparently, left town in a hurry. Then the war came and Max joined the army. 'He must have met up with Verity in the late forties and the whole thing started up again.'

'Where is Whitby?' asked Meg, feeling as if things were suddenly moving very fast. And, once again, she regretted not looking at a map.

'It's on the other side of England,' admitted Emma, 'but it's where England's at its narrowest. I don't think it would take more than three hours in a car.'

'But we haven't got a car,' said Meg.

Emma pointed at a sign hanging outside a depressed-looking building opposite. 'Jimmy's Motors: Repairs and Car Hire'.

'It's meant,' said Emma, with that smile again.

Meg looked doubtfully at the garage. It was really just a wooden shack between two derelict houses. The concrete forecourt smelled pleasantly of petrol and the only car visible was a Vauxhall Viva raised up on wooden blocks. Meg's father and brother were both motor mechanics but she thought that even they would give Jimmy's a wide berth.

But Emma marched straight up to the open door. 'Excuse me,' Meg heard her say to a burly man in overalls. 'Are you Jimmy?' Meg sighed and made her way across the oily courtyard.

'You want to hire a car?' Jimmy had a high voice which made his Liverpudlian accent sound even more pronounced. 'Have you got a licence?'

Emma held out her driving licence.

'Emma Stephens,' Jimmy read out slowly. 'Mrs. Have you got your husband's permission, love?'

'I don't need it,' said Emma, her voice becoming several times more Roedean. 'I can pay.'

'Can you, love?' Jimmy crossed his arms, clearly preparing to enjoy himself. 'Why don't you ring your old man, just the same?' Behind Jimmy's ear, a topless woman smiled from a pile of tyres. Miss October 1965.

Meg took out her warrant card. 'We're police officers,' she said. 'Have you got a car that we can hire? Just until tomorrow.'

Jimmy gaped at them. 'Police officers?' he said. 'But you're—'

'Women. Yes,' said Meg. 'I'm WDC Meg Connolly from the Brighton police. You can't ring my husband because I don't have one.'

Jimmy looked as if this didn't surprise him. But he unfolded his arms and said, 'I might have a Ford Cortina out back.'

EIGHTEEN

They stopped at the first phone box so that Meg could ring the DI. She steeled herself for a reprimand, perhaps even an order not to go to Whitby. But, instead, the DI said, 'That might be an idea. You can interview Seth Billington. We've had some new information about him.' He told her about the fingerprints on the letter, warned her not to stay more than one night and to drive carefully ('the roads are very rough up north'). Then it was Emma's turn to telephone. She got back in the car looking thoughtful.

'Edgar says he's having a fantastic day with the kids. He's even thinking of baking a cake.'

'Well, he doesn't have to do it every day, does he?' said Meg. 'Mind you, I can't remember my dad ever looking after us.'

'Never?'

'Never.' Was this odd? thought Meg, as she manoeuvred the unfamiliar car through the unfamiliar streets (they had agreed that Meg would drive to Whitby and Emma would drive back). Meg loved her dad, he was a benign presence in the house, but she could not remember him ever cooking a meal for his children. Her mother did everything; all the cooking, cleaning, caring, and all the shouting and disciplining too. Meg was eleven when Connor was born and she remembered being roped in to change nappies from the start. She had never seen her father do it though.

'My dad didn't help around the house either,' said Emma. 'But, then again, my mother didn't do much housework herself.'

'I suppose you had servants,' said Meg. She'd read about houses like this. Aisling used to have a magazine that was full of stories about scullery maids marrying lords. Their houses were chock-a-block with uniformed servants, all bowing and curtsying like mad.

'Well, we had a housekeeper, Ada,' said Emma, sounding defensive. 'But she was more like a friend really. And we had a cook.'

More like a friend, thought Meg. She wondered if Ada would say the same. But she didn't answer because they were caught in a maze of streets that suddenly, and terrifyingly, turned into a road that soared into the sky, the docks and the factories far below. There were signs everywhere and it was only at the last minute that Emma saw one for Leeds.

'That's the right direction,' she said. 'Left here.'

Meg saw a gap in the traffic and wove through. A tunnel, another bewildering junction and then they were on a wide, clear road with hills on either side.

'Well done,' said Emma. 'You're a great driver.'

'I love driving,' said Meg. 'But I don't often get the chance.'

'Of course, women aren't allowed to drive police cars,' said Emma, 'what with us being such sensitive flowers and all that.'

'I wish I could drive instead of DI Willis,' said Meg. 'He's *so* slow.'

Emma laughed. 'I don't think I've ever been in a car with Bob but I can imagine. Who taught you to drive?'

'My dad. He's a mechanic so he knows all about cars. He taught me when I was seventeen.'

'My dad taught me too,' said Emma.

'In the Rolls?' said Meg, with a sideways glance.

There was a brief silence and then Emma said, 'Yes, actually.' Meg started laughing and, a few seconds later, Emma joined in.

In the end the drive took more like four hours. Some of it was surprisingly beautiful, with open countryside all around them and dark hills – almost mountains – in the background. 'The Pennine Way,' Emma said. But they also passed sprawling cities and factories spewing smoke. They stopped at a roadside café outside York and ate sandwiches and drank black coffee at a rickety picnic table.

Then they crossed the moors, dark with heather and the shadows of clouds. It was the longest drive Meg had ever undertaken and, by the time they saw signs for Whitby, her back ached and her foot had cramp from pressing on the accelerator.

'Not far now,' said Emma. She passed Meg a wine gum, another roadside purchase. They had got into a comfortable rhythm now, talking for stretches then staying silent for miles, having a wine gum every ten minutes. They had talked about the case, about their families and the unfair way women were treated in the police force (that had lasted from Huddersfield to Leeds). Now they were onto Max Mephisto. Meg had met him briefly last year, but she'd been in the middle of catching a killer so she hadn't been able to concentrate. She just had a vague memory of a tall figure racing up some stairs.

'Max is very charming,' said Emma. 'I mean really charming, not slimy in the way some men are. He really listens to you and seems interested in you. But somehow it's hard to get to know him. You can never really tell what he's thinking. Ed's been friends with Max since the war and they've been through a lot together. I think he's as close to him as anyone is but he doesn't really know him.'

'Does Edgar … Superintendent Stephens … know Lydia Lamont too?'

'Hardly. The four of us had lunch together but it's not as if we're all mates.' Emma paused for a minute before saying, 'Lydia came to see me, you know.'

'Came to see you?' said Meg, squinting as the low sun reflected on the windscreen. 'When? Where?'

'She came into the office,' said Emma. 'Said she wanted to help with the case.'

'Help with the case? How?'

'By being our eyes and ears in Whitby. She also implied that the mafia were out to get Bert.'

'The mafia? Did you tell the super?'

'No,' said Emma. 'I mean, it was obviously nonsense.' But Meg thought that she sounded rather defensive.

'How come Max married Lydia Lamont anyway?' she asked. 'Did he go to America?'

'Yes,' said Emma. 'He got a part in a Hollywood film. Lydia was in it too and they fell in love.' She paused. 'Max wanted to get away from England. There was a woman he was in love with. Florence, her name was. She was on the stage, in one of those tableau acts.'

'Like the DI's wife?'

'Betty? Yes. Actually, Florence was in the same troupe and she was truly beautiful. Like a film star. Like Vivien Leigh. Anyway, she was murdered. It was a horrible case. A few weeks after it happened, Max went to America and the next thing we knew he was starring in films and he'd married Lydia.'

'Do you really think that Max had an affair with Verity?' said Meg.

'Yes, I do,' said Emma. She had some theory about Max fancying older women because his mother died when he was young. Meg wasn't quite sure it was as simple as that. After all, this Florence person wasn't old. Nor was Lydia Lamont. 'I can't see him trying to kill Bert, though,' Emma carried on. 'For one thing, he was in a Bert Billington panto in Brighton in 1951. *Aladdin*.'

'I went to see it,' said Meg, unaccountably excited. 'Boxing Day treat with the Knights of St Columba. Max was Abanazar, wasn't he? I thought he was amazing. A bit scary but amazing. Of course, I was only six.'

Emma was silent for a while and Meg wondered if she was offended by this reminder of their age difference. Then Emma said, looking out of the window, 'That was the Christmas that two children were killed. I can't think of the pantomime without thinking of that.'

'I remember,' said Meg. 'Hansel and Gretel, they called them. I can remember my mum and dad talking about it when they thought we were asleep. They were really scared, they even stopped letting us go out to play in the street.'

'We caught the man who did it,' said Emma. 'But it was . . . tough. I've never forgotten it.'

'Was DI Willis involved in that case?'

'Bob? Yes. It was the first big case we worked together. He was really affected by it. We both were. We got to know the children's families really well.'

'It must have been awful,' said Meg.

'It was,' said Emma. Then, after a slight pause, she added, 'It was a nightmare but, in a horrible way, it was exciting. That was when I realised that being a detective was all I wanted to do.'

'I know what you mean,' said Meg. 'I felt like that about the kidnapping case last year. It's dreadful for the people involved but there's nothing like it when you're on the chase.'

'On the chase,' said Emma with a laugh. 'That's us now.'

It was seven o'clock and nearly dark when they reached the outskirts of Whitby. They crossed a bridge and suddenly there was the town, a string of lights ending at the blackness that was the sea. Looking up, Meg saw what looked like a huge castle on a hill, lit by the baleful glow of a rising moon.

'What's that?' she said.

'Whitby Abbey,' said Emma. 'Beautiful, isn't it?'

Meg wasn't sure that was the right word. The building looked ominous and unreal, staring down at the town as if it had come from a different century, or a different universe. Maybe it was actually a spaceship, waiting to take Dracula back to his home planet. Emma started to direct them to the hotel where Max was staying, the ever-present map open on her lap.

The Royal Whitby Hotel was, of course, extremely grand, a square white building high above the sea, looking across to the abbey ruins on the next hill. Every light seemed to be blazing and Meg imagined the guests sitting down to dine, wearing evening dress and pearls, while a string quartet played in the background. She got out of the car, feeling stiff and grubby. Most of her hair seemed to have escaped from its ponytail and she knew that the lipstick and powder she had applied so carefully at seven a.m. in Brighton had evaporated long ago. She saw Emma smoothing back her hair and realised that her sophisticated companion was having exactly the same thoughts.

'Let's find a ladies' before we find Max,' said Emma.

Meg agreed enthusiastically and they made their way across the car park, following the signs to 'Reception'. It was now very dark and Meg was aware of the ruined abbey watching them, the moon shining through its empty windows. There were trees on one side of the hotel and dark shapes that Meg suddenly realised were tombstones, angels and crosses silhouetted against the night sky. She had to fight a ridiculous urge to hold Emma's hand. As it was, they moved closer together as they passed the graveyard. The wind picked up, making the trees moan and sigh. The moon disappeared behind a cloud and, in the sudden blackness, they heard a gate creak open. And saw Dracula in front of them, his pale face lit by a smile that seem to welcome them to their doom.

Meg screamed. She apologised afterwards but she just couldn't help it. Even Emma gave a gasp of terror.

Dracula said, 'I'm terribly sorry. I was taking a shortcut.'

'Seth?' said Emma.

'I'm sorry,' Dracula said again. 'Do I know you?'

Torchlight gleamed on a white shirt. Another figure loomed out of the dark and a voice said, 'Emma? What are you doing here?'

It was Max Mephisto. He was dressed, like Seth, in white tie and tails, covered by a cloak. Vampires were always so well-dressed, thought Meg. Max was accompanied by an older woman in ordinary clothes.

'Emma?' said Seth. 'Emma Holmes?'

'Hallo, Seth,' said Meg. She thought it was about time that they noticed her too.

Seth peered at her. He still looked very Transylvanian but Meg was pleased that he wasn't wearing his fangs.

'Aren't you the policewoman?' he said.

Once seen, never forgotten, thought Meg. 'Yes,' she said. 'We'd like to have a word with you. And with Mr Mephisto too.'

'Have you come all the way from Brighton?' asked Max.

'From Liverpool,' said Meg. 'We've been following a lead.' She rather liked the sound of this.

'Oh, I love Liverpool,' said the woman. 'But it's a long drive from there to Whitby. Why don't we go inside, out of the cold? I'm Irene, by the way. I'm the wardrobe mistress.'

Theatrical titles were very odd, thought Meg. Wardrobe mistress sounded dodgy somehow. But she liked the idea of leaving the graveyard gate.

'Yes, let's go in,' said Max. 'We've just finished filming.

Another midnight scene. Seth and I didn't bother to get changed. We didn't think we'd be meeting anyone.'

'It's not midnight,' said Meg, thinking, too late, how stupid this sounded.

'It's always midnight in horror films,' said Max.

They walked round to the front of the hotel. It seemed a different world, brightly lit, with sweeping steps leading to revolving doors.

In the lobby – red carpets, marble columns – Max said, 'I need to get changed. Then, why don't you come up to my room for that chat?'

'Is Mrs Mephisto with you?' asked Meg. It sounded wrong. Wasn't his wife Lady something?

'No, she's gone home to see the children,' said Max. 'Just give me ten minutes.'

'Can we talk to you too, Mr Billington?' said Meg.

'All right,' said Seth. 'Meet you in the bar in an hour?'

'I think we'd better talk in private,' said Emma.

NINETEEN

It was strange, thought Emma, seeing Max in his hotel room. There was his coat on the back of the door, his cigarette case and gloves on the table. The wardrobe was slightly open and she could see a dark suit hanging inside. Had Lydia taken all her clothes with her when she left 'to see the children'? Lydia hadn't mentioned any such visit when she'd spoken to Emma on Monday.

Max's Dracula costume was thrown onto one of the chairs. He was now wearing pin-striped trousers and an open-necked white shirt with the sleeves rolled up. It was the most casual Emma had ever seen him look. She supposed that he hadn't had time to put on cufflinks.

Max sat in the other chair. Emma and Meg sat side by side on the bed. It seemed an odd way to conduct an investigation but, then again, everything about today had been odd: the long journey to Liverpool, the slightly disturbing interview with the Gillespies, Jimmy's car hire, Meg's heroic drive across the Pennines, the meeting in the graveyard.

She realised that Meg was waiting for her to start, maybe because she knew Max better. Don't take over, Emma had told herself all day. She had expected (maybe even hoped?) that Meg would be intimidated by her, just because Emma was older, married to the super and had once been the youngest woman detective in Britain, etc., etc. And, at first, Meg *had* seemed a bit overawed, she'd clearly never been far from her native town and seemed to find Liverpool and its inhabitants rather bewildering. But, from the moment that Meg had flourished her warrant card at Jimmy, Emma had seen a different side to the WDC. Meg had then taken the wheel and driven calmly and competently across the breadth of England. But, when they arrived at the hotel, Emma thought she saw her companion shrink a little, intimidated by the Royal Whitby. Running into Dracula probably hadn't helped either.

Emma took a deep breath. 'We've just been to see Sandra and Norman Gillespie, the parents of Glenda Gillespie.'

Max grimaced. 'That poor girl. I remember when it happened.'

'Sandra said that you'd had an affair with Verity Malone. Is that true?' Lydia had said it too, but Emma didn't think she would mention that.

Max sighed. He opened his cigarette case and looked at its contents but didn't light up. Then he said, 'It was a long time ago. Before you were born probably.'

'Really?' Emma had certainly been alive in 1949, which was when Glenda had died.

'I'd just started out in the business,' said Max. 'I was lucky to get a Bert Billington show. Very low billing, but still. Verity gave a sort of tea party for all the artistes. I fell in love at first sight. She was so beautiful in those days.'

'How old were you?'

'Eighteen. She was thirty-eight.'

'And you had an affair with her?'

'Yes. She was my first love, in a way. I'd had girlfriends before but she was different.'

'How long did the affair go on?'

'All through that run and the next. Then Bert got suspicious and I had to leave town in a hurry.'

'Did the affair carry on?'

'No. We went our different ways. I met Emerald, Ruby's mother. Then the war came. I didn't see Verity again until I was appearing in Manchester in 1949. Verity was in Liverpool. She asked to see me. She was upset about Bert. He was carrying on with one of the showgirls as usual. Barbara something.'

'Sandra said Glenda walked in on you and Verity,' said Emma.

'I was just giving her a hug,' said Max. 'She was upset and I was comforting her. Glenda – God rest her soul – was the sort who liked to exaggerate everything. It seemed to have been inherited.'

'Sandra also said that you tried to kill Bert when a piece of scenery fell on him.'

Max gave a bark of laughter. 'That was a genuine

accident. I wasn't that good with the props in those days. Bert was furious with me for a few years. I thought it would ruin my career. But he forgave me in the end. Or he realised that I was still good box office. He cast me in his pantomime in Brighton. *Aladdin*. Do you remember?'

'How could I forget?' Emma held his gaze.

'Bert Billington was an actor once,' said Meg suddenly. 'Eric Prentice told me. He played Layer something in *Hamlet* before the First World War.'

'Laertes,' said Max. 'Well, I suppose that's fitting.'

'Why?' asked Meg. Emma admired the way that Meg never minded admitting when she didn't know things.

'Because Laertes was poisoned,' said Max. 'Stabbed with a poisoned sword that was meant for Hamlet. "I am justly killed by mine own treachery." Something like that anyway.'

'Mr Mephisto,' said Meg. 'Who do you think killed Bert Billington?'

Max turned to look at Meg but Emma thought that he wasn't really seeing her. Which face from his past was he conjuring?

'Lots of people hated Bert,' he said at last. 'But a few people loved him. I'd concentrate on them, if I were you.'

After talking to Max, they moved three doors along the corridor to interview Seth. Max had urged them to stay in Whitby for the night. 'It's far too late to drive back to

Liverpool now. I'll ring down and see if they can find you a twin room.' Emma had been tempted, she wasn't looking forward to driving across country for four hours in the dark. But Meg had sounded shocked. 'We've got rooms booked in Liverpool. Paid for and everything.'

'Then they won't mind if you turn up or not,' said Max. 'I can ask Irene to get you some night stuff.' Meg had blushed dark red at that.

Emma was surprised that Seth's room, though comfortable, was smaller than Max's suite. But she supposed that Max and Lydia together outranked even Seth Billington. Where *was* Lydia?

Seth was also casually dressed in dark trousers and a soft grey jumper. His hair looked like it was wet from the shower. The thought of Seth in the shower made Emma feel slightly embarrassed and she was annoyed at herself. She was a happily married mother of three, she shouldn't be fantasising about film stars. Meg had said that her younger sisters were mad about Seth but they were teenagers, they had an excuse for being silly. Although, watching Meg watching Seth, Emma thought that her companion wasn't immune either.

This time, Meg took the lead. 'Mr Billington,' she began.

'Seth, please.' Seth smiled at her. 'Were your sisters pleased with the autographs?'

Meg blushed again but she kept her tone businesslike. 'Yes, they were. Thank you very much. Seth, did you know that your mother received an anonymous message after the death of Alma Saunders?'

Seth's face clouded. 'Poor old Alma. I still can't believe it.'

'Did your mother tell you about it?' asked Meg. 'It was a flyer for *Dick Whittington* with "King Rat" written on it.'

'King Rat?' Seth's look of bemusement was perfect.

'Yes. It was an advertisement for a show in 1949. When your father played King Rat.'

'I remember,' said Seth.

'But you don't know who sent that flyer?'

'No. Why are you asking about it?'

'Because your fingerprints were on the envelope.'

It was very well done. The words fell between them like a stone in a deep pool. Emma felt as if she was watching the ripples getting wider and wider.

'That's impossible,' said Seth at last.

Emma and Meg just looked at him.

'I mean,' said Seth, running his fingers through his damp hair. 'Why would I do a thing like that?'

'You tell us,' said Meg.

'Mr Billington,' said Emma. 'Where were you on Tuesday night?'

'Tuesday night? Surely you can't think—'

'It's a simple question,' said Meg.

Seth gave her a look that seemed to change his face completely. Just for a second, he looked not unlike the Prince of Darkness himself.

'I stayed at the Old Ship.'

'In Brighton?' said Meg in surprise.

'Yes.'

'Why didn't you stay with your mother?' asked Emma.

'Why do you think?' said Seth. 'Because I was with a woman, of course.'

'Ruby French?' said Emma.

Now Seth really did stare at her. 'How the hell did you know that?'

TWENTY

When they went back downstairs, the receptionist informed them that there was a twin-bedded room reserved for them and that Mr Mephisto was waiting for them in the dining room. Meg didn't know which announcement disturbed her more. She didn't have the money to pay for half a hotel room at the Royal Whitby, she probably didn't have enough money in her entire bank account for that. And she'd never eaten a meal in a smart restaurant, let alone in the company of a famous person. She looked helplessly at Emma, who said, 'Shall we take the room?'

Meg lowered her voice. 'I don't have ... I couldn't pay ...'

The receptionist coughed discreetly. 'Mr Mephisto asked us to put the room on his account.'

'No,' said Emma. 'I'll pay.' She steered Meg away. 'Max is a great picker-up of bills,' she said. 'I think he does it to be in control. Well, partly anyway. Look, I'll pay for the room. It's my fault. I just couldn't face driving all that way in the dark. We'll go back to Liverpool first thing, collect our cases and be on the midday train to London.'

It sounded so easy put like that, thought Meg. How simple the world was if you had money.

'Thank you,' was all she said.

'Now let's go to the ladies' and freshen up,' said Emma. 'I don't know about you but I feel like something unearthed from Tutankhamun's tomb.'

Meg agreed even though she only had the vaguest idea about what had been found in the pharaoh's tomb. It was discovered in the 1920s, she knew, and everyone involved had died mysteriously. She couldn't suppress a slight shiver as she followed Emma towards the doors displaying a silhouette of a woman in Victorian dress.

The loos were bigger than Meg's house, with flock wallpaper, sinks with gilt taps and one of those velvet sofas without a back. Meg washed her face and tried to get her hair back in its ponytail.

'Shall I do you a French plait?' said Emma. 'I've been practising on Marianne.'

Marianne was Emma's eldest daughter. Meg knew that from their conversation in the car. It felt odd having Emma comb her hair and tease the strands into order. She could see their reflections in the mirror; Emma concentrating, frowning slightly, Meg looking rather scared. They could almost be mother and daughter, except that Meg was so much taller.

'There,' said Emma. 'What do you think?'

Meg's dark hair had been arranged in a complicated plait that started on the top of her head. It made her look older, smarter and – Meg thought – richer.

'I love it,' she said, truthfully. 'You'll have to show me how to do it.'

'It's easier on someone else,' said Emma. She twisted her own hair into a knot, stuck in a couple of hairpins and created a very neat bun. Then she got lipstick out of her bag and applied it. She offered it to Meg, who shook her head. It was one thing to let Emma do her hair, another to borrow her lipstick. Meg would just have to go for the fresh-faced look.

They went through into the restaurant and Max Mephisto stood up to greet them. He was now wearing a jacket and tie, cufflinks gleaming at his wrists. What would her parents say if they could see her now? wondered Meg. Their daughter, her hair in a complicated braid, sitting down to dine with a film star. Her nerves had vanished and now she felt an almost dreamlike confidence. The waiter offered them an aperitif. Emma ordered a martini and Meg asked for the same. The drink came in a shallow glass with an olive bobbing on top. Meg took a sip and felt her eyes watering.

'The food's quite good here,' said Max. He ordered a bottle of wine and the waiter poured some in his glass to taste. Max saw Meg staring and smiled. 'My father just used to sniff the cork but that always struck me as strange.'

'Very strange,' said Meg, taking another sip of martini.

'Isn't Seth joining us?' asked Emma. Meg hadn't expected Seth to emerge from his room, not after she'd practically accused him of being involved in Alma's murder. She assumed that Emma was asking to ascertain how much Max knew.

'No,' said Max. 'We mostly keep ourselves to ourselves off set.'

'I gather that Seth stayed in Brighton for a few days,' said Emma. 'He says that he only got back to Whitby on Wednesday night.'

'That's right.' Max raised his eyebrows. 'He wasn't needed for filming until Thursday. Is that somehow significant?'

'Maybe,' said Emma.

Seth had been with Ruby on Tuesday night. Ruby was Max's daughter. The complications were making Meg's head swim. Although that could be the martini.

Meg got through the menu by copying Emma again. She wasn't sure what she had ordered – half the words seemed to be in French – but it turned out to be roast lamb. And delicious.

Meg found herself enjoying the meal. As Emma had said, Max was very charming. He asked her about growing up in Brighton ('one of my favourite cities') and about life in the police force.

'I imagine Emma blazed a trail for women officers.'

'They still talk about her,' said Meg. 'She's a legend in Brighton.' She would never have dared to say this normally.

The martini, now combined with a glass of wine, seemed to have loosened her tongue.

'I changed nothing,' said Emma. 'Women are still side-lined into domestic cases. They can't even drive panda cars.'

'I've been involved with two murder cases,' said Meg.

'You're lucky,' said Emma.

'I'm lucky because of you,' said Meg, talking another gulp of wine. 'And DI Willis, I suppose.'

'Bob's a good chap,' said Max. 'A little slow on the uptake, perhaps, but a solid citizen.'

'Don't underestimate Bob,' said Emma. Meg was surprised to hear her sounding quite angry.

Neither Max nor Emma wanted pudding, but Meg was now bold enough to strike out on her own and ordered the Black Forest gateau. Over a glass of brandy, Max told them about his children.

'Rocco loves books. He spends hours in the library at home. I don't think anyone ever read the books in there before. My father didn't. I didn't. They're kept behind a grille, as if they're dangerous. Elena's a firecracker like Ruby. She always wants to be where the action is.'

'You must miss them,' said Emma. Her attitude seemed to have softened too. She smiled into the dregs of her wine. Was she thinking about her children? Meg was trying to concentrate on the undercurrents around the table but was momentarily distracted by the arrival of her cake, a glistening slice of chocolate sponge, oozing cream and cherry jam.

'Lydia must be missing them too,' Emma went on. 'Is that why she's gone back?' Meg had misjudged her colleague. Emma wasn't softening, she was luring Max into a trap.

'Of course she's missing them,' said Max, sharply. 'It's hard for a mother.' This was a counter blow.

'I think it's just as hard for fathers,' said Emma. 'I often feel sorry for Ed. He sees so little of the children. That's why he has enjoyed today so much.'

Max laughed. 'Is that so? I rang him earlier and he seemed completely frazzled. Jonathan had smeared jam all over the television or something like that.'

To Meg's surprise, Emma gave a shout of laughter. 'Really? And Ed doesn't like the children watching TV.' She seemed happier than she had been all day. At any rate she didn't ask what, to Meg, was the obvious question. Why had Max been telephoning the super?

Meg finished her cake, resisting the temptation to run her finger over the remaining crumbs.

'I can't believe Ruby's your daughter,' she said to Max. 'I love *Iris Investigates*. You must have been very young when she was born.'

'I was twenty,' said Max. 'But I'm afraid I didn't know of her existence until years later. I'm fifty-five now and I've got two young children. I've been trying to catch up ever since.'

Meg had never been good at mental arithmetic and the alcohol didn't help. She tried to take Seth's age (gleaned from *Film Frolics*) from Max's to see if the answer was eighteen. Looking at Emma, she thought that she was working on the same sum.

Irene the wardrobe mistress had left a package for them in reception. It contained two voluminous nightdresses. 'The best I could do, I'm afraid,' said the accompanying note. 'These were worn by the girls who get turned into vampires in the film but I hope they'll be cosy enough!' There was also a paper bag containing toothpaste and soap.

The room was large and comfortable with two beds a good distance apart. Meg had never stayed in a hotel before and she was enchanted with it all: the fluffy towels, the bedside lights in the shape of flowers, their own bathroom with its little bottles of shampoo and body lotion.

Meg bounced on her bed. 'Were you thinking the same as me?' she said. 'About Max and Seth?'

'About whether Max is his father?' said Emma. 'I must admit, it did occur to me. Seth is thirty-six, Max is fifty-five.'

'Which means Seth was born when Max was nineteen.'

'Yes,' said Emma. 'You know, when we saw them today, in the graveyard, I thought how alike they were.'

'That's because they were both dressed up as vampires.'

'Dracula and Son. That's what Max calls the film. I wonder if he knows?'

'He must suspect, surely?'

'The question is,' said Emma, 'did Bert suspect?'

Meg had a fit of the giggles when Emma emerged from the bathroom in the big white dress, like a Victorian bride. On her, the nightdress didn't quite come to the floor and was a little tight across the shoulders.

'We look like lunatics,' said Meg, still giggling as she got into bed.

'Sounds as if the film is full of undead girls in their nightdresses,' said Emma. 'How depressing.'

'What actually happens in *Dracula*?' said Meg, settling herself on the pillows.

'It's a long time since I've read it,' said Emma, 'but it starts when an English solicitor called Jonathan Harker visits a castle owned by a Transylvanian count called Dracula. All sorts of weird things happen, including Dracula climbing up the walls like a spider, and Jonathan realises that Dracula is a vampire, someone who never dies but goes around looking for human blood to drink. I can't remember how Jonathan escapes, but he does. Then Dracula comes to England looking for new blood and ends up in Whitby. Dracula spends a lot of time pursuing Jonathan's fiancée, Lucy. Van Helsing, a sort of vampire expert, tries to save Lucy by giving her garlic to wear but she's killed anyway. Van Helsing puts a crucifix on her body but a servant steals it so Lucy becomes a vampire. Local children report seeing a beautiful woman – a "boofer lady" – in white, stalking them. Eventually Van Helsing and Lucy's friend Mina defeat Dracula and Jonathan marries Mina. Dracula turns into dust, I think.'

'There was garlic in my supper,' said Meg, who'd been impressed by this. 'I'm safe.'

'It's just a story,' said Emma. 'The author, Bram Stoker, was fascinated by actors. That explains a lot, in my opinion. Goodnight, Meg.'

It might have been just a story, but Meg thought that Emma remembered it pretty well, down to all the characters' names. She must have been more affected by the book than she admitted. The narrative kept slithering around in Meg's mind. She'd been awake since before six and thought she'd go to sleep immediately but images kept flashing up, like one of those old black-and-white films, the sort that ends with the girl tied to the railway tracks and the piano music rising to a crescendo. A cloaked figure in a graveyard, a man climbing a wall like a spider, a woman in a long white dress, bones crumbling to dust. She could hear her watch ticking under her pillow and Emma breathing steadily in the next bed. Then there was another sound, a sort of scrabble that stopped and then started again, gradually coming closer. Was it the sort of noise a Transylvanian count would make trying to scale a hotel wall? Meg got up and went to the window. She pulled the curtains and saw the moonlight shining on the white tombs. And, staring up at her, Count Dracula, once again smiling that dreadful smile of welcome.

TWENTY-ONE

'She was really scared,' said Emma. 'Her scream woke me up.'

'Were you scared?' said Edgar.

'I was a bit,' admitted Emma. 'He just stood there, gazing at us, then he whisked off through the graves, his cloak billowing around him. It was all very B-movie. But effective all the same.'

They were in their basement kitchen. Edgar had opened a bottle of wine as a welcome home treat. The children were all in bed and Emma felt relaxed and happy. She had arrived back in Brighton at six p.m., to an ecstatic welcome from all the family. 'I should go away more often,' she said, not entirely joking.

Edgar and the girls had made spaghetti bolognaise for supper. Marianne and Sophie were thrilled with their efforts, watching Emma's face as she ate. Jonathan joyfully threw chopped-up pasta strands across the table. But, when the children were in bed, Edgar said, pouring wine, 'I'm exhausted. I don't know how you cope with the three of them. I let them watch television all day today, even though most of it was quite unsuitable.' Emma had to hide her smile of satisfaction.

Now her thoughts were back on the case. 'I suppose it must have been Seth,' she said. 'Max said he gave his costume back to the wardrobe mistress but Seth must have kept his. It doesn't explain why he was wearing it at midnight in the graveyard though.'

'Max rang me on Friday,' said Edgar. 'It was at rather a tricky moment actually. Jonathan was intent on destroying the TV. Anyway, it was a bit odd. Max wanted to know if I'd seen Seth in Brighton on Tuesday. I said I assumed he'd gone back to Whitby on Monday, like Max.'

'Seth was in Brighton on Tuesday,' said Emma. 'He was at the Old Ship Hotel with Ruby.'

She watched Edgar closely as she said this but she couldn't detect any longing for his former fiancée. Instead he said, 'So Seth *was* here. Is he having an affair with Ruby?'

'I think so,' said Emma. 'She hinted as much when she came for lunch.'

'Does Max know?'

'Maybe he suspects.'

'If Seth was in Brighton on Tuesday,' said Edgar, 'he was here when Alma was killed.'

'Exactly,' said Emma. Then, after a pause in which they both sipped their wine thoughtfully, 'Meg and I were wondering if Max could be Seth's father,' said Emma. 'The dates match up. Max was sleeping with Verity when he was eighteen. He's nineteen years older than Seth.'

'That's a thought,' said Edgar. 'And it would explain why Max wouldn't want Seth seeing Ruby. Because she's his half-sister.'

'Max swears that the affair with Verity didn't continue after the war,' said Emma. 'But Glenda – the girl who died – says she saw them together in Liverpool in 1949. That was the year that Bert played King Rat in Dick Whittington. Max was performing at Manchester.'

' "Max Mephisto mesmerises in Manchester",' said Edgar.

'What?'

'It was a newspaper cutting I once found in the possession of a dead girl,' said Edgar. 'I lost contact with Max after the war. We met again in 1950. He certainly wasn't seeing Verity then.'

'And in 1951 Bert Billington cast him in *Aladdin*.'

'That doesn't necessarily mean anything,' said Edgar. 'They're a hard-nosed lot, show-business people. And they don't hold grudges. I learnt that in the Magic Men. Bert might still have given Max the role, even if he suspected him of sleeping with his wife. Max is good box office.'

This was almost exactly what Max had said, Emma remembered. And it might be true. But it didn't alter the fact that someone in Bert's life *had* held a grudge. And that person had killed him.

'I've got the list of Bert's girlfriends somewhere,' said Emma, getting up.

'I can't believe Verity gave you that,' said Edgar.

'She offered,' said Emma. She went to the desk where she kept her Holmes and Collins files.

'And what about Seth's fingerprints being on the envelope of the King Rat flyer?' said Edgar. 'How did he explain that?'

'He didn't really,' said Emma, riffling through pages. 'Meg put it to him straight. She did it very well actually. But he just denied it.'

'It's not enough to charge Seth,' said Edgar. 'But it's certainly evidence against him. If we can prove that he was in Rottingdean on Tuesday . . .'

'Maybe Seth was the woman in the brown coat,' said Emma. 'He certainly seems to like dressing up. Here it is.' She brought the handwritten list to the table and they both peered at it. Edgar refilled their glasses.

Jenny Wilkins, early 1920s
Beryl Simmonds, around 1928
Joan (?) war-years
Rita Edwards — 1945. Had child, Christopher (Kit).
Glenda Gillespie (RIP). Had child, Angela (RIP).
Barbara (Babs) 1949. Query dead?
Louise Henshaw, 1950s. Had child, Daisy.
Pamela Curtis??

'Blimey,' said Edgar. 'She's even given dates.'

'Rita was the woman who turned up when Seth was

staying with his mother,' said Emma. 'He said Verity gave her money to go away. David, the oldest son, paid off some of the others. Apparently, he tried to give money to the Gillespie family but they wouldn't take it.'

'Pamela Curtis,' said Edgar. 'Wasn't she Bert's assistant?'

'Yes. I don't know why she's on the list. She told me and Sam that she wasn't interested in men.'

'Maybe Verity ended up suspecting everyone. I'll ask Bob to trace all these women. Every one of them had a motive, after all.'

'He'll just get Meg to do it,' said Emma.

'Well, it is her job,' said Edgar.

'She's really good,' said Emma. 'She'll be a DI one day.' Unless she gets married and has to leave the force, she added silently.

'She's a bright girl,' said Edgar abstractedly. He was looking at the names on the list. 'Glenda Gillespie,' he said. 'RIP. She doesn't feel very peaceful, somehow.'

Max was also enjoying an early evening drink with his wife. They were in the drawing room at Massingham Hall, with a fire burning and cooking smells drifting from the kitchen. Lydia, wrapped in a cashmere shawl (despite the fire the house was still extremely cold), sat with her legs tucked under her, sipping a glass of white wine. Max drank his whisky and felt, unusually for him, entirely at peace.

The idea of going home had come to Max when he was woken in his suite at the hotel by a car idling outside. He'd gone to the window to see a rather rusty Ford Cortina by the main entrance, clouds of blue smoke around it. Emma was at the wheel, her hair tied back in a scarf. Then Meg came out, hurrying as if she'd forgotten something. Her hair was loose and she looked younger than she had last night. She got in the car and the two women drove away.

It was only seven a.m. but Max didn't feel like getting back into bed. It was a bright but misty morning. In the distance Whitby Abbey was doing its atmospheric thing again. Saturday and Sunday stretched ahead of him. There was no filming this weekend. What would he do? Play golf with Wilbur, the director? Drink too much in the hotel bar? He thought of Emma and Meg disappearing in a puff of smoke, like one of his own magic tricks. If Emma could drive to Liverpool, he could drive home to Somerset. If he left now, he'd be there at midday. And he would be in his newly serviced Jaguar, not some rickety hired car. Besides, said the old touring pro inside him, Sunday is changeover day. He should be on the move.

He'd arrived at Massingham Hall at three o'clock. Parking in front of the double staircase that formed a ridiculously grand entrance, he was surprised to see orange spheres on every step. Getting closer he saw that they were pumpkins, each one hollowed out to contain a candle. What was this? He didn't have time to wonder because a dog started barking inside the house and, a few seconds later, the doors burst open and Elena and Rocco tumbled out.

'Daddy!'

He tried to sweep them both into his arms. The dog, a crazy black-and-white spaniel, danced around them in hysterical joy. Max still missed his Alsatian, Caesar (Bob to his friends), who had been left behind in California in the care of their former housekeeper. This creature was too needy, too undiscerning. Plus, he'd let his children christen it Panda.

'Are you staying home now, Daddy?' said Elena, hanging on his arm.

'I've got to go back tomorrow,' said Max. 'But there's only two weeks of filming after that. Then I'll be home.' Until the next job, he thought.

Rocco wanted to carry his bag but they compromised on a handle each. As they sidled into the hall, Max asked where Lydia was.

'She's in the playroom,' said Elena. 'We're making American things called jack lanterns.'

'Jack-o'-lanterns,' said Rocco.

The playroom had once been Max's father's study. Even now, Max couldn't enter the room without imagining the old man at his desk, looking up, annoyed at any interruption. What had he been doing in there for hours every evening? Alastair Massingham hadn't been a great reader and he only acquired a television in later life, when his granddaughter started appearing on it. Surely he couldn't have spent all his time polishing his gun collection and writing angry letters to the *Telegraph*? The room was now pleasant and airy, with squashy chairs and a parquet floor decorated with Rocco's train track and Elena's farm animals. There was also what Lydia called a 'craft table', covered with a plastic cloth. She was there now, using a knife to cut shapes out of a pumpkin.

'Max!' She looked up. 'This is a nice surprise.'

Lydia was wearing jeans and an old sweater. Her hair was skewered carelessly on top of her head. She looked very beautiful and slightly wary.

Max came over to kiss her. 'I missed you. I wanted a weekend with my family.'

'The weekend's half over,' said Lydia. But she had kissed him back and, briefly, rested her head against his shoulder.

Now, he said, reaching out to pat Panda who was panting at his feet. 'What's with all the pumpkins?' There was even one by the fire, candlelight glittering in its eyes.

'It's an American tradition,' said Lydia. 'For Hallowe'en. All the kids dress up and they go from house to house saying, "Trick or treat." The neighbours give them candy. If a house is decorated with a lighted pumpkin, it means the kids can call in. It's a sort of signal.'

Max vaguely remembered Hallowe'en in California. His children had been too young to dress up then – and the houses too far apart for walking, especially in car-centric

America – but he could recall seeing some decorations in the shops. He didn't know quite where Lydia's delightful vision came from. She'd spent her early years in a trailer park. He couldn't exactly imagine the fellow residents doling out sweets to winsome children. Hard drugs, yes. Candy, no.

'Isn't Hallowe'en at the end of the month?' he said. 'And isn't it all about witchcraft?'

'That's in England,' said Lydia. 'In America it's a family holiday.'

'I wish the children were eating with us,' said Max.

'They're quite happy with Nanny.'

'Mary Poppins?' This was Max's name for the nanny because they'd seen the Disney film last year, but all Mary Painswick shared with that magical creature was a first name.

'Besides,' said Lydia, 'I want some time alone with you.'

She smiled at Max, reaching over to touch him lightly on the arm. He was beginning to look forward to the evening.

TWENTY-TWO

After the excitement of Liverpool and Whitby, Meg found it rather dull to be back in the underground CID offices on Monday. She wanted to tell everyone about her adventures but no one even asked how she'd got on. She supposed that she'd only been off work for one day and her colleagues weren't to know that she'd had supper with a film star and seen Dracula in a graveyard. It was annoying though.

Even the DI hadn't asked many questions, although he had been interested to learn that Seth hadn't made it back to Whitby until the day after Alma's murder. They didn't have enough to charge Seth, he said, but it was 'potentially useful information'. He told Meg to get on with tracing the women who supposedly had had affairs with Bert Billington. Emma had copied out the names for her, a list originally supplied by Verity Malone.

Jenny Wilkins, early 1920s
Beryl Simmonds, around 1928
Joan (?) war-years
Rita Edwards – 1945. Had child, Christopher (Kit).
Glenda Gillespie (RIP). Had child, Angela (RIP).
Barbara (Babs) 1949. Query dead?
Louise Henshaw, 1950s. Had child, Daisy.
Pamela Curtis??

Meg couldn't believe how many names there were. Pinned to the noticeboard was a photo of the dead impresario: thin white hair, small eyes, narrow mouth. How on earth had he managed to sleep with so many women? 'Money talks,' her mother would say, but did it really speak that loudly?

She had to look at this logically. Emma thought that Rita had called on Verity when Bert was in hospital and that Verity had given her money for her son, Kit, now about eighteen. Barbara was the girl who had supplanted Glenda in Bert's affections, if affection was the word, which Meg thought it wasn't. Mrs Gillespie had thought that Barbara might be dead. They needed to be sure but it was hard without a surname. The same went for Joan(?). Meg could look in the census for the other women or maybe even visit Somerset House in London to look at the records for births, marriages and deaths. She perked up at the idea of another trip. She was becoming quite the traveller, she thought.

She'd also heard of something called a microfiche, which had records of every newspaper article ever printed. Maybe she could ask the DI if she could search the microfiche at the Dome. It was time that she got over her fear of libraries.

Looking at the list again, Meg thought that there was one person she could interview immediately. Pamela Curtis lived in Hove, only about ten minutes' walk away. Emma had said that Pamela was unlikely to have had an affair with Bert because she was, as she put it, 'not that way inclined'. This explained the two question marks against her name and made Meg even more curious to meet Bert's former assistant. Why had Verity put Pamela on the list?

Meg reached for her hat.

Sam was also in the office, the headquarters of Holmes and Collins Detective Agency. It was rare for her to be there without Emma but her colleague was once more encumbered by childcare. Her babysitter was out of hospital but Emma didn't like to leave her with Jonathan too long, 'not while he's in such a destructive phase'. As far as Sam could see, this phase had started at birth and would probably continue until Jonathan was at least thirty. Sam liked children – she especially liked Emma's children – but after spending a day with them she tended to feel better about her childless, unmarried state.

When she was at UCL, Sam sometimes heard female students talking about 'getting their MRS degree', in other words bagging an eligible husband. The idea had seemed ludicrous to her, even at the time. Sam had studied English so that, when she graduated, she would get a better job. The fact that she'd ended up doing dogsbody work at the Croydon *Echo* still hadn't taken the gloss off those university years. Sam had told Pamela Curtis that men were overrated but, actually, she was rather fond of the male species. She'd had several boyfriends and, when she'd lost her virginity to a history student called Jimmy, she regarded that as another milestone passed and therefore ticked off her list. Jimmy, though, had other ideas and had pursued her for several weeks, even making an embarrassing midnight visit to her digs, proposing marriage. After Sam had declined that kind offer, he had – thank goodness – left her alone and eventually married a trainee teacher from Goldsmiths.

Sam's parents had generally been supportive about her life choices. She knew that her mother would have liked her to be married with children by now but she was good enough not to mention this too often. Luckily Sam's brother Luke had married and produced two children so, as Sam's father put it, 'the line continues'. Sam was not quite sure why this was so important; it wasn't as if Collins were an unusual name or that the family were aristocrats or business moguls. But she was glad that her parents were happy.

Sam sat at the partner desk and thought about the case. Two people were dead now and she agreed with Emma that the murders of Bert Billington and Alma Saunders must be connected. What would she be doing if she were approaching the deaths from a journalistic point of view? She'd be looking for a story. Where was the story here? Was it glamorous Verity Malone marrying rich Bert Billington? Was it Glenda Gillespie meeting an older man who would ruin her life? Was it David Billington coming back from the war and joining the family business? Was it Aaron Billington buying a new motorbike or Seth Billington playing the prince of darkness? Sam kicked off her shoes, tucked her legs under her and started to scribble.

She was surprised, half an hour later, to find the floor littered with paper and, on the desk in front of her, an apple core floating in a cold cup of coffee. She really must clear up before Emma came in. Sam was just starting to tidy her notes, many of them mysteriously coffee-stained, when there was a loud knock on the door. She hoped it wasn't Emma and Jonathan, one bent on order and the other on chaos. But Emma would have a key, wouldn't she? Sam descended the stairs. There was a bulky shape visible through the bubbled glass. A man. Sam felt an unexpected twinge of fear.

The man was a stranger, tall and heavily built, wearing a dark suit that made him look even more threatening.

'Emma Holmes?'

'No.' Don't give anything away, Sam told herself.

'Sam Collins then?'

'Yes.'

'I'm Frederick Saunders. Fred. I wondered if I could have a word.'

Sam thought back to her notes, to her web of connections. Frederick was Alma's eldest son. That explained the black suit, at least.

Sam led Fred into the office, picking up papers as she went. She offered coffee which, surprisingly, he accepted. This, at least, gave her several minutes in the tiny kitchen waiting for the kettle to boil. Enough time to compose herself.

When she carried the mugs into the main room, Fred was holding the china horse.

'This looks like one of Mum's,' he said.

'It is,' said Sam. 'Alma gave it to Emma. My partner.' And, as if to prove it, she took her seat at the partner desk.

'I'm so sorry about your mum,' she said.

Fred just grunted and frowned into his coffee. Sam didn't blame him, the milk was slightly off and it looked quite nasty. 'I've just been to see Verity,' he said. 'She said that she'd engaged your agency to investigate Bert's death.'

'That's right,' said Sam, trying to look like the joint head of a thriving detective agency. She wished she hadn't taken her shoes off.

'Do you think that Bert was killed then?'

'Yes,' said Sam. 'Traces of rat poison were found in his blood. My partner spoke to the pathologist.' And a creepy bloke he was too, by all accounts. Useful though.

'And do you think the same person killed my mum?' His voice shook on the last word and Sam found herself feeling sorry for her visitor.

'It's a possibility,' she said. 'I'm sorry.'

'I just can't . . .' Fred stopped and started again. 'I just can't believe anyone would hurt Mum. Everyone loved her. Including Bert Billington.'

He looked at Sam. There was no doubting the implication of his words. Sam said, trying to keep her voice cool and impersonal, 'Did your mother have an affair with Bert?'

'You could call it that,' said Fred. 'Apparently it went on for years. Of course, we didn't know at the time. But then, a few Christmases ago, David's wife told my brother Barry.'

'Sheena?'

'Yes. She does the bookkeeping at the firm. She told Barry that there were regular payments to my mum, aside from her salary, going back years. He confronted Mum and she denied it, of course. But Barry thought it was true. Sheena said that it started when they went to live in Lytham.'

Sam looked at Fred Saunders. At first glance he didn't resemble careworn David, heart-throb Seth or sulky

Aaron but, like the Billington brothers, he was tall and dark-haired. Could Fred and Barry be Bert's sons? She wished she could remember the timeline of Alma's life. When exactly did she move to Lytham? She'd have to ask Emma.

'Did your father know?' she asked.

'I don't know,' said Fred. 'I hope not. He and Mum always seemed happy but you can never tell as a kid, can you? I did wonder why they didn't move to Surrey when Bert and Verity did, but I thought Dad just wanted to be near Gran and Granddad. Me and Barry had left home by then.'

'Did Verity know?' asked Sam.

'If she didn't, you can be sure Sheena told her,' said Fred, with a grim laugh. 'She's a prize bitch, that one.'

'Why are you telling me this?' asked Sam.

'Because someone killed Bert and someone killed Mum,' said Fred. 'Stands to reason it's someone who knew them both.'

Someone who knew them both, thought Sam, and someone who hated them both.

Meg enjoyed the walk along the seafront. It was a bright autumn day and the sea was breaking in companionable little waves against the pebbles. As she passed the peace statue, she saw a group of hippies – freaks, they called themselves – burning something on the beach. When she got nearer, she saw it was the American flag. Were they protesting about Vietnam or something else? Meg was still on chapter one of *The Feminine Mystique* but she was beginning to discover that America was a more complicated place than she had realised.

She turned right into First Avenue, just as the freaks burst into song. It was, of course, the Beatles. *All you need is love.* Meg was still humming it as she knocked on the door of Pamela Curtis's basement flat.

'A uniformed policewoman,' said Pamela. 'I am honoured.'

Meg wasn't quite sure how to take this. It sounded sarcastic but the older woman seemed friendly enough.

'We're investigating Bert Billington's murder,' she said. 'I understand that you used to work for him. I just wondered if you could answer a few questions.'

'I've already spoken to the dynamic duo,' said Pamela, 'the private detectives. I don't know if I have anything else to add.'

'It's just routine,' said Meg. *Dynamic duo.* Emma would love that.

Pamela ushered her into a room full of the weirdest paintings Meg had ever seen in her life. She literally didn't know where to look. On one side there was a woman with three breasts, on the other a naked man sitting on a giant tortoise. She compromised with looking at her hostess, who was smiling as if she knew exactly what Meg was thinking.

Meg asked a few questions about when Pamela started working for Bert and when she last saw him.

'It was a couple of years ago, walking along the seafront. He was with Aaron. I was with a girlfriend. We just passed the time of day.' Someone else had used this phrase recently. Who was it?

Pamela's casual mention of a girlfriend threw Meg slightly. Did she mean more than a friend who was a girl? Well, that wasn't relevant here.

'Miss Curtis,' she said. 'Someone recently told us that you'd had an affair with Bert. Is this true?'

In answer, Pamela threw back her head and laughed. She laughed for so long that Meg was reduced to staring at the triple-breasted woman again.

'No, dear,' said Pamela at last. 'It's not true. For one thing, I prefer women. For another, I wouldn't have slept with Bert Billington if he was the last man alive.'

Meg could readily believe this.

'Why would someone say that you did then?' she asked.

'It depends who that someone was,' said Pamela, still chuckling. 'And whether they were trying to divert attention elsewhere.'

'Misdirection,' said Meg. The word had come up when she and Emma were discussing Max.

'Exactly,' said Pamela. 'Who's performing this trick?'

Emma arrived in the early afternoon, accompanied by a frighteningly cheerful Jonathan.

'I can't stay long,' she said. 'I've got to pick the girls up from school at three-thirty.' She looked around the room. 'Have you been tidying?'

'Yes,' said Sam, pleased she'd noticed. She'd started clearing up when Frederick left and had got rather carried away. She'd even used the carpet sweeper

'Are you feeling all right?' asked Emma, letting go of Jonathan's hand with the air of one releasing a grenade.

'Fine,' said Sam. 'Coffee? I've washed all the cups although they're still that weird brown colour inside.'

'Washing the cups? Have you had a visitor?'

Oh, Emma was good. You couldn't get anything past her. Sam told Emma about Frederick Saunders. Her partner listened intently while Jonathan edged his hand towards the china horse.

'Alma Saunders and Bert Billington. Do you think Verity knew? Alma made out that she was so loyal to her.'

'Fred was pretty sure that Sheena would have told her too.'

'Why would Sheena do that?'

'Just to stir things up, maybe. Fred called her a prize bitch.'

'Hmm,' said Emma. 'Funny how animal metaphors are always insulting when applied to women.'

'Hilarious,' said Sam. 'The question is, does this give Verity a motive for killing Alma? Verity could easily have been the woman in the brown coat.'

'It's certainly possible,' said Emma. 'Verity didn't put

Alma on the list of Bert's girlfriends though. I wonder why?'

'Because she didn't want us to know,' said Sam. 'Because it gives her a motive.'

'That's true,' said Emma. 'And, if Verity had only recently found out about the affair, that answers the question about why Bert and Alma were killed now. That's what's been worrying me about the Glenda Gillespie motive. As Edgar said, fourteen years is a long time to wait for revenge.'

Sam thought about jealousy. It had always seemed a pointless emotion to her but there was no doubt that in some people it boiled to a murderous temperature. Emma seemed absorbed in trying to extricate the horse from Jonathan's grasp but Sam wondered if she was thinking along the same lines. They both jumped when the telephone rang. It was still rare to get a call at the office.

Emma picked up the receiver. 'Holmes and Collins. Oh, hi. Yes, she's here. I'll pass you over.'

She handed the phone to Sam. It was Don, the editor of the *Evening Argus*. He never sounded animated but today there was a note of grim excitement in his voice.

'You know the murder of that young man in Manchester? A woman has been arrested now. Name of Myra Hindley. Police think she and Brady may have killed many more people. Children too. You need to go up there, Sam.'

TWENTY-THREE

Wednesday, 27 October

The Moors Murders, as they came to be called, dominated the news for the next few weeks. Brady and Hindley stared out from newspapers and television screens, terrifying Meg's younger brother when he saw them on the early evening news. Once again Meg's parents were talking in hushed voices when they thought their children weren't listening. Although Meg, for one, probably knew more about the case than they did. It was all anyone talked about at Bartholomew Street police station.

Meg knew that Emma's friend, Sam Collins, was in Manchester, covering the story as a freelance reporter for the local paper. According to Emma, the truth was actually worse than the lurid headlines. Emma had told Meg this when she came into the station with some new information on the Billington case. Emma had asked to talk to Meg and the DI. At least Meg had assumed that Emma had asked for her, otherwise she was sure that she would have been excluded from the meeting. Emma's information was that Alma Saunders' son, Frederick, had claimed that Alma Saunders had been another of Bert's lovers. The DI had rubbed his hands together. 'This gives Verity Malone a motive for Alma,' he had said. 'I'm not so sure,' Emma had replied.

Meg wasn't sure either. She still thought that the answer lay in the past. Which was why she was sitting in the incident room on a cold October morning, going through the names of Bert Billington's paramours, as the DI called them.

Meg had made some progress over the last two weeks. The annotated list was in front of her.

Jenny Wilkins: Died in 1953. Cancer, according to her daughter.

Beryl Simmonds: Married and living in Scotland.

Joan (?) war-years.

Rita Edwards: Lives in Newhaven. Son Kit working as a plumber (Verity gave money for apprenticeship).

Glenda Gillespie: died in 1949

Barbara (Babs). Query dead?

Louise Henshaw: Married and living in Bristol. Has two other children.

Pamela Curtis: says she wouldn't have slept with Bert if he was the last man alive.

Only Joan and Barbara remained elusive. It was almost impossible without surnames, thought Meg. She'd been to the library and used the microfiche but she could hardly look through every copy of *The Times* published since the war. Today she was writing up her notes in her careful round handwriting. Emma said that doing this often produced hidden patterns. 'It's like automatic writing,' she had said. 'The message goes from your brain to your hand to the paper.' But all Meg was getting was cramp.

'What are you doing?' PC Danny Black appeared in the doorway. The room got almost no natural light and it was a shock for Meg to see that Danny was in his outdoor clothes. Was it lunchtime already?

'I'm having a séance,' said Meg. Then she wished she hadn't said that. The station was meant to be haunted and although, in theory, Meg didn't believe in ghosts, it seemed a bad idea to taunt them. A fellow WPC had reported seeing a tall black shape walking through the subterranean corridors at night. Was it Henry Solomon, a former police chief murdered at his desk in 1844? Meg didn't know and she didn't want to find out.

'Well you can stop, whatever you're doing,' said Danny. 'I'm going to take you for a ride.'

Meg sat up. Danny was smiling but she didn't quite trust him. Was he teasing her? She knew that some of her colleagues thought that she fancied Danny. She didn't

– he was shorter than her for one thing – but she didn't want to agree to something that would make her look stupid. After all, wasn't that what being taken for a ride meant? The police were fond of practical jokes and, in her early days, Meg seemed to be the butt of most of them. She still remembered going up to Sergeant O'Neill with the message, 'There's a Mr I. P. Knightly on the phone for you.'

But it seemed that Danny was on official business. 'Her ladyship. Verity Malone. She wants to see you. The DI asked me to drive you to Rottingdean. Get your coat.'

Meg wasn't sure that she liked his tone but she got up readily enough. Anything was better than more automatic writing.

Verity met them at the door of Tudor Close. She was wearing a strange knitted garment that was either a dressing gown or some other sort of robe. It was red, which made Meg think of Father Christmas.

Verity greeted Meg warmly but looked Danny up and down.

'Shall we let him in, Meg?'

'I suppose so,' said Meg. 'It's a bit cold to wait outside.'

'It's definitely a bit parky today,' said Verity, standing aside to let them pass. 'Winter's nearly here.'

She led Meg and Danny into the low-ceilinged sitting room. Verity sat in the armchair and gestured for the police officers to take the sofa. There were photos scattered on the coffee table, as if Verity had been trying to organise them. In pride of place was a framed colour photograph of a group of people standing in front of what looked like Whitby Abbey. Just seeing it made Meg shiver, remembering the graveyard and the caped figure staring up at her.

Verity saw her looking. 'Seth sent me that,' she said. 'It's a photograph of them all on the set of *The Prince of Darkness*. They finished filming last week.'

She offered the picture to Meg who look it rather hesitantly. There seemed to be lots of people in the photo, all of them smiling and waving. Seth was in the middle with Max beside him. Meg thought she saw Irene, the wardrobe mistress, at the end of the line. Danny peered over her shoulder. 'When's the film out?' he said. 'I'll take my girl to see it.' This was the first Meg had heard of a girlfriend.

Verity didn't seem impressed. 'No idea,' she said. 'I haven't liked films since they've had talking in them. Anyway, I didn't ask you here to chat about the cinema. I want to know how the investigation is going. It's been nearly three weeks since Alma was murdered. You know, they've only just released her body for burial. The funeral's on Friday.'

Meg knew. The DI said that they should attend, partly out of respect and partly because 'the murderer often attends the funeral'. Meg suspected him of reading this in a book somewhere.

'We're following up a few leads,' said Meg, thinking how weak this sounded. 'Going through the names on the list of . . . on the list you gave Emma.'

'The list of Bert's fancy women?' said Verity. 'That's what I wanted to talk to you about. I've got something to show you. I was sorting out some old pictures. There's no need to keep everything. I'm not one for sentiment. But I thought the grandchildren might be interested in some of the old ones. Anyway, I found this.'

She held out a photograph of an elderly man in a dinner jacket between two young women, an arm round each of them. Both were scantily dressed. With a twinge of revulsion, Meg realised that the man was Bert Billington. He was peering into one of the girls' cleavages and you could see the indentations where his fingers dug into the women's flesh.

'Bert,' said Verity, her voice expressionless. 'With Glenda and Babs.'

Meg recognised Glenda from the picture on the Gillespies' television. Her bright blonde hair and wide smile made her look the epitome of a showgirl. Barbara was dark and her eyes were looking at something out of camera shot. She was smiling too but her eyes looked frightened. She was carrying a basket of flowers.

'Babs was the rose girl,' said Verity. 'They often have

them in panto. She went into the auditorium and threw flowers at the audience. It gives the stagehands time to prepare for the Reveal.'

'I've been trying to track Barbara down,' said Meg, still looking at the photograph. 'You don't know her surname, do you?'

'It came to me yesterday,' said Verity. 'Dobson. Or Dodson. One of those names.'

'Do you know what happened to her?'

'I think she ended up in Hastings,' said Verity. 'We all do, in the end.'

What did that mean? thought Meg, as they drove back along the coast road. She remembered the super once mentioning Aleister Crowley, the writer, artist and supposed devil-worshipper, who was said to have cursed Hastings because they wouldn't let him be buried there. As a young policeman, the super had been sent to observe Crowley's funeral in Brighton. Had the necromancer really put a spell on the neighbouring town?

Danny persuaded her to stop for fish and chips on the beach, so it was two o'clock before Meg got back to the station. The first thing she did was telephone the *Hastings Gazette*. And, in the end, it was easy. A small item dated August 1965. 'Inquest into the death of prostitute, Barbara Dodson, found dead in her Hastings flat.'

TWENTY-FOUR

Meg felt slightly awkward when she learnt that she was to travel to Alma's funeral with the DI, the super and Emma. After Whitby she felt that Emma was almost a friend but it would be strange to see her in this company, Meg in her uncomfortable dress uniform, Emma with her husband, who was Meg's boss's boss. The car stopped in Kemp Town to pick Emma up. She came running down the steps of a tall, thin house, wearing a black coat and no hat. The day was sunny and her hair looked almost shockingly bright. Meg, her hat rammed down around her ears, felt more ridiculous than ever.

'Hallo, Meg,' said Emma, getting into the back seat beside her. 'Ready for another road trip?'

'It's St Margaret's Church in Rottingdean,' said the super. 'Let's not get excited.'

'Just getting out of the house is a treat for me,' said Emma.

'Who's babysitting Jonathan today?' said Meg. Her

sister Collette had babysat for the Stephenses a few times now. She said that the children were lovely but exhausting. The oldest daughter insisted on putting on plays all the time and the baby had torn two chapters out of one of Collette's schoolbooks.

'My friend Astarte,' said Emma. She turned to Meg. 'Astarte is a fortune-teller. She's a got a caravan on Brighton pier.'

'Gosh,' was all Meg could say.

'She's very fond of the children,' said the super.

'She told Bob's fortune once,' said Emma. 'She said that he'd marry a beautiful woman. And he did.'

In the front seat beside the driver, the DI's ears were bright red.

St Margaret's was the church next door to Tudor Close. It was properly old and exactly Meg's idea of what a church should be: a solid building with a bell tower looking out over the pond and the village green. The police car drew up on the grass outside just as the hearse rounded the corner. Meg and her colleagues hurried under the lychgate and into the church. Inside it was dark and smelt of flowers and damp. The only light filtered in through elaborate stained-glass windows. The place seemed very full and the police contingent took their seats near the back. Meg's view was hampered by a stone pillar but she could see Verity's yellow hair in one of the front pews. There were tall men on either side of her. Was one of them Seth? Alma was honoured, if so. But David had said that Alma was like a second mother to the Billington boys so maybe it was no wonder that they were all in attendance. At the end of the row was a leather jacket that could only belong to Aaron.

Meg had never been to a Church of England service before and was surprised to find that it was very like a Catholic mass. The same prayers and hymns, even a recital of the Our Father, although with some extra words at the end which caught Meg out. The vicar said that Alma had been a stalwart of the parish and would be much missed. There was no mention of the manner of her death. Alma's son Frederick paid tribute to 'the best mum anyone ever had'. At this, Meg saw a flurry of white from Verity's pew as if someone had taken out a handkerchief. Then more prayers, 'Abide with Me', and Alma's coffin was borne out of the church. There was a wreath of red roses on the polished wood.

As they walked through the graveyard, Meg found herself next to an elderly man with a face like an eager gnome.

'Are you a policewoman?' he asked.

No, I'm just wearing these clothes for a bet, Meg wanted to say. She admitted that she was a police officer.

'I expect you're here because of the *murder*,' said the man, giving the word what seemed to be unnecessary relish. 'What a terrible thing.' He leered up at her. His head was level with Meg's shiny epaulettes.

'Really terrible,' said Meg. 'How did you know Mrs Saunders?'

'I'm a sidesman at the church,' said the man. The job meant nothing to Meg but the word had a sneaky, sidling quality that seemed appropriate. 'Leonard's the name. Leonard Holt. David, Alma's husband, was a sidesman too. Alma did the flowers. Lovely people. Salt of the earth.'

Meg had heard this phrase before and noticed that it was only used by people who considered themselves of a higher social status than the salty ones.

'Alma was in *showbiz*, you know,' said Leonard, giving the word the same lip-smacking treatment as 'murder'. He trotted along at Meg's side as they made their way to the spot, under an oak tree, where the gravediggers awaited. 'Lots of show-business folk buried in this graveyard.'

'Really?'

'Yes. Tudor Close, the place next door, used to be a hotel. They all stayed there, all the Hollywood stars. Well, there's a film star here today. Seth Billington. Over there.' Meg followed the shaky finger and saw that Seth, David and Aaron were flanking their mother at the graveside. 'He's famous.'

'I know,' said Meg. 'He gave me his autograph once.'

'He was very fond of Alma. I think she used to be his nanny. He often used to visit, busy as he was. You know, I saw him coming out of her cottage on the evening that she died.'

Meg stopped still on the gravel path. 'What?'

Her mother would be furious. She thought 'What?' was very common and always insisted on her children saying 'Pardon?'

Emma stood at the graveside, holding Edgar's arm. There was something ageless and tragic about the scene: the wintery trees, the men in black lowering the coffin into the earth, the seagulls crying from the sea. Emma could see Meg, very noticeable in her uniform, walking from the church accompanied by a small man with a bald head and white beard. He looked like one of the dwarves in *The Hobbit*. Meg was bending her head as if she was interested in what Thorin Oakenshield had to say. When he left her, walking surprisingly quickly to join the other mourners, Meg got out her notebook and wrote something down. Emma applauded her silently for having pen and paper to hand.

Alma's two sons and their wives scattered earth on the coffin. Then the undertaker offered the tray to Verity, who took it between her gloved hands. Verity was wearing a black coat with an enormous fur collar. It made her small, bewigged head look as if it were resting on a platter. Anne Boleyn, albeit rather an elderly version. Seth watched his mother anxiously. Aaron stared at the ground. David and his wife, Emma noticed with interest, had gone to stand with the Saunders family. Frederick Saunders had spoken in the church, his voice choking with emotion. Did he still suspect one of the Billingtons of murdering his mother? Fred was now whispering to Sheena, whom he professed to hate. As Emma watched, Eric Prentice came over to join the group. Emma would have given anything to know what was being discussed.

Verity took a handful of soil and threw it into the grave. Emma heard the small stones clattering on the wood. Verity looked distressed and Seth put his arm round her. This must bring back memories of Bert's funeral, thought Emma. Presumably he too was buried in this graveyard. A final prayer, the words lost in the wind, and the congregation dispersed, leaving the grave-diggers to their work.

The police car was waiting around the corner. The doors were barely shut when Meg said, 'Guess what I've just heard?'

'Was it the old man?' said Emma. 'The one who looked like a goblin?'

'Yes,' said Meg. 'He said that he saw Seth Billington leaving Alma's house on the evening that she was killed.'

'What?' Bob twisted round in his seat. 'Did you believe him?'

'Yes, I did,' said Meg. 'He seemed like the sort of person who knew everything that goes on in a village. His name's Leonard Holt and he's a sidesman at the church. I took his address.'

'Good work,' said Bob. 'If we get a statement, we might have enough to arrest Billington.'

'Yes, good work,' said Edgar. 'I think you should go back to the funeral, WDC Connolly. Go to the wake. Mingle.'

'Mingle?' said Meg, as if she'd never heard the word before. Admittedly, it was a strange choice for Edgar.

'Chat to the family and friends,' said Edgar, 'see if you can find out more.'

Meg looked at Emma as if asking for support. Emma smiled encouragingly. Meg squared her shoulders – already very square in her best uniform – and got out of the car. Emma watched her walking through the gravestones on her way to the church hall, where the wake was being held. She wished she could follow her. She thought of Seth in the garden of his mother's house, all charm in his fisherman's jumper; she thought of him looming out of the darkness in his Dracula cloak; of his face when Meg told him that his fingerprints were on the King Rat flyer. Could Seth, the actor whose face could change in the blink of an eye, really be a murderer?

When the car stopped outside her house, Emma was tempted to ask if she could go on to the station, so that they could discuss this latest development. But, of course, she needed to relieve Astarte. And, in a few hours' time, she would be collecting the girls from school. So she got out, turning to wave when she reached the front door. It was essential to put on a happy face in front of Bob and, especially, Edgar.

When she opened the door, she heard a strange and haunting tune coming from the sitting room. There she found Jonathan sitting entranced while Astarte played to him on Marianne's school recorder, eliciting sounds never before heard from the much-maligned instrument. Also sitting on the floor, constructing an elaborate train track, was Sam.

Sam looked up. 'Hi! How was it? You look nice in that coat.'

'Thank you.' The coat was new, one of the shorter 'swing' designs, so Emma was pleased that someone had noticed.

'It was OK. Potentially interesting. That was lovely, Astarte. Where did you learn to play the recorder?'

'My grandmother taught me on a penny whistle. It's a Romany tradition.'

Jonathan reached out eagerly for the instrument. 'No, pet,' said Astarte. 'You might break it.' To Emma's amazement, Jonathan accepted this, staring lovingly at his babysitter.

'I thought you were busy with the Moors Murders,' said Emma to Sam.

'I am. I just needed a break. It's so grim. Those two are pure evil.'

'His heart is black,' said Astarte, 'and hers is black when she's with him. I'm afraid they'll find more victims. When I saw Brady on the news I thought of earth, cold earth, fathoms of it.'

Emma shivered. 'Well, wait till I tell you the latest on our case.' She told Sam about the sighting of Seth on the night of Alma's murder. Astarte picked up the order of service for the funeral, which Emma had thrown onto a chair. She made a small exclamation.

'What is it?' said Emma. Jonathan looked worriedly at Astarte and reached out a hand to pat her cheek.

'Who's this?' Astarte pointed at the face on the cover, a colour photograph of the deceased.

'That's Alma Saunders,' said Emma.

'It's also the woman who came to see me for a reading,' said Astarte. 'Giving her name as Verity Malone.'

TWENTY-FIVE

Emma stared at her friend.

'You mean, you saw Alma and not Verity?'

'I saw this woman.' Astarte pointed at the photograph on the order of service. 'She came to see me for several private readings.'

'You said that Verity Malone was capable of violence,' said Emma. 'Did you mean Alma was capable of violence?'

'Honestly, Emma,' said Astarte. 'Do you remember every word everyone says?'

'When I'm on a case I do. Can you remember what Alma said to you? You can't be worried about confidentiality now. She's dead.'

'You think the dead can't hear us?' said Astarte. She smiled at Emma and they both jumped as Sam sent the train whizzing around the track, under a bridge and through the complicated points system. Jonathan laughed delightedly although Emma thought that he was dying to pull the thing apart and enact another great train crash.

'Mission accomplished,' said Sam. She arranged herself more comfortably on the floor and grinned up at Astarte. 'Spill the beans,' she said.

'There's not really much to say,' said Astarte. 'Verity – Alma – just wanted to know the usual things. What the future held for her and her family. Of course, it's not that simple . . .'

Of course it isn't, thought Emma. But she said nothing. She'd consulted Astarte herself once.

'But I do remember that Verity – the woman I thought was Verity – was very worried about one of her sons. And I sensed that he was on a dark path.'

'Which son?' asked Emma.

'The oldest one.'

'David?'

'No,' said Sam. 'Frederick.'

They looked at each other as the toy train continued to circle the track.

'If Alma was pretending to be Verity,' said Emma, 'was she talking about her son or Alma's?'

'She wasn't pretending to be Verity,' said Sam. 'She was just using her name. That's very different.'

They both turned to Astarte, who was sitting serenely on the sofa, recorder in her lap. Jonathan was still staring at her adoringly.

'The spirits don't work in that way,' she said. 'They don't care about names. If I was talking to Alma Saunders, then it was her aura I was seeing. She'd brought in something belonging to her son – a cigarette case – and I sensed his aura from that.'

Emma shook her head to clear it from the pleasant but bewildering miasma that Astarte often induced.

'The point is that Alma was worried enough to ask a medium about her son. This might have been because Fred had just found out about the affair with Bert. Could she have been worried that Fred would kill him?'

'Fred might have killed Bert,' said Sam, setting the engine in motion again. 'I thought that he might be a tough customer if roused. But I can't see him killing his own mother.'

'It happens,' said Emma.

'I know,' said Sam. 'I've covered stories like that. But to strangle his own mother because of an affair? I can't see it. Besides, Bert might have been his father.'

'Do you really think so?'

'It's possible. You saw him at the funeral today. Did you see a resemblance?'

Emma thought back to the figure in the pulpit. She was ashamed to say that Fred's accent, a strange mixture of Lancashire and Cockney, had prevented her from noting any resemblance to the Billington brothers. But he had been as tall as they were. She thought back to the tableau by the graveside.

'Fred was talking to Sheena,' she said. 'Whispering almost. I thought that was odd. I mean, you said that he seemed to hate her. He called her a bitch.'

'Love and hate are sometimes interchangeable,' said Astarte.

Meg was trying to mingle. She was standing by the refreshment table in the village hall, balancing a cup of tea and a rock cake. The room, which was either genuinely old like the church or pretend old like Tudor Close, seemed very full of people. The Saunders family were surrounded by other mourners. Meg wondered whether she should insert herself into the group but she felt embarrassed about being in uniform. What had seemed appropriate for the service now seemed out of place in a social gathering. Besides, the stiff collar was chafing her neck.

As she raised her cup to her lips, she heard a voice say, 'Where's the bloody alcohol?'

This was very much what Meg had been thinking. At her grandfather's funeral, the Guinness had flowed like water. She thought she recognised the voice and turned slightly in its direction. Yes, it was Aaron Billington in his leather jacket, looking sulkily at the tea urn. He was talking to his older brother, David.

'Fred said that no one was getting drunk at his mother's funeral,' said David.

'Stupid bastard,' said Aaron.

'I bet Mum's having a glass of something now,' said David. 'I didn't buy that story about her suddenly feeling overwhelmed. And Seth was only too keen to go back to the house with her.'

'Probably afraid of people asking him for his autograph,' said Aaron. 'What with him being so famous and all. Conceited bastard.'

'Hallo,' said Meg. 'Do you remember me?' She tried a friendly smile.

'Well, the uniform is a bit of a giveaway,' said Aaron.

'It's WDC Connolly, isn't it?' said David. 'You came up to London to talk to me and Sheena.' Meg was impressed by his remembering her name. She looked around for Sheena and thought she saw her sleek head in the group around the Saunders brothers.

'It's very sad about Mrs Saunders,' said Meg, trying to sound sincere and not simply inquisitive. 'You must have known her well.'

'Yes,' said David. 'Dear old Alma. She practically brought us up. Especially in Lytham when Mum and Dad were too busy.'

'Dad was running the company,' said Aaron.

David sighed, as if he knew what *that* was like. 'He was busy, like I said.'

'I can't think what Mum was busy doing,' said Aaron.

Was Verity busy having an affair with Max Mephisto? wondered Meg. He'd said that, after the war, they were just friends but men seemed to have a different definition of friendship. Meg remembered Sheena saying that Alma had known everyone's secrets. She wondered what she'd known about David. And Aaron.

'You must know Alma's sons too,' she said. 'Frederick and Barry.'

Did the brothers exchange a quick glance, a flicker that suddenly made them look very alike?

'We know them,' said David. 'I mean, we grew up together in a way but we weren't exactly close. They went to different schools.'

Meg could believe this.

'Seth and Barry were quite friendly for a while,' said Aaron.

David looked over at Fred and Barry, the other fraternal grouping. Meg followed his gaze. Barry was shorter than Fred and far stockier. He also had bushy sideburns that made him look rather wolfish. Meg thought she'd heard that he was a fireman.

'I don't see Seth comforting Barry today,' said David.

As if sensing her husband's scrutiny, Sheena came over to join them. She was wearing a black dress with a boat neckline and looked far more glamorous than she had in London.

'Hallo, WDC Connolly,' she said. 'Keeping us all under scrutiny.' So both the Billingtons remembered Meg. Maybe they'd discussed her?

'I came here as a mark of respect,' said Meg.

'How commendable,' said Sheena. She blew cigarette smoke away from Meg's face in a way that was almost more insulting than letting it choke her.

'How was Fred?' asked David. There was definitely a note of something in his voice but Meg wasn't sure what. Anger? Jealousy? Warning?

'Completely broken,' said Sheena. As she spoke, Fred's loud laugh echoed across the room. Sheena took a drag of her cigarette. 'Where's Seth?'

'He's gone back to the house with Mum.'

'Is that wise?' said Sheena.

Meg started to edge away. She thought that it was time she caught up with Verity Malone.

'We need to go and see this Leonard Holt,' said Edgar. 'And take a proper statement. If he's a credible witness – and WDC Connolly thinks he is – then we need to bring Seth Billington in for questioning.'

'Have we got enough to arrest him?' asked DS O'Neill. They were all crowded into Edgar's office: Bob, Sergeant O'Neill, the other DS, a lugubrious individual called Barker but inexplicably known as Chubby, and DC Black. Henry Solomon looked down sorrowfully from his portrait over the mantelpiece.

'I don't think so yet,' said Edgar. 'But we've got his fingerprints on the envelope of the flyer sent to Verity Malone and he's been placed at the scene of the second murder. If we bring him in for questioning, we might get something out of him.'

O'Neill cracked his knuckles. Edgar had heard rumours about O'Neill intimidating witnesses. He resolved that Bob and Meg should interview Seth.

'Let's concentrate on building a case against Seth,' said Edgar. 'Bob, you and O'Neill go and see Leonard Holt. I'll come with you. If his statement holds up, we'll go straight round and bring Seth in.'

'Where's WDC Connolly?' asked the young policeman, Danny Black, suddenly.

'She's attending the wake,' said Edgar. 'I told her to mingle with the family, see what she can find out.'

O'Neill whispered something to Barker, who sniggered. Black went red but Edgar was pleased to see that he ignored the older officer's comment. Edgar was counting the weeks until O'Neill retired.

Meg walked through the graveyard with its ominous mound of freshly turned soil. It was only two o'clock but already it seemed as if the shadows were deepening. Seagulls, very white in the gathering gloom, were swooping down in search of worms. Meg opened the gate that led into the gardens of Tudor Close. She wasn't sure why she was taking this route, except that it was the quickest and the most discreet. As she walked across the lawns – beautifully maintained by Ted Grange – she heard a deep bark from inside one of the houses. Was that Lola? She'd seen Eric Prentice at the funeral but hadn't spoken to him. She didn't think he'd been at the wake.

Meg had meant to go round to the front entrance but, as she passed Verity's French windows, someone called her name. Her actual name, not her rank.

'Meg!'

It was Seth Billington, standing in the doorway

smoking a cigarette. He was still in his black suit but his collar was loose and his tie was undone. Meg thought about the time when she and Emma had interviewed Seth in his hotel room, actually sitting on his bed. Oh God, she was sure that she was blushing.

'Hi.' Meg came closer, trying for a casual yet professional tone. Channelling Emma, in fact. 'Just came to see how Verity was.'

'She's all right,' said Seth. 'But the funeral was a strain. Alma was her best friend.'

He stood aside to let Meg pass, his voice full of warm concern. But a witness had seen Seth leaving Alma's house on the night she had died. If the DI was satisfied with Leonard Holt's statement, he might well be on his way to Tudor Close to arrest Seth. Meg might be there when this happened, a traitor in the heart of the family.

Verity was sitting on the sofa with a glass of brandy in her hand.

'Ah, Meg. How nice of you to come. How was the wake? Pretty grisly, I expect.'

'It didn't seem much fun,' said Meg.

'Barry told me there wasn't going to be any alcohol,' said Seth. He too was holding a glass. 'So Ma and I escaped.'

'Yes,' said Meg. 'I'd heard that you and Barry were friendly.'

'Who did you hear that from?' said Seth. He sounded

amused. 'From one of my loving brothers, I expect. They could never understand why I'd be friends with the char's son.'

'Seth,' said Verity, on a note of reproof. 'Alma was more than a char.'

Much more, according to Fred Saunders, thought Meg.

'I'm sorry,' said Seth. 'Alma was a wonderful woman.' He turned to Meg. 'Have you got any idea who could have done this awful thing?'

'We're following a few leads,' said Meg.

Edgar waited in the car while Bob and O'Neill disappeared into the neat cottage called The Old Forge. They emerged half an hour later, carrying the completed paperwork.

'Pretty good witness,' said Bob, getting into the car. 'Very convinced that he saw Billington coming out of the house at ten p.m. on the night of Tuesday, the fifth of October.'

'Why didn't he go to the police?' said Edgar.

'Didn't think anything of it,' said Bob. 'He knew of the connection between the families. Even when it came out that Mrs Stephens had been murdered, he still didn't think it could be Seth.'

'Just because he's a film star doesn't mean that he can't be a murderer too,' said Edgar. 'Carter thought that Alma Saunders had been killed between nine p.m. and midnight on the fifth, so the timings fit.'

'What about the woman seen entering the house at eleven p.m.?' said Bob. 'The one in the brown coat.'

'We haven't been able to trace her,' said Edgar. The mysterious woman in brown was one of the many frustrating aspects of the case. 'Let's go and have a word with Seth.'

The photographs were still on the coffee table.

'I've been sorting through them,' said Verity. Meg sat next to her. Some of the pictures were in albums – fat velvet affairs with gold tassels – but most were loose. Seth put a glass of whisky in front of Meg but she didn't think she should drink it. She was on duty and in uniform. Besides, she would need her wits about her.

Seth left the room and Verity continued to leaf through the black-and-white images. Occasionally she held up a picture to show Meg. 'Trixie Tupman, she was gorgeous. Letty Lane, the Purley Princess.' But the beauty of these women, if it had ever existed, did not survive the stilted poses and out-of-focus photography. They seemed almost comical with their black lipstick and firmly corseted figures. Only the young Verity seemed undimmed by time and fashion, smiling gaily over her shoulder or blowing kisses into the air.

'My dad's got a picture of you,' said Meg. 'My mum was ever so cross when she found it.'

Verity was delighted. 'I'll send him a signed photo,' she said. 'But tell your mum, men who look seldom touch.'

Meg tried, and failed, to imagine saying this to her mother.

'I saw Alma's sons at the wake,' she said. 'Is Seth still friendly with Barry Saunders?'

Verity was peering at a picture of a chorus line. 'My first job,' she said. 'Dancing was hard work in those days. Two shows a night, sometimes a different town every day. Weekly rep was a luxury. The head girl was so strict. Your costume had to be perfect, seams straight, feathers at the right angle, even if nobody saw you. Sometimes the stages were so small that, if you were at the end of the line, you were high kicking away in the wings. Still, it was better than home.'

Meg repeated her question.

'I don't think so, dear,' said Verity. 'But they were quite close when they were young. The boys were brought up together really, well the older ones were. Seth and Barry were alike, both little daredevils. David and Fred were more serious.'

It was funny, thought Meg, how words sometimes came back to you. As clear as day, she remembered sitting in this room and Verity describing the last time she'd seen Alma. *I said, 'See you later, alligator.' It was a joke we had. David and Fred used to love Bill Haley and the Comets.* So the older boys hadn't been all that serious and they *had* been friends. Or, at any rate, close enough to share musical tastes which, Meg knew from her brothers, was an even better currency than football.

'Your daughter-in-law Sheena was talking to Fred and Barry at the wake,' she said.

'I've no doubt she was,' said Verity.

Meg waited for her to say more and, after a few minutes of rather aimless shifting through photographs, Verity said, 'Sheena always liked Barry. He's a good-looking devil. But not as much as she likes Seth.'

'Sheena likes Seth?'

'Well, everyone likes Seth,' said Verity. 'Look at you, going red every time he talks to you. But Sheena's got a bit of a thing for him. She sees all his films and collects his press cuttings. I think it drives David mad. He's a patient man but no one likes their wife lusting after another man. Especially not their own brother.'

The word 'lusting' had a very old-fashioned sound, thought Meg. Like something you'd hear in the Bible. She decided to ask the question that had been troubling her for the last few weeks, ever since Emma had visited the police station. Perhaps the day of Alma's funeral wasn't the right time to ask but when would she get a better chance, sitting alone with Verity surrounded by memories of the past?

'Apparently Sheena told Fred that Alma had had an affair with Bert,' she said.

Verity continued to rearrange the photographs, like a magician shuffling a pack of cards.

'Who told you that?' she said.

'Fred told Sam Collins, Emma's partner.'

'Oh, the journalist. She's a smart girl. Like Emma. Like you.'

Meg waited, although she couldn't resist storing up this nugget of praise to examine later.

'Sheena hinted as much to me,' said Verity, 'but I don't believe it. I'll never believe it. Alma would never betray me. She was my best friend.'

Now Verity looked Meg straight in the eye. Meg believed her. Well, she believed that Verity believed it.

'Why would Sheena say that if it wasn't true?' said Meg.

'Because Sheena's a vindictive cow, that's why.'

Verity's voice had the carrying quality of one used to being heard in the stalls and dress circle. When, a few minutes later, Sheena entered the room, Meg wondered if she'd caught this ringing endorsement. Sheena was accompanied by David and Aaron and carrying a covered tray of sandwiches.

'Hallo, Mother,' she said. 'Fred sent these for you. They've got far too much food.'

'Mother' surprised Meg. Was this what you called your mother-in-law? Her older sister, Marie, was married but her husband, Terry, had called Meg's mother 'Mrs Connolly' right up until their wedding day. Now Meg rather thought that he avoided addressing her directly.

'That's kind,' said Verity. 'But I'm not hungry. Meg might like one though.'

Sheena seemed to register her presence for the first time.

'What are you doing here, WDC Connolly?'

'Just checking in on Verity,' said Meg.

'That's very kind,' said Sheena. 'But we're here now.'

There was a definite implication that it was time for Meg to leave but Verity said, 'We haven't finished looking through the pictures yet. I know you're not interested in this stuff, Sheena.'

Sheena looked for a second as if she was going to argue but she picked up the tray and walked out of the room. Aaron came to sit in the armchair beside his mother and David brought him a beer. He didn't offer a drink to Verity or Meg. There was no sign of Seth.

It was the first time Edgar had been to Tudor Close, described by Bob as 'a palace' and Emma as 'an art-deco nightmare'. Edgar could see both aspects. The house looked mellow and picturesque today, the low roofs golden in the late afternoon light, but there was still a strange atmosphere to the place, something heightened and unreal, the timbered walls and the many windows looking inwards as they crossed the lawn. Behind them was the church where they'd had the funeral earlier but Edgar had the weird feeling that if he went to the gate that led into the churchyard he wouldn't be able to go through, as if Tudor Close was held in its own force field. I've been watching too much *Dr Who*, he told himself. Edgar was a convert to television drama and a big fan of the science fiction programme. The girls were terrified of the opening music and always hid behind the sofa when it came on.

The door was opened by a dark man in a black suit. To

Edgar, he could have been any one of the sons, so he was pleased to hear Bob address the man as David. That was the eldest. The one who ran the business.

'Can we come in?' said Bob.

David looked doubtfully at Edgar and even more so at O'Neill, who looked bulkier and more intimidating than ever surrounded by the hobbit-sized doors, but he ushered them into the house.

At first sight the sitting room seemed full but, when Edgar's eyes had adjusted themselves to the proportions of the place, he saw that there were actually only four people there, surrounded by looming pieces of furniture. Verity Malone was sitting on a sofa, still in her black dress and pearls but with a woollen cardigan over her shoulders. Next to her sat WDC Connolly, an incongruous figure in her dark uniform, gold buttons twinkling in the dim light. Meg looked up when they came in, her glance apprehensive and rather scared. It looked as if the two women had been going through old photographs as there were several albums open on the coffee table. The mechanic brother sat in an armchair nursing a pint glass. Another woman – David's wife, Edgar presumed – was standing by the door.

'What's going on?' she said.

'It's the police, Sheena,' said David. There was a definite note of warning in his voice.

'Mrs Billington?' Edgar addressed himself to Verity. 'I'm Superintendent Edgar Stephens.'

'The superintendent?' said Verity. 'We are honoured. And it's Verity, if you please.' Her voice was slightly slurred, and Edgar wondered if she was a bit drunk.

'You're Emma's husband, aren't you?' said Verity, suddenly sharpening as if he was coming into focus.

Edgar said that he was.

'I like Emma,' said Verity. 'She's very clever. I bet she's cleverer than you.'

'She is,' said Edgar. He didn't look at Bob or WDC Connolly.

'We've come to talk to Seth,' he added. 'Is he here?'

'What do you want with Seth?' said the mechanic. What was his name? Aaron. 'You can't just barge in like this. My mother's upset. We're in mourning.'

'Aaron . . .' said the daughter-in-law warningly.

'Don't take on, Sheena,' said Verity. 'He can't talk to Seth because he's not here.'

Meg turned to her. 'What do you mean?'

'He's gone,' said Verity, picking up a velvet-covered book and peering myopically at the contents.

'What are you talking about, Mother?' said David. 'Seth hasn't gone. He's upstairs or in the garden having a smoke.'

'He's gone,' repeated Verity. 'He left half an hour ago.'

'He didn't tell us he was leaving,' said Sheena.

'Seth's an actor,' said Verity. 'He's good at exits.' And she closed her eyes as if readying herself for a refreshing nap.

TWENTY-SIX

Max was in one of his favourite places, the bar of the Strand Palace Hotel in London, drinking a whisky on the rocks. Filming was finished and he was going to rejoin his family tomorrow. Now he was about to have lunch with his eldest daughter. Given all this, Max wondered why he wasn't feeling happier. Partly, it was the melancholy that always accompanied the end of a project. He hadn't particularly enjoyed filming *The Prince of Darkness* but, for a short time, the cast and crew had been a unit and now they wouldn't see each other again until the premiere, if there was one. He'd miss Irene and Wilbur and some of the others. Even Seth had been companionable at times. At least the job had given him a sense of purpose, but now he was back to the old game of wondering what on earth he was doing with his life. He was a magician who didn't do magic any more. He was an actor who couldn't really act. He was Lord Massingham, whatever the hell that meant. For his father it had been his entire identity but to Max the title sounded ridiculous, like the name of a suspect in a murder mystery play. *Enter Lord Massingham, looking shifty.*

Draining his whisky, Max suddenly heard Sam Collins speaking in his head. She had a nice voice, he remembered, rather low-pitched and often seeming on the edge of laughter. *But it's not such a bad thing to be a movie star. I'm sure it beats being a jobbing reporter.* Sam was right; he was being self-pitying. He had work and he had his family. That was enough.

Thinking of his family crystallised the other vague anxiety that had been forming in his head all morning. Ruby had requested this meeting. This was unusual. Ruby must have something to tell him and she'd chosen a very public place to make the announcement.

He knew, without looking round, that Ruby had entered the room. There was a change to the electricity. People put down their papers and stopped their conversations. The barman stood motionless with a cocktail shaker in his hand. Max turned and saw his daughter pausing in the doorway as if acknowledging this appreciation. Ruby was wearing a black-and-white checked dress with a short black jacket, her hair swung glossily at her ears and she looked somehow radiant, as if a light were shining through her. Max felt his heart lurch.

'Hallo, darling.' Max kissed Ruby on her cheek, which felt cold. The weather had been getting progressively colder all week. 'Would you like a cocktail?'

'No thanks. Can we just go through to the restaurant?'

After they had ordered, Ruby took off her jacket, smoothed her hair and said, 'Just so as you know, I won't be having any of the wine.' Max had asked for a cold bottle of Chablis.

'Why?' said Max. But he knew. He'd known as soon as he saw her in the doorway.

'I'm pregnant,' said Ruby. She favoured him with a dazzling smile that made the approaching waiter almost drop his ice bucket. She waited until the wine had been poured before saying, 'The baby's due in April. I'm very happy about it and I'm not going to marry the father.'

'Who is the father?' said Max.

'Dex,' said Ruby. 'Were you worried it was Seth?'

'Slightly,' said Max.

'Why? Is he your son?'

Max took a long drink of wine. 'I've sometimes wondered but, on balance, I don't think so.'

'On balance?' said Ruby. 'Good thing I didn't sleep with him then.'

'I know you met him in Brighton that time.' Max didn't add that he'd rung Edgar to ask when Seth had returned to Whitby.

'Are you checking up on me?' said Ruby. She didn't actually look displeased at the thought. 'I just met Seth for lunch. Some reporters saw us though, which was annoying. I don't think Seth minded. Maybe he's looking for a little misdirection.'

'What about Dex?' said Max. 'Is he pleased about the baby?'

'He's delighted,' said Ruby. 'He wants us to get married but I really don't want to be anyone's wife. I do want to be a mother though.'

'What does *your* mother think?'

'Oh, she's horrified, though she pretends not to be. She actually said the baby would be a half-caste. Such a horrid term. Dex says mixed race, so I will too.'

'I wish you well.' Max raised his glass to her. 'But it'll be hard work.'

'I know,' said Ruby. 'But I won't have it as hard as some women. I've got money, for one thing. And I've got a nice flat, though I might look for somewhere with a garden. I'm going to take a couple of years off work.'

'You've got it all worked out.'

'That's what Dex said. He thinks I don't realise that babies don't always go to plan. He's got two children of his own, you know.'

'I didn't know.'

'He's divorced but he still sees them regularly. This baby's going to have a very complicated family. Just think, Rocco and Elena will be an uncle and aunt.' Rather to everyone's surprise, Ruby was devoted to her half-brother and sister.

Max laughed. 'They'll love it. I'll be a grandfather. I'm not too sure about that.'

'And Lydia will be a grandmother,' said Ruby. 'Can't wait.'

After lunch they took a taxi to Kensington Gardens. Ruby wanted some fresh air and the park was within walking distance of her flat. Neither of them contemplated getting the bus. It was very pleasant, Max thought, walking with his daughter on a late autumn afternoon. Soon it would be winter. If Ruby had wanted a wholesome picture of motherhood, she could hardly have done better than the park famously featured in the *Peter Pan* stories. Children were everywhere: sailing boats on the Round Pond, pulling toy dogs on wheels, jumping up to catch falling leaves. They passed a mother pushing a pram and holding the hand of a stout toddler in a duffel coat who, in turn, was holding a fluffy white dog on a lead. Two children, who had obviously just finished school for the day, were chasing each other round the statue of the Boy Who Never Grew Up. Two others were swinging their satchels against horse chestnut branches to bring down conkers.

'Don't say it,' said Ruby.

'Say what?' said Max.

'That'll be me in a few years' time.' The mother of the schoolchildren was shouting in vain for them to stop.

'You've got a few more years before my grandchild starts school.'

'So it's *your* grandchild now, is it? Dex says "my son", which is even worse. I'm sure it's a girl.'

'Lydia says that women always think they'll have a girl first because you expect a mini version of yourself. She was very surprised when Rocco turned out to be a boy. But, when they're born, you can't really imagine them any different.'

'I never really think of Lydia as a mother.'

Max thought of Lydia cutting faces into pumpkins, of the conker collections and splashy paintings in the playroom. 'She's a good mother,' he said. 'She really loves doing things with the children.'

'My mum was a good mother,' said Ruby, swerving to avoid a child on roller skates. 'But she didn't really like playing.'

'Emerald's a very serious person,' said Max. This had been true even when she was a twenty-two-year-old snake-charmer.

'Maybe I'll be serious when I'm a mother,' said Ruby. 'But I doubt it somehow. I'm really looking forward to having fun with this baby.'

'You'll be wonderful,' said Max, suddenly sure of it. 'He or she is a very lucky baby.' He had some vague memories of his mother laughing with him, playing cards, taking him for walks in the woods. The actual events were hazy but the accompanying emotions seemed untouched by time. He had been happy at Massingham Hall then, he realised.

They walked to Ruby's flat, off Kensington Church Street. Ruby didn't invite Max in, saying that she was exhausted. She didn't look even slightly tired and Max wondered whether Dex would be coming round later. More likely Ruby would sit on her green velvet sofa (the flat was redecorated every year), with her Siamese cat on her lap, hugging her secret to her.

Max hailed a taxi on Kensington High Street. He would go back to the hotel, play a few games of patience and drink a toast to Ruby and his grandchild. He felt very proud of her, his brilliant, unknowable, independent daughter. It wouldn't be plain sailing. Life was hard for what the papers called 'unmarried mothers', even if the mother in question was wealthy and famous. And it wouldn't be easy having a baby that people would call half-caste. But Max had no doubt that Ruby would rise above these challenges as she had risen to become one of the biggest TV stars in England. She must get some of that from him, surely? Although, to be fair, Emerald had been a mesmerising performer too. And there was something of the snake-charmer about Ruby.

The receptionist called out to him as he went past. 'Two messages for you, Mr Mephisto.' Max took the piece of paper which had a picture of a telephone on it. He assumed the calls were from Lydia who often phoned several times a day. He smiled. Today's revelation had made him feel very affectionate towards the mother of his children.

But there were two other names on the note, both with numbers beside them. *Irene* and *Edgar*.

Max made his way to the telephone booth in the lobby. Why on earth would Irene the wardrobe mistress be calling him? He decided to ring her first.

'Oh, Max.' Irene sounded slightly flustered. 'I hope you don't mind me ringing but you said that you always stayed at the Strand Palace.'

'Of course I don't mind. Is anything wrong?'

'Not wrong exactly.' There was a pause. Max could hear crackling over the telephone lines. Then Irene continued. 'It was something Lydia said at the end-of-shoot party. I've been thinking about it and it's been worrying me. We were talking about Bert Billington. About how he died. How he was killed. And Lydia said, "I know who did it." I thought she was joking but I asked her, "Who?" And she said, "I've got someone else I need to tell first." Well, like I said, I didn't think she was serious, but I've been thinking about it and I thought I ought to tell you.'

'Thank you,' said Max.

'Do you know who she meant?'

'No,' said Max. 'No, I don't.'

Max telephoned Edgar next. He could hear voices in the background and imagined the dingy police offices, Bob and the others milling around ineffectually. 'I thought you should know,' said Edgar. 'We want to question Seth Billington about the death of Alma Saunders.'

'My God. Really?'

'Yes. We had a credible witness who placed him at the scene. Seth was in Rottingdean today for Alma's funeral so we went round to Tudor Close this afternoon. Seth had gone.'

'Made a run for it?'

'Looks that way. None of the family seemed to know where he was heading. Or they pretended not to. But we asked around. Seth drives a flashy green Aston Martin which made it easier. Anyway, the garage on the seafront said that he'd filled up with petrol there at about three p.m. And he'd bought a map. A map of Somerset.'

Somerset. The place where Max had grown up. And where his wife and children now lived.

TWENTY-SEVEN

Max telephoned Lydia but there was no answer. This wasn't unusual. The telephone was in the old servants' quarters and its ringing often went unheard. But he couldn't just sit in the hotel doing nothing. Max went to the porter's cubbyhole and asked for his car to be brought round. Seth had left Brighton at three. It would take him at least four hours to drive to Somerset, even in an Aston Martin. It was now five o'clock. If Max left immediately, he might just catch him up. It was a longer journey from Brighton and Seth might easily get lost, despite the hastily bought map. When the Jaguar came to the door, Max tipped the porter and practically sprinted to the driving seat. He had driven down the Strand and was over Waterloo Bridge before he had really thought what he was doing. Was Seth really on his way to Massingham Hall? But why else would he be going to Somerset? And did Lydia really know who had killed Bert? And was that person Seth?

It was Friday night and the streets were filling up with

people. Max cursed at every red light and every wandering pedestrian. He was heading south: Richmond, Aldershot, Basingstoke. It was a good thing that he knew the route so well because he was aware of driving on automatic pilot. With any luck, Seth would get caught up in the London traffic. Max thought about the man he had worked with for the past three months. Seth was a pleasant presence on set, punctual, prepared, always polite even to the most lowly member of the crew. Could he really have murdered his father and that woman, Alma Whatsit? He thought of Seth saying, 'My dad could be a bit of a bastard.' At the time it had seemed a fairly light-hearted comment and Max had replied in kind. He'd always been wary of discussing Bert because of his own history with Verity. But what if Seth had hated his father, hated him enough to kill him? Max could picture Seth's handsome face, that evening in the bar, radiating only concern for his mother. But if Seth was anything, he was a very good actor.

Max had sometimes wondered whether Seth could be his son. Not at the time. Conception hadn't crossed his mind when, as an eighteen-year-old, he'd slept with the goddess that had been Verity Malone. She told him not to worry about 'all that' and he hadn't. He'd parted company with Bert Billington Productions shortly afterwards and, when he'd learnt that Verity had a second child, he'd assumed that this was a sign she had reconciled with her husband. God, he'd been a fool in those days, thought Max, overtaking a bus with very little room to spare. Two years later he'd had an affair with Emerald and she hadn't told him that they'd conceived a daughter until Ruby turned up in Brighton, wanting to be his assistant. It was really only the film, *The Prince of Darkness*, that had made him think about Seth's parentage. People kept commenting on their supposed resemblance although that was really just because they were both tall and dark and dressed as vampires. 'You're not old enough to be his dad,' Irene had said loyally but Max knew that he was. That was why he had been worried when it seemed that Seth might be interested in Ruby. What was it that Ruby had said? *Maybe he's looking for a little misdirection.*

Max drove faster, freeing himself from the suburbs of London.

'We need to watch the house,' said Edgar. 'Seth could well come back. He might not be heading for Somerset after all.' He wondered if he'd been too hasty in telling Max Seth's supposed destination. He'd alerted the Somerset police and asked for an officer to visit Massingham Hall. Because where else could Seth be heading? If he knew Max, he'd be on his way there too, speeding across country in his ludicrously expensive car.

'I'll send a car to wait outside Tudor Close,' said Bob. They were in Edgar's office having what Edgar called a strategy meeting. Bob was looking worried but then he often did when he was in the middle of a case. Edgar thought the word 'strategy' made him nervous.

'Make it an unmarked car,' said Edgar. 'We don't want them to get alarmed.'

He thought of the Billingtons, gathered in that strangely eerie house. Did they really not know why Seth had left? Was Verity covering up for him? Emma had said that Seth seemed to be her favourite son. 'Well, to be fair, he's everyone's favourite,' she'd said.

Meg was obviously embarrassed that Seth had disappeared on her watch. 'I thought he'd just gone upstairs,' she said. 'David, Sheena and Aaron had got back from the wake. Sheena was fussing about sandwiches and David and Aaron were drinking beer. Verity was showing me pictures of old variety stars. Seth didn't tell anyone he was going, unless he'd told Verity earlier. I'm so sorry.' Edgar didn't blame Meg. There was nothing she could have done to stop Seth leaving, after all, and maybe it was more important that she had developed a rapport with Verity.

'Let's send WDC Connolly to Tudor Close in the morning,' said Edgar. 'She seems to get on well with Mrs Billington. Verity. We'll see if she can get any more out of her.'

'Wilco,' said Bob. He often used phrases that he thought were RAF slang. Edgar wondered if it came from being in the shadow of his pilot officer brother.

When Bob had left, Edgar made a few phone calls and then prepared to leave for the day. There was nothing much he could do until tomorrow. Bob would let him know if anything happened at Tudor Close and he very much hoped that Max would telephone when he arrived in Somerset. Edgar gathered up his things, nodded at the portrait of Henry Solomon on the wall and left the office. Most of the day staff had left but, when he passed the incident room, he saw that Meg Connolly was still there, writing what looked like a letter.

'Working late?' he said.

Meg flushed guiltily but she was the sort of girl who often blushed when spoken to. Despite this, she wasn't shy exactly.

'Did DI Willis explain about going to Tudor Close tomorrow?' he asked.

'Yes, sir.'

'We thought you could keep the place under surveillance in case Seth Billington turns up. You've done well to establish friendly relations with the family.'

He'd meant to be encouraging but he realised that he had used about twenty words where one or two would have sufficed. *Well done* or *Good work*. *Whizzo*, as Bob's RAF brother would probably say. Meg looked a bit bemused but it turned out that her mind was on other things.

'Sir?'

'Yes?'

'I've been writing up my notes on the women who were . . . who had affairs with Bert Billington.'

'Oh yes?' He remembered Emma showing him the list.

'I just wondered . . . could you show them to Emma?

Mrs Stephens? She's so good at finding patterns and clues. I thought she might see something I'd missed.'

She was holding out the folded pages. Edgar was torn between thinking it was rather a cheek to use him as a postal service and admiration for Meg's diligence. He also felt rather proud of his clever wife (cleverer than him, as Verity had pointed out earlier). Meg was right, Emma *was* brilliant at looking at a tangle of information and finding a way through it. Of course, Meg would have got to know Emma well on their road trip.

'I'll show Emma,' he said.

'Thank you,' said Meg.

Edgar walked back along the coast road. The clocks had gone back the previous weekend and it was pitch dark at six p.m. A full moon was rising over the sea, illuminating the clouds around it. A Gothic sky, thought Edgar. Emma had reminded him that Sunday night was Hallowe'en, All Hallows' Eve, the day when the dead walk the streets. If you look in a mirror on Hallowe'en night, Emma had said, you're meant to see the face of the man you were going to marry. Or else you see your own death. Edgar thought that she'd probably got that from Astarte. He wondered whether it was such a good idea, after all, to let Astarte babysit the children.

And it seemed that Astarte had struck again. As soon as he opened the door, Emma was telling him that Alma Saunders had apparently visited Astarte for a reading, claiming to be Verity Malone.

'Why would she do that?' said Edgar, taking off his coat.

'I don't know,' said Emma. 'But it's interesting, isn't it? Apparently, Verity, or Alma pretending to be Verity, said she was worried about her oldest son.'

'David?' said Edgar, remembering the man who had opened the door at Tudor Close.

'No,' said Emma. 'Frederick. Alma's oldest son. Astarte said it was his aura she sensed.'

She was smiling, as if inviting him to share the joke, but Edgar knew that she was desperate to discuss the case. Her face was glowing in a way that made Edgar remember the young DS Holmes. He found this touching, but he also wanted to have his supper and forget murder for a while. Marianne and Sophie came racing downstairs full of news about school and what somebody did to somebody else when Miss Hobden wasn't looking.

'Sam's made this amazing railway track,' said Sophie. 'Come and see.' She dragged him into the sitting room where the trains now ran under the sofa, through the nest of tables and ended in a terminus by the television set. Even Jonathan seemed entranced by it, although Edgar noticed that he was chewing one of the signalmen. Should he stop him? Was that lead paint?

'Was Sam here?' he said, stooping down to look at the locomotives. He couldn't resist sending one on its way.

'Yes,' said Emma. 'She wanted to talk about the case.' There was a definite edge to her voice now.

'Can we talk about it later?' said Edgar. 'When the children are in bed?'

'It's that *pas devant* thing again,' said Marianne to Sophie. 'I think it's very rude.'

'Ruby said we'd probably like a good murder,' said Sophie.

This didn't surprise Edgar at all. He turned to Emma, hoping to share the joke, but she was still watching the train circling the track.

Max made good time through Aldershot and Winchester and then he was driving over Salisbury Plain. There was darkness on either side of him, although occasionally he saw faint wavery lights on the horizon. Stonehenge was out there somewhere, monolithic and solemn, unaffected by his petty problems. He'd taken Lydia and the children to see it last year. Rocco and Elena had played hide-and-seek through the stones, pretending to be Heidi and Peter. He'd tried to tell them about the Stone Age and the people who had transported the stones so many miles to this deserted spot, but he was hampered by their lack of interest and his own lack of knowledge. Lydia had said the place was dreary and could do with a few shops.

Max hurtled on through the Neolithic landscape.

Meg was lucky enough to catch the 1A bus just as it was leaving the Old Steine. That meant she wouldn't have to walk up Wilson Avenue, which always seemed longer in the dark. She leant her head against the window, watching the people scurrying across the road, heads down against the wind. When you're walking, the lights of a bus seem the epitome of good cheer but, looking out, Meg found herself thinking wistfully about the people going past and those living behind the windows of the smart houses on Marine Parade. Occasionally she saw a chandelier or a draped curtain. She liked it at Christmas when lots of the flats had decorations that could be seen from the road. Only another two months until Christmas.

Meg's forehead bumped against the glass. She thought of the funeral that morning, of Leonard Holt saying, 'Lots of show-business folk buried in this graveyard.' She thought of Barbara Dodson dying alone in Hastings and of Aleister Crowley who had cursed the town. She thought of the Gillespies and the picture over their TV, the smiling blonde woman and her angelic baby. She thought of Whitby and the ruined abbey and the cloaked figure staring up at her. There was something about this case, she thought, that went beyond the usual domestic tragedy, wives killing husbands, husbands killing wives. This was about retribution, she was sure of it. She thought of the DI's strange quotation. *Ellum she hateth mankind, and waiteth.* The words of a song came into her head, a song that had been in the charts that summer. She couldn't remember much of it, just the chorus about waiting until the midnight hour. The lyrics were meant to be somewhat risqué – some radio stations had refused to play the track – but now the phrase came back to Meg with another meaning. Bert could escape his crimes for years but there would come an hour, the midnight hour, when he would have to pay.

Edgar offered to read to the girls. Usually he was the favoured reader because he did different voices for all the characters but tonight he kept getting the dwarves' names wrong and was prompted by Marianne, at first with a laugh and then with an exaggerated sigh. He left them locked up in the Elf King's dungeons and went downstairs to find Emma reading Meg's notes at the kitchen table.

'Tea?' he said. He knew that she was still annoyed about his refusal to discuss the case earlier.

'I'd rather have a glass of wine,' said Emma. 'Have we got any?'

'I think we've got a bottle of red somewhere.' He found it in the cupboard, pulled the cork and poured them both a glass. He sat opposite Emma at the table and prepared himself to make an effort.

'Anything interesting from Meg?'

'Don't worry,' said Emma. 'I know you don't want to talk about work.'

She put a slight emphasis on the last word. Was she implying that to her it wasn't just work? wondered Edgar.

'I was thinking today,' said Edgar, 'how good you were at sifting through evidence and finding things that the rest of us have missed, finding a pattern.'

'Are you trying to get round me?' said Emma.

'Yes,' said Edgar.

Emma made a dismissive noise but she took a sip of wine and, after a few seconds, said, 'Meg's very good. Very thorough. I hope Bob appreciates her.'

'I'm sure he does,' said Edgar. But he thought of O'Neill whispering to Barker and resolved to make sure that Meg was looked after.

'I've been thinking about the Billington brothers,' said Emma. 'I think we should look at David. He might have wanted to get his father out of the way so that he had complete control of the business. It can't have been easy, having Bert breathing down his neck. To say nothing of having to pay off all of Bert's mistresses.'

'What about Alma Saunders?'

'Maybe she knew something. Sheena said that she knew all the family secrets. It's in Meg's notes.'

'But it was Seth that was seen leaving the house.'

'Are you sure?' said Emma. She fixed him with one of her uncomfortably direct looks. 'The brothers look very alike.'

And Edgar thought of David opening the door at Tudor Close and how, for a few minutes, he hadn't been sure which brother he was facing.

Max shot through Yeovil – luckily the streets were empty – then he was on the narrow country roads. The wind had picked up and the trees creaked ominously overhead.

Occasionally he saw a full moon riding across the sky. *The hag is astride, this night for to ride.* Lydia might think that Hallowe'en was a charming family holiday but Max tended towards the darker version. *The graves stood tenantless and the sheeted dead Did squeak and gibber in the Roman streets.* His car headlights illuminated hedgerows, cottages, a signpost like a white hand at a crossroads. He was nearly there now. He had walked these lanes as a boy, ridden them on his pony, spluttered past in his first car, desperate to escape. And there was the sign. Massingham Hall. Max took the corner almost on two wheels and then had to make an emergency stop. A police car was parked by the gates.

Max got out. 'What's going on?' He winced at how like his father he sounded, every inch the outraged landowner.

Two policemen got out of the car. One of them had a torch and it reflected his white face and peaked cap. He touched the brim now and said, 'Lord Massingham?' Just for a second, Max thought that the policeman too was thinking of his father. Then he remembered that this strange supporting character was now him.

'We had a call from the Brighton police, sir,' said the officer. 'They asked us to check that everything was all right at the hall. We've just called in and Lady Massingham assured us that all was well. We'll just keep watch for a little bit longer if it's all the same to you, sir.'

'Yes,' said Max. 'Very good. Thank you.'

He was breathing a little easier when he got back in his car but, all the same, he wanted to see for himself that all was well. He could see the lights of the house as he drove nearer and that, too, reassured him. He was about to park by the front steps when something told him to drive round to the stable block where the garages now were.

And he was just in time to see a green Aston Martin driving away.

TWENTY-EIGHT

Max was used to disappearing acts. They had, once, been his speciality. The vanishing box, the phantom, the empty cabinet. The girl on the table, the drapes thrown over her – casually concealing the hidden trapdoor – the reveal, the double-take, the gasps from the stalls. But this version, he reflected as he walked towards the house, had been imperfectly performed. Ideally, he should not have seen the car or, better still, Seth should have remained in the house, pretending that he was there to see Max. It was the escape that proved his guilt. The question was, how would Lydia play her part? As Max often said: in vanishing tricks, everything depends on the girl.

As he climbed the stairs to the front door, Max saw the pumpkins on each step, each one glowing with an inner light. 'If a house is decorated with a lighted pumpkin,' Lydia had said, 'it means the kids can call in. It's a sort of signal.' Had these been a signal to her lover? A sign that the coast was clear?

Max could hear Panda barking inside the house. He felt irrationally irritated with the dog. Caesar would have defended his house better. He betted that Panda had fawned all over Seth and now the stupid animal was barking at his master.

Lydia was waiting for him in the hall. Max noticed immediately that she was casually, but carefully, dressed in slacks and a cashmere jumper. She was wearing make-up too, but subtly applied so as to look as if she wasn't. Panda came frisking up to Max but even he looked rather embarrassed.

'Max,' said Lydia. 'This is a nice surprise. I wasn't expecting you until tomorrow.'

She was a good actress but her eyes were wary. Max didn't think he could stand much more of this. 'I saw Seth's car,' he said.

'Oh yes,' said Lydia. 'He was in the area and he popped in, hoping to see you.'

Max looked at her. Just wait, that's what the old pros always said, count to ten before you say the line. That way you can be sure that the audience is listening.

'Seth was in Brighton at three o'clock this afternoon,' he said at last. 'I wonder what brought him here in such a hurry?'

Lydia shrugged. 'I didn't ask him.'

'So he drove for four hours just on the off-chance of seeing me?' said Max. 'I never knew he was such a devoted friend. Strange, though, having made such an effort, that he should drive away just as I arrive.'

Now it was Lydia's turn to stay silent.

'How long have you been having an affair with Seth?' asked Max, in a conversational tone.

Even so, Lydia backed away. 'I'm not—'

'Oh, for God's sake!' said Max. 'Don't lie about it.' Panda, alarmed by his raised voice, started to whine. Max reached down to pat him. 'It's OK, boy.'

He straightened up to face Lydia, keeping his tone conversational. 'If the police hadn't come round, I would probably have caught you in bed together, wouldn't I? Like some French farce.' He suddenly thought of something. 'Where are the children?'

'In the playroom,' said Lydia. 'Watching a cinefilm with Nanny.'

'Jesus,' said Max. 'You thought of everything.'

Lydia raised her chin. 'Not quite everything. I didn't think you'd be here. I suppose your policeman friend tipped you off.'

'Sorry to inconvenience you,' said Max. 'How long have you been sleeping with Seth?'

'It's not what you think,' said Lydia. 'We're in love.'

'You know he could be my son. Was that part of the attraction?'

'He asked his mother,' said Lydia, 'and she says you're not his father. It was Bert Billington. The one who was murdered.'

'You know the police think that Seth murdered him?'

'That's not true!' Lydia fired up immediately. Maybe she

did love Seth. 'He was in Whitby when his father died and with me in Brighton when that woman was killed, the cleaner.'

Didn't Edgar say that Seth had been seen leaving the victim's house? But Max couldn't think about that now. He looked at Lydia. Her face was pale and her eyes wide with trepidation. Max thought that she'd never looked more beautiful. Suddenly he felt old and tired.

'I'm going to see the children,' he said, 'and then I'll sleep in the spare room.'

'Max,' said Lydia. 'We have to talk.'

'There's nothing left to say,' said Max. And he began to walk up the stairs, Panda following at his heels.

Verity started her bedtime preparations early. The evenings were very long at this time of the year and she got her best sleep before midnight. She usually woke up several times in the early hours and sometimes came downstairs to drink tea and read a book. Anything to get away from the voices in her head.

Tonight she was especially tired. People had stayed so long after the funeral. David and Sheena hadn't left until seven. Sheena even offered to cook her supper. 'I don't eat much in the evening,' Verity had said, with perfect truth. Anyway, even if she were starving, nothing would induce her to eat a meal cooked by Sheena. Verity went upstairs as soon as she heard their car starting up outside. First, she took off her false eyelashes. They were so heavy that it was quite hard to keep her eyes open. Then she took off her make-up using the routine taught to her as a young pro: cold cream, hot water, cold water, night cream. Unadorned, her face looked bland and unwary. She knew that she looked old too but her long sight wasn't good and so the vision in the mirror was comfortably blurred. Then she took off her wig, sighing with relief as she put it on its stand. Underneath, her hair was white and distressingly thin. Verity thought that this was because she had spent so many years curling it and dyeing it. Thinking of her golden mane made her sad though. When she'd looked at those old photographs of herself today it had been like looking at a deceased friend. Who was this radiant creature? Well, she didn't exist now.

In her nightdress and dressing gown, Verity went to the window and looked out. The full moon was shining over the graveyard. Only a few hundred yards away Alma was lying in the earth. Bert too, of course. The silvery light glittered on the flint walls of the church; in the distance the windmill was a black cross against the sky. As Verity watched, she thought she saw something moving through the tombstones, a crouching black shape that looked somehow not animal and not human. It moved towards the gate with a horrible, loping stride and then disappeared into the trees. Verity drew the curtains.

It was Hallowe'en in two days' time. Verity remembered attending a Hallowe'en party years ago. She'd gone as a witch, which allowed her to wear a tight black dress.

They'd played one of her old records, 'Something Wicked'. How did it go? *Something wicked in my heart. Something wicked in my mind. La la la put a spell. La la la heaven or hell.* Alma would have remembered. She knew all the words of all Verity's songs. Sometimes they used to sing them together while Alma cleaned the house. *Something wicked at the door. Something wicked asks for more.* Of course, the lyricist had meant 'wicked' in the sense of being roguish, a little bit naughty. But now, looking out over the moon-lit graveyard, Verity felt the other meaning of the words.

Something wicked at the door.

Max got through the evening somehow. The children were delighted to see him, and he sat with them to watch the end of *The Hundred and One Dalmatians*. When the weirdly anthropomorphised animals had made their way home in time for Christmas, Max had been surprised to find tears in his eyes. Why was he crying? Because his children's perfect family home no longer existed? Because his marriage was not as good as Pongo and Perdita's? Panda sat on the sofa with them, sighing occasionally. Perhaps he was sad too.

Max ate supper with the children and their nanny. Lydia did not put in an appearance. After Rocco and Elena had gone to bed, Max took Panda out for a last walk. How dark the countryside was. Max felt that he would have given anything to see the lights of a theatre or even a taxi. The only illuminations in the rural gloom were the guttering candles in Lydia's pumpkins and a single light from the marital bedroom. The children's rooms were on the other side of the house. What was Lydia thinking, alone up there? Was she dreaming of her demon lover? Or was she expecting Max to join her? She'd have a long wait if so, thought Max. Knowing Lydia, though, she was probably just engrossed in her night-time skincare regime.

Max had intended to sleep in the guest room, but he'd forgotten that it now contained his father's old four-poster bed. Had Lydia been planning to disport herself there with Seth? For his part, Max could not bring himself to sleep in the old master suite. Lydia had redecorated when they moved in and got rid of Alastair's faded parrot wallpaper and worn draperies but, even so, the room still seemed to belong to Max's father and not to him. So he decamped to his childhood bedroom at the end of the passage. It contained only a single bed, a wardrobe and a chest of drawers but it was, unquestionably, his.

Max lay on the bed and stared at the ceiling. There was still the mark there that looked like the ace of hearts. The blood card. When he'd come back to this house after his father's death he'd found the four of hearts stuck into the skirting boards in this room. At the time, he'd tried to make this significant but it wasn't a card that had much glamour to it. The four of hearts was something to be chosen at random from the pack, to be produced again from the punter's waistcoat pocket. Four was a smug number, it had none of the mystery of three. Husband, wife and two children. Well, now, four would become three. Unless Lydia married Seth and he became the children's stepfather. They were in love, Lydia had said. But did Seth feel the same? It was quite a commitment to take on another man's children. And where would they live? If Max divorced Lydia for adultery, he would probably get custody, but was that fair on Rocco and Elena? Should he take the gentleman's way out and pretend the fault was on his side? But, if the children went with their mother, would Max live on in this mausoleum alone, just like his father? It was the children's home; he couldn't uproot them. Did that mean giving Seth his house as well as his wife?

A scratch on the door made him jump. Was it the old man's ghost come back to haunt him? No, it was that ridiculous dog. Max got up, let Panda in and resumed his contemplation of the plasterwork. The spaniel sniffed every corner of the room before heaving himself onto the bed. There wasn't really room for the two of them but Max was glad of the animal's warmth. The bed wasn't properly made, just a blanket over a bare mattress, and it was cold in the upstairs rooms. It reminded him of theatrical digs, which were always icy in the winter. He remembered Mrs M's boarding house and how cold it had been in the attic bedroom until he made the trip downstairs to share the landlady's boudoir. He had treated Mrs M badly. He had treated lots of women badly and maybe he was getting his just deserts now.

Should he go back on the circuit? But the variety circuit didn't exist any more. Everything was about television now and, unlike Ruby, Max had never taken to the small screen. He thought of Ruby. Had she guessed about Lydia and Seth? Was that what she had meant by 'misdirection'?

God, he was never going to get to sleep. Max sat up and lit a cigarette. Panda sighed and buried his nose under his tail. Don't you start, Max told the animal silently. What the hell was he going to do with the rest of his life? He was fifty-five, fifty-six next month, there were at least another twenty years to get through. The melancholy that he'd felt that lunchtime while waiting for Ruby at the Strand Palace Hotel (was it really still the same day?) now washed over him again. He was no longer a magician and now he was no longer a husband. Max blew a smoke ring up to the pockmarked ceiling. And suddenly, like a scene from a magic lantern, he saw Brighton Pier with the snow falling. And he saw himself walking beside a woman in a duffel coat and woolly hat. He couldn't see her face but he thought he knew who it was.

TWENTY-NINE

Meg got a lift to Rottingdean on the back of Patrick's bike. She hadn't mentioned this form of transport to the DI because she was pretty sure that riding on motorbikes was one of the many things that amounted to 'disrespecting the uniform'. But Patrick had a job in Peacehaven and, when he offered to drop Meg off on the way, she had leapt at the chance. Anything was better than waiting for the 1A in the cold. There was frost on the ground this morning. And it was exciting to follow the racecourse, clinging to Patrick's leather jacket, feeling as if she was on a galloping steed of her own.

Patrick dropped her at the bottom of Dean Court Road.

'Bye, sis. Don't do anything I wouldn't do.'

That left a lot of leeway, thought Meg, as she took off the helmet and replaced it with her cap. Although, in family lore, Patrick was 'the steady one' and Declan was 'the wild one'. Patrick tied the spare helmet to his handlebars and roared off, causing an elderly lady walking her dog to clutch her chest in horror. Don't have a heart attack, Meg told her silently, smiling politely as she stood aside to let them past. The street was peaceful in the morning sunshine. It was Saturday and no one was going anywhere. The detached houses were smug behind their hedges and the only sign of life was an errand boy whistling as he carried a parcel.

Meg pushed open the fretwork gate that led to Tudor Close.

Verity actually looked rather pleased to see her. She was wearing a curly wig this morning and it wasn't on quite straight. Her make-up, too, looked hastily applied, and one false eyelash was coming adrift.

'I was hoping they'd send you,' said Verity. 'I assume you're here to check that Seth doesn't come back?'

'I'm just here to keep an eye on you,' said Meg. 'It's quite nice for me though. Better than being at the station.'

'What's it like being a woman policeman?' said Verity. 'Do the old guard give you a hard time? I remember, when I was a young pro, the old music hall types did everything they could to make things difficult for me. They'd tell me the wrong time for band call, give me apple-pie beds, put spiders in my dressing room. Most of the men made passes too. I was pleased when Alma started to travel with me. She protected me.'

That's what Eric had said, Meg remembered. *She was always there. Always with Verity. Protecting her.* What had Alma felt when Verity had then married the biggest lech of all? And did Alma really have an affair with her employer's husband? With the husband of the woman she clearly adored? But maybe Alma hadn't had much choice in the matter. Meg had never met Bert Billington but she imagined he wouldn't be averse to pressurising women to sleep with him. She thought of the list of paramours. Surely they hadn't all fallen for his bright eyes and sparkling conversation?

Maybe there had been security in being married to Bert. David had described his father as the most powerful man in show business. Presumably the old guard treated Verity with more respect when she was Mrs Billington. But what had Verity said the first time Meg met her? 'I never answer to Mrs Billington.'

'Some of the male officers do tease me,' she said, wondering if 'tease' was exactly the right word. 'About being tall and so on. But I ignore them.'

'Good for you. I expect they feel threatened. You'll be the boss one day. I was reading about it in the paper. Women's liberation is on its way. Have you read a book called *The Feminine Mystique*?'

'Some of it,' said Meg. Aisling had provided her with a precis last week. There was a lot of unintelligible stuff about psychoanalysis and 'self-actualisation' but the message seemed to be that women didn't have to stay in the kitchen.

'Let's have a good chat about it later,' said Verity. 'But now why don't you make us a nice cup of tea?'

The irony of being asked to perform domestic tasks

aside, Meg was quite happy to have a chance to nose around Verity's kitchen. She thought it was very smart, with blue Formica units and a gas stove with an eye-level grill. There was a fridge too – something Meg's family had only recently acquired – and even a twin-tub washing machine. All the surfaces were clear apart from some sandwiches under a tea towel. They had probably been left over from yesterday and were curling at the edges, though Meg was still quite tempted to eat one. 'Get yourself a biscuit,' Verity had said and Meg found a tin on top of the cupboard. Everything in Verity's kitchen was in the right place: tea, coffee and sugar all in marked containers. In Meg's house, the tea caddy contained small screwdrivers and Mary's spare rosary.

She ate a biscuit while she made the tea and took two cups and a plate of garibaldis back into the sitting room. Verity was in the armchair, looking out over the garden. The table was once more covered with old photographs.

'Ted's coming later,' she said, and Meg realised she meant the gardener. 'He normally comes on a Sunday but he said last week that he'd be here on Saturday. He'll have his tea and two chocolate biscuits. I keep them in a special tin with guardsmen on.'

Meg wished that she'd come upon this tin rather than the one containing the garibaldis. She noted that, once again, Verity seemed to expect her to do the catering. Women's liberation might be on its way, but it didn't seem to have arrived yet.

*

Edgar had been pleased to get a call from Max. He'd been slightly worried when Max hadn't telephoned last night, although the Somerset police had reported that all seemed well at the house. But now Edgar put down the receiver feeling shaken. It seemed that all was not well. Lydia was having an affair with Seth. 'It appears to have been going on for some time,' Max had said, in the clipped voice he used when he didn't want to be questioned any further. 'They met on the set of a film a few years ago. Being in Whitby together seems to have fanned the flames.'

Edgar felt very sorry for his friend – not that he'd dream of expressing sympathy because he knew this was the last thing Max wanted – but he also couldn't help thinking of the implications for the case. Seth had been with Lydia on the night of Tuesday, 5 October, the night when Alma Saunders had been killed. 'Lydia said they were together all evening,' said Max. 'I assume that's of interest to you?' Well, it was. Leonard Holt had said that he'd seen Seth leaving Alma's house at ten o'clock. If Lydia was to be believed, Seth couldn't have been in Rottingdean at that time. Could it have been, as Emma had suggested, one of the other brothers? They really did look very alike.

Edgar went into the incident room where he found Bob looking at pictures of the crime scene. This was a recent innovation; in the past officers had been forced to rely on their memories and handwritten notes. As a young DI,

Edgar had been one of the first to photograph murder victims, something his then boss had described as 'morbid'. Maybe so but there was nothing like a photograph to concentrate the mind. Bob was looking at Alma Saunders, upright in her chair. From her position, they had concluded that she had known her attacker, had been relaxed enough to sit down in their presence. Was it one of her surrogate sons, David, Seth or Aaron?

As succinctly as possible, Edgar told Bob about Seth's alibi.

Bob whistled softly. 'Lydia Lamont, eh?' But he knew not to say more.

'WDC Connolly is at Tudor Close now,' he said. 'She's keeping a watch on the place. I've told her to phone in from the local station at midday.'

'We need to find this mysterious brown-coated woman,' said Edgar. 'Do you think Meg could find an excuse to look in Verity's wardrobe?'

'I'm sure she could,' said Bob. 'She's got enough nerve for anything.'

But he said it admiringly.

Ted arrived at ten, coming through the house to reach the back garden. He was an elderly man but with a spry energy that reminded Meg of her father. He carried his boots in his hand and stopped when he saw Meg.

'Verity's just popped upstairs,' she said. 'Do you want a cup of tea?'

'Yes, please,' said Ted, making his way towards the French windows. 'With two biscuits,' he added.

'I know,' said Meg. At this rate, she could get a job as a waitress. She'd done it once in the school holidays but had been sacked for being too clumsy. Aisling, on the other hand, was a dab hand with the teapot and sugar tongs.

In the kitchen, Meg ate another biscuit while the tea brewed. She looked around the tidy room, trying to get a sense of the people who lived here. There was a calendar of Lancashire scenes on the wall. Where had she seen something similar? On the kitchen table, the sort with sides that folded down, was a large wireless set. Could she turn it on and listen to some music? Better not. She was on duty after all.

Meg poured the tea into a mug ('Ted won't drink out of a cup and saucer') and carried it, with the regulation biscuits, into the sitting room.

To find Ted lifeless on the floor.

THIRTY

Meg didn't scream. She was quite proud of herself for that. She bent over the body on the floor, registering the open doors and the boots left outside. Ted lay motionless, with blood haloing his head, but she could feel a faint pulse. She ran into the hall where she'd seen a telephone. She called for an ambulance and for police back-up and then opened the front door and looked outside. The court-yard was quiet and, as usual, all the doors were shut. She went to the gate and looked up and down the street, but Dean Court Road was completely empty.

Meg ran around the side of the house and through the door that led to the communal gardens. She met Verity walking across the lawn from the direction of the church. What was she doing? Meg could have sworn she said she was going upstairs.

'Meg!' said Verity, catching sight of her face. 'What's up?'

'It's Ted,' panted Meg. 'He's been attacked. Can you

wait by the front door? The ambulance should be here soon.'

'Attacked?' said Verity. 'By whom?'

That's the question, thought Meg. Verity looked bemused but she went to wait by the door. Meg went back into the sitting room. She knew that she shouldn't move Ted, who was now making faint bubbling sounds. She also thought that she should leave the room exactly as she found it. The super was very strict about not touching evidence, something Barker and O'Neill often mocked him about. 'Does he think he can find the killer from a spot of blood on a carpet?'

Meg looked around her. There was no sign of a weapon. Ted had fallen into the coffee table and the photographs were scattered on the floor. There was a vase of roses on another table and their petals lay like confetti on the patterned carpet. The mug of tea she had been carrying was on top of the television set. Otherwise the room was exactly as it had been.

She heard voices in the hall and then the nice sergeant from Rottingdean police station appeared.

'What's going on? Lady at the door said there'd been an accident.'

Meg had hardly finished explaining when the ambulance men arrived, closely followed by the DI and the super. Verity was hovering in the background. Ted was lifted onto a stretcher and carried out through the garden to avoid the low ceilings and beams. Meg saw one of the other front doors open and wasn't entirely surprised, a few seconds later, to see Eric Prentice at the French windows, accompanied by Lola.

'Don't bring that dog in here,' said Verity. She had collapsed onto the sofa and was holding the super's hand. He looked very uncomfortable.

'What's going on?' said Eric, standing by the open door, holding Lola's collar. 'Is there anything I can do?'

'The gardener has been taken ill,' said Meg. She thought that was the safest thing to say.

'Ted?' said Eric. 'Is he all right?'

'He's been taken to hospital,' said Meg.

The super extracted himself from Verity and stood up.

'I'm Superintendent Edgar Stephens,' he said to Eric.

'Eric Prentice.' The little man seemed to stand up taller, as if remembering his army training. 'I'm a neighbour.'

'Did you see anyone in the garden a few minutes ago?' asked the super.

'Only Verity,' said Eric. He seemed to be struggling to prevent Lola from getting into the room. Meg thought the dog had her eye on Ted's biscuits. 'She walked past a few minutes ago.'

'I was going to the church,' said Verity. 'I wanted to look at Alma's grave.'

'I thought you were upstairs,' said Meg.

'Upstairs?' said Verity vaguely. 'No, dear.'

But Meg was sure Verity had said she was going upstairs, something about 'a call of nature'. She'd certainly left the room. Had she gone out of the front door, skirted the house and headed for the church across the back lawn? But why take such a convoluted route when the French doors were wide open? Had she been trying to avoid someone? The gardener? Eric Prentice?

'Did you see anything suspicious, WDC Connolly?' asked the super.

'No,' said Meg, feeling extremely stupid. A man was attacked while she was actually in the house. She'd never hear the end of this. 'I went to make Ted, the gardener, a cup of tea. When I came back in, he was lying on the floor, bleeding from the head.'

'Did you see anyone when you walked to the church?' Superintendent Stephens asked Verity. 'You had to cross the garden, didn't you?'

'No,' said Verity. 'The first thing I saw was Meg running round from the front of the house.'

'I'd been to check the road,' said Meg.

The DI, who had accompanied Ted's stretcher to the ambulance, now came back into the room.

'Will Ted be all right?' asked Verity. 'He's a funny old thing but he means well. It's so awful to think of someone hurting him.'

'The ambulance crew thought he'd pull through,' said the DI. 'I'll call the hospital and find out more in a little while. In the meantime, is there someone we should be contacting? Do you know who his next of kin is?'

'He has a daughter,' said Verity. 'But I can't remember her name. One of those modern names. Sharon or Tracy.'

'I'll ask Emma,' said the super. 'I know she interviewed Ted a few weeks ago.'

Meg was sure that Emma would have made a note; she made a note of everything.

'I'll send another officer to guard the house,' said the DI. 'I don't think the assailant will be back but just to be on the safe side.'

Meg wasn't at all sure that the assailant wouldn't be back. It was a horrible thought that someone was watching the quiet property in the quiet street, just waiting for their moment to strike.

'I don't need anyone else,' said Verity. 'I'm quite safe with Meg. Shall we have another cup of tea?'

Emma put down the phone, feeling thoughtful. She had, of course, made a note of Ted's daughter's name but, before he rang off, she'd made Edgar take her through the attack step by step. Ted had arrived to do the gardening. Meg Connolly went into the kitchen to make him a cup of tea and Verity Malone had supposedly gone upstairs but was later seen in the garden, walking from the direction of the church. Meg had come back into the sitting room to find Ted on the floor, bleeding from a head wound. Eric Prentice had then appeared, asking what was going on. Ted was in hospital but Bob thought he'd pull through. Meg was still at the house with Verity. Oh, and Lydia Lamont was having an affair with Seth Billington, which meant that he had an alibi for Alma's murder. It was a lot to take in.

Sam was in Manchester, covering the Moors Murders. Ian Brady and Myra Hindley had been in court again and the list of victims was growing. Emma knew how much Sam hated this sort of work and she missed her partner. But, on the plus side, when she'd visited Mavis yesterday, her neighbour had said that she was well enough to baby-sit again. The girls were tired from horse-riding and even Jonathan was looking rather sleepy. Emma telephoned Mavis who said that she'd be happy to come round for an hour or so. 'Working on a Saturday, love? It's not right.' But Edgar was working, thought Emma, and no one questioned that. She just wanted some time alone with her thoughts. Edgar had said that she was good at finding patterns. Admittedly, he had been trying to placate her but Emma thought that he had also meant it. Could she see a pattern in the recent events at Tudor Close?

Leaving Mavis and the children in front of the television, Emma walked to the Lanes. As she let herself into the room above Midas and Sons, she thought of the time when Lydia had visited, gliding up the stairs in a scented cloud of fur.

Why had Lydia called on her that day? Was she worried that Seth might be accused of his father's murder or was she worried that he'd done it? In retrospect, Lydia had certainly been indulging in a spot of misdirection, hence all that talk of hit men and debts. But was there a nugget of something more substantial in her B-movie scenarios? Lydia had told Emma about Max's affair with Verity, which turned out to be true. Lydia had wanted to be involved in the case, to be Emma's 'sleeping partner' but she'd never contacted her again. What else had Lydia said when she visited the office above Midas and Sons? That Verity might have killed her husband, probably helped by her son David, whom Lydia described as 'creepy'. Emma had never spoken to David but Sam had liked him and she trusted Sam's judgement. But likeable people sometimes do terrible things. And why had Alma Saunders consulted Astarte about her own eldest son, Fred? Sheena had said that Alma was obsessed with the occult but Emma hadn't seen, or sensed, any sign of this when she had visited Alma's cottage in Rottingdean.

Sheena was another mystery. She'd told Barry Saunders that his mother was having an affair with Bert. Fred thought that she'd told the same story to Verity. But, at the funeral, Fred and Sheena had seemed quite friendly. In her notes Meg had commented that Sheena had been talking to Fred and Barry at the wake, also that Seth and Barry had once been friends. Was there something about the two families that Emma was missing?

Facing Emma across the partner desk was the little horse that Alma had given to Jonathan. Alma was a kind woman, she was sure of it, someone who had cared about the Billington family. Why, then, had Alma been killed? Had it been revenge for Alma's supposed affair with Bert or was it because she knew something about his death? It all came back to the mysterious woman in the brown coat. But, as Meg had said, the woman might not be a woman at all. 'Anyone can wear a coat.' Actors and acting. Costume and disguise. Emma thought of the Dracula story that she had told Meg in Whitby. *Local children report seeing a beautiful woman – a 'boofer lady' – in white, stalking them.* Verity's visitor hadn't been described as beautiful but there was certainly something unearthly about her, forever lurking just out of sight, a mysterious shape in the darkness.

Emma took out Meg's notes and began to read them again. The china horse grazed contentedly on the leather blotter.

By evening, Meg was beginning to get seriously spooked. She was doing her best to look after Verity. She'd made them both boiled eggs for lunch and then they'd sat down and listened to *Mrs Dale's Diary* on the radio. Meg had picked up all the photographs and helped Verity put them back in order. She'd seen so many women in evening dresses and men in bow ties that they started to merge together in her mind.

'That was Dolly O'Rourke, she had an act with a performing monkey, horrid little animal . . . Ravik and Renee, they were a devoted couple, both dead now . . . The Great

Diablo, he was a character, used to take a hip-flask on stage . . . Cecily Harmond, she had an act with a swing, the men used to go wild . . . The Diller Twins, they weren't even sisters really . . .'

But now Verity was dozing in her chair and Meg was watching the shadows outside. The DI had sent a squad car but they were parked on the street, at the front of the house. Meg was sure that the assailant had come the other way, from the direction of the church. Just before Verity had fallen asleep, she had said something about an animal prowling about the graveyard. Could it have been Lola? But the hound never seemed to leave Eric's side. Meg couldn't help thinking about Whitby and the story Emma had told her. *All sorts of weird things happen, including Dracula climbing up the walls like a spider, and Jonathan realises that Dracula is a vampire, someone who never dies but goes around looking for human blood to drink . . .*

'Vampires don't exist,' Meg said aloud. *It's Hallowe'en tomorrow though*, said a voice in her head, a voice which, disconcertingly, sounded like her mother. All sorts of creatures prowl the earth on Hallowe'en. Verity opened her eyes. 'Alma would never do that to me,' she said.

Was she talking about Alma's affair with Bert or was Verity still lost in the past?

'Do what?' said Meg. She thought how uncouth she sounded. Verity had even managed to say 'whom' when asking who had attacked Ted.

'She'd never sleep with Bert. She told Aaron.'

'When did she tell Aaron?' asked Meg. But Verity was asleep again. Meg thought of Pamela Curtis. *I wouldn't have slept with Bert Billington if he was the last man alive.* Strange how people use the word sleep to mean sex, which was surely the opposite of sleeping. Meg wouldn't know; she'd never tried it herself. The closest she'd come was with Paddy Malloy behind the bumper cars on the pier. And, even if Declan and his pals hadn't arrived at precisely the wrong moment, Meg doubted that she'd have gone 'all the way', as her schoolfriends used to say. All the way was a very long way when you came to think about it.

Verity murmured something about figs, or maybe wigs. Where was she going this time? Meg waited but Verity's breathing deepened and her chin dropped to her chest. Meg went to the French windows. The neat garden looked very different at night: all sorts of shapes appeared which Meg hadn't noticed in the daylight. Was that tree always there? And what was that animal crouching just by the window? Maybe she should draw the curtains? It would stop her trying to turn the topiary hedges into werewolves and men in cloaks. She pulled the velvet drapes and instantly everything seemed safer but also more enclosed. She could hear the clock ticking from the hallway and the mechanical whirr of the fridge. Upstairs, a floorboard creaked. Of course, Tudor Close was an old house – even if it wasn't actually Tudor: you'd expect a few creaks and groans. But even so, the sound made Meg feel uneasy.

The room suddenly seemed much darker. Meg lit the fringed standard lamp and, as she did so, she saw something poking out from under the sofa. It must be one of the photographs dislodged by Ted's fall. Meg pulled it out. It was the group shot from the film, *The Prince of Darkness*. There was a dirty thumbprint on the frame. Ted must have been holding this picture when he was attacked.

'So now you know,' said Verity.

THIRTY-ONE

'What?' said Meg. 'What do I know?'

'You know who killed them,' said Verity.

'What do you mean?' said Meg. She felt as if she was frozen to the spot, standing by the lamp with the photograph in her hand. 'Who killed them?'

'I did,' said a voice from the doorway.

Meg didn't at first recognise the woman, though she did register that she was wearing a brown coat. It was only when she said, 'Hallo again, Meg,' that the picture came into focus: Whitby, the graveyard, Dracula, the two other figures looming out of the mist, one of them a woman. *Why don't we go inside, out of the cold?*

'Irene?' said Meg.

'I almost dressed up as Dracula again,' said Irene. 'But I didn't have the heart.'

'That was you,' said Meg. 'In Whitby? In the graveyard at night?'

'Yes,' said Irene. 'That's the thing about being in charge of the wardrobe. You have all the costumes.'

Meg remembered Irene lending them the Victorian nightdresses to sleep in. She'd seemed a kindly woman then, a comforting presence. But she'd taken Max and Seth's Dracula clothes away, only to change into them later.

'Did you kill Bert?' she said.

'Yes,' said Irene. 'He killed my daughter, you see.'

'Glenda?' said Meg. But that wasn't right. Glenda's mother was Sandra Gillespie.

'Barbara,' said Irene. 'After he abandoned her, she lost all hope. She went downhill, drink, drugs, you name it. There was nothing her father or I could do. My husband died of a broken heart. In a way, Bert killed him too.'

'Barbara died in August, didn't she?'

'Oh, you knew that?' Irene looked almost pleased. 'I didn't think anyone was interested in poor Babs. Yes, she died, penniless, on the streets. As soon as I heard, I knew he had to pay. I wrote to Verity and told her so.'

'You came here the day he died, didn't you?' If she yelled, wondered Meg, would the policemen outside hear her? If only she could get past Irene . . .

'Yes. I just popped in to administer a dose of poison,' said Irene. 'Unfortunately, Alma saw me. So I had to kill her too.'

Verity gave a soft moan. 'Poor Alma. She didn't deserve that.' Meg noticed that she'd said nothing about her husband not deserving to die.

'I had to,' said Irene. 'I felt bad about it though.'

'Alma wouldn't have told anyone,' said Verity. 'She didn't even tell me.'

But Verity had known all the same, thought Meg. Had she known that Irene was actually in the house? Presumably Irene had come across Ted looking at the photograph and realised that he, too, would recognise her? Had she meant to kill him or just to silence him? Had she run upstairs afterwards? Meg couldn't believe that no one had thought to search the bedrooms.

But there was no time to think about any of that. Meg had to escape, to get help. The French windows would be easiest. Meg started to back away but, quicker than she would have thought possible, Irene had crossed the room and grabbed her arm.

'Oh no you don't.'

'Don't hurt Meg,' said Verity. 'I like her.' But she didn't move from her chair.

Meg fought to get free. She was strong, used to play-fighting with her brothers, but Irene was almost a match for her. Eventually Meg gave Irene a push that knocked her to the floor. Then Meg was unlocking the French windows and running for her life across the lawn.

'Help!' she shouted. 'Help!'

She ran round to the side of the house but the door was locked. Was that Irene's work or was it always locked at night? After kicking at it and rattling the latch, Meg doubled back across the garden, heading for the gate that led to the church. She could hear loud piano music coming from somewhere in the house. Eric certainly wasn't going to come to her aid. Meg ran into the darkness and fell over almost at once. She scrambled to her feet and then something hit her in the back and she was knocked face down in the mud. She tried to get up but now there was a dead weight on top of her. Meg smelt perfume, something suffocatingly sweet, and then two hands were round her neck, squeezing, throttling.

Meg fought desperately and, somehow, she got free. She staggered across the grass just as the moon came out from behind the clouds and she saw the church tower and, blessedly near, the gate. She fumbled with the latch and then she was running through the tombstones, white in the moonlight. Was Alma's newly dug grave somewhere nearby? The soil would still be loose. Would she fall into it? She heard the gate opening again and, turning, tripped over a fallen gravestone. The dreadful weight was on her again, the hands round her neck. Was this how she was going to die? In a graveyard at Hallowe'en? How embarrassing. But her thoughts were becoming jumbled, this time she couldn't find the strength to fight off her attacker. It almost felt easier to sink into the earth and close her eyes. And then, out of the depths, she heard a sound.

A dreadful, unearthly howling.

Irene heard it too and, just for a second, she relaxed her grip on Meg's neck. Meg hit back with her elbow and managed to twist round, trying to stand. Then, two things happened. A creature, a vast animal, threw itself on Meg's attacker. And a wonderfully familiar voice shouted, 'Stop! Police!'

'Emma?' croaked Meg.

Emma Holmes, pale hair gleaming, stood over Irene's body. The animal, which seemed to be a large dog, was standing guard, panting.

'Irene Dodson, you're under arrest for the murders of Bert Billington and Alma Saunders,' Emma was saying. 'You have the right to remain silent . . .'

'Help!' shouted Meg. 'Help!' And then there were flash-lights and running feet. Meg sank back onto the ground, her head resting against stone. Emma was crouching beside her. 'Are you all right, Meg? It's OK. The police have arrested Irene.'

'How did you know?' Meg struggled to form the words. 'How did you know it was her?'

'It was all in your notes,' said Emma. 'I came as soon as I worked it out.'

'And the dog?' Meg thought she saw the super in the background but she couldn't be sure. All the faces were blurry and unreal. She almost thought that she saw Drac-ula too and Bert Billington in his dinner jacket, his arms round two scantily dressed girls.

'I think he's a lost dog called Tiny,' said Emma. 'Another case closed.'

She seemed to be laughing but Meg closed her eyes and heard no more.

THIRTY-TWO

Afterwards all she remembered was a jumble of lights and voices. 'Possible concussion ... keep her still ... telephone her parents ... Can you hear me, Meg? What's the pain like on a scale of one to ten, Meg?' There were people in uniform and other faces who couldn't possibly be there: Irene, Verity, Bert Billington, Count Dracula, her own dead grandfather. There were blue lights in the night sky and then someone was saying, 'Take her up to the ward.' Meg wanted to say that she could walk but the words wouldn't come. Sirens, fluorescent tubes, lift doors opening and closing.

When she opened her eyes again, she was lying between crisp sheets and her mother was saying, 'Whatever have you done to yourself, Meg?'

This seemed incredibly unfair. Meg thought for a minute about how to answer. 'I caught a murderer,' she said at last.

'From what I hear, the murderer nearly caught you,'

said her mother, but she stroked Meg's hair, which hurt rather but was nice all the same.

'I dreamt about Grandda,' said Meg. Or maybe she didn't. Maybe she was dreaming again. This time, when she opened her eyes, Emma was sitting by her bed.

'So,' she said, 'do you want to hear what happened next?'

Meg nodded as she struggled to sit up but a nurse appeared and told her to lie flat. 'You've got concussion,' she told her, as if this was something that Meg had brought into the ward on the sole of her shoe.

'I won't excite her,' said Emma. 'I promise.' Her voice seemed to pacify the sister. The wonders of a posh accent.

'Irene has confessed to the murders of Bert and Alma,' said Emma, settling more comfortably in the visitor's chair.

'She confessed to me too,' said Meg. 'But, then, I think she was planning to kill me so she must have thought it didn't matter.' She thought of running through the graveyard, knowing that her attacker was close behind her. She thought of Irene's weight bringing her to the ground.

'She was awfully strong,' she said. 'I mean, she must be in her seventies.'

'Max says that she used to have a strong-woman act,' said Emma. 'Edgar rang him just now. Irene also had an act with her husband where she dressed up as a young boy.'

'I saw an errand boy in Dean Court Road this morning,' said Meg. 'Do you think that was her?'

'It's possible,' said Emma. 'It turns out she only lives nearby. In Newhaven. It would have been easy for her to catch the bus into Rottingdean. But Irene did seem to enjoy dressing up. I'm sure she was the person we saw in the graveyard at Whitby, dressed as Dracula.'

'It was,' said Meg. 'She said so. I wonder why she did that?'

'Perhaps to point suspicion towards Seth,' said Emma. 'Irene rang Max yesterday and told him that Lydia knew who the murderer was. I think that was meant to make him think it was Seth. Max drove like a madman to Somerset and found Seth there. With Lydia.'

'Golly,' said Meg. It seemed an inadequate response. She tried to imagine the scene but it ended up being like an illustration in one of Aisling's magazines. Would Max have challenged Seth to a duel? No, that was another sort of story altogether.

'Lydia gave Seth an alibi for Alma's death,' said Emma. 'That's what made me think it must be someone else.'

'How did you guess it was Irene? I didn't realise even when I saw her standing there, in Verity's sitting room. I couldn't believe it. Verity didn't seem surprised though.'

'I didn't guess for ages. Until I was at home putting the children to bed. Edgar had told me that Ted had been attacked and I thought it must be because he'd recognised the woman in the brown coat. I looked back through your notes. You'd included a transcript of Barbara's birth certificate. I saw the mother's name. Irene Dodson. And I remembered Sandra saying that Barbara's mother was in the business too.'

'There were roses on the table,' said Meg. 'Verity said that Barbara used to be called the rose girl. Verity was cutting roses on the day that Bert died.'

'Verity was talking about roses when Edgar went round there tonight,' said Emma. 'He thought that she seemed completely out of it. Aaron's looking after her now.'

'Aaron,' said Meg. 'I think he was the person who called on Alma the night she died.'

'Why do you think that?'

'Something Verity said. She said that Alma told Aaron that she didn't sleep with Bert. Mind you, she was half asleep at the time.' Or maybe Meg herself was half asleep. She struggled to sound coherent.

'What happened next? How come you rescued me?'

'I knew you were at Tudor Close,' said Emma, 'and I knew you were in danger. Edgar had told me about the gardener being attacked. I guessed that the attacker was still lurking somewhere.'

'In an upstairs room,' said Meg. 'Irene must have hidden there after trying to kill Ted. I feel so stupid. The murderer was actually in the house.'

'Don't blame yourself,' said Emma. 'You never expected the killer to be so close. Well, I was worried about you. I rang Edgar and, of course, he told me to stay home. He'd handle it. Et cetera.' From her prone position, Meg couldn't see Emma's face very well but she heard the irritation in her voice. 'But I couldn't just stay behind,' Emma went on. 'I asked my neighbour to look after the children and I drove straight to Dean Court Road. I knew the police would go to the front of the house so I thought I'd take the route through the graveyard. I'm glad I did.'

'You just appeared like an angel. Then I heard you reading Irene her rights.'

Meg thought Emma sounded embarrassed. 'I forgot I wasn't a police officer for a minute.'

Meg's head was still aching and she was starting to see the flashing lights again but she wanted to get all the details while she had the chance. 'What about the dog?' she said. 'Where did that come from? How did you know its name?'

Emma laughed. 'Sam and I were asked to look for a lost dog called Tiny. There were some sightings in the Rottingdean area. I just put two and two together. He's a St Bernard, the breed that rescues people lost in the mountains, and he seemed to think it was his job to save you.'

'Have you taken him back to his owners?'

'Yes. I dropped him off on the way here. They were very grateful.'

'I'd like to have a dog again,' said Meg. 'We've only got a budgie. Padre Pio.'

Emma must have thought that she was rambling because she said, 'I should leave you to rest. I'm sure Bob will visit tomorrow. After all, you did catch the murderer. You're a heroine.'

It was a comforting thought and it carried Meg onto a wave of sleep.

Emma left the ward, thanking the night sister profusely, and found Edgar waiting outside.

'Is she OK?' he said.

'Yes,' said Emma. 'The nurses say that she's got concussion and a few cuts and bruises. They'll keep her in for a night and discharge her tomorrow.'

'I checked up on Ted Grange, the gardener,' said Edgar. 'Looks like he'll make a full recovery too. He was lucky. Irene was interrupted by WDC Connolly before she had time to kill him.'

'Meg thinks that Irene hid upstairs,' said Emma.

'Let's hope the press never get to hear of that,' said Edgar. 'We'd look such fools.'

'I won't even tell Sam,' said Emma.

They started to walk along the corridor, a chilly expanse of parquet, the walls painted green to waist height and cream above.

'It reminds me of visiting you in hospital,' said Edgar. 'That time you got hit over the head. I remember rushing here, frantic with worry.'

'And Daddy threatened to sue you,' said Emma. 'I remember.' She was glad that Edgar had resurrected this memory. It meant that he wasn't angry about her leaving the children to come to Meg's rescue. It also reminded her of the days when she was intrepid DS Holmes.

'The matron was a real dragon,' said Edgar. 'She only let me stay with you for a few minutes.'

Emma remembered. She also remembered that Edgar had been with Ruby that night. She'd come to the hospital too although she'd waited outside. Emma could still feel the wave of despair that had swept over her after Edgar had left, knowing that he was going home with Ruby. Emma took her husband's arm. 'You proposed to me when I was in hospital too,' she said. That had been another case and another injury.

'You were a liability,' said Edgar, but there was laughter in his voice. They descended the staircase – a grand affair more suited to a posh hotel than a hospital; it reminded her of the Royal Whitby – and made their way out through the main entrance. An ambulance drew up outside the Casualty Department and two doctors emerged to greet the stretcher. A few feet away a couple of nurses were smoking cigarettes in the porch. The calm chaos of a hospital at night. As they crossed the forecourt, a clock struck midnight. It was Hallowe'en at last, thought Emma.

Emma had parked her car on one of the double yellow lines that had recently appeared all over Brighton but traffic wardens seemed to have left it alone. Emma was delighted to see its snub-nosed shape. It was only a short walk back to their house but she suddenly felt very tired.

'I called in at home earlier,' said Edgar. 'Mavis said that she was happy to stay the night.'

'That's very kind of her.'

'She said she'd missed looking after them.'

'Wonders will never cease. Do you want to drive?'

'No,' said Edgar. 'You drive.' He folded his long legs into the passenger seat.

Emma got behind the wheel. 'Bob must be pleased to have the case tied up,' she said.

'Ish,' said Edgar. 'You know Bob. He's worried about WDC Connolly. Thinks it was his fault that she was attacked.'

'She'll be OK,' said Emma, putting the car into gear. 'Women are tough.'

'They certainly are,' said Edgar.

THIRTY-THREE

'I hear you solved the case in the end,' said Verity.

Verity looked remarkably well, thought Emma, for a woman in her seventies who had, only yesterday, come face to face with her husband's murderer. This morning, Verity's wig was a neat bobbed affair and she wasn't wearing her false eyelashes. She was also wearing trousers for the first time in their acquaintance. They suited her slim-hipped figure. It was Sunday morning and the bells were ringing from St Margaret's.

'I was almost too late,' said Emma. 'I only realised about Irene when I saw Barbara's birth certificate.'

'Poor Babs,' said Verity. 'She was such a pretty girl. I thought about her when I found the photograph the other day. The one of Bert with Babs and Glenda. I showed it to you, didn't I? No, that was Meg. I get the two of you mixed up.'

Hard to do, thought Emma, when she was blonde and Meg was dark. Not to mention Meg being over a head taller.

Then she thought of the waitress in Liverpool thinking they were sisters. Maybe there was a resemblance somewhere.

'You told Meg that Barbara used to be called the rose girl,' said Emma. She looked across the room to where pink roses were displayed in a silver bowl. They looked as if they'd been freshly picked.

'Yes,' said Verity. 'She threw roses into the audience. Funny how pantomime audiences love things being thrown at them. I knew that Bert had his eye on her when he gave her that part. Then, one day, he had a rose in his buttonhole. Silly old fool.'

'And Glenda found out about it?'

'Yes. She was living in Liverpool with the child. She came to the theatre one day and found Bert with Babs. And, well, you know the rest.'

Emma wasn't sure that she did. She knew that Glenda had gone home, got into bed and gassed herself and her child. She knew that her parents still grieved for her. And she knew that, years later, Barbara had died alone in her little flat in Hastings. 'Death brought on by the effects of drink and drugs,' according to the coroner.

'Babs really loved Bert,' said Verity. 'I thought it was strange at the time.'

And that was a very strange remark, thought Emma. There was a brief silence. Outside, Emma could see Aaron Billington mowing the lawn. He appeared to have taken it upon himself to replace the injured gardener and Emma thought that the arrangement seemed to suit mother and son rather well. Aaron looked happy and perhaps was pleased to be able to do something practical to help his mother. Verity went as far as to call Aaron 'a treasure', a term Emma suspected had hitherto been reserved for Seth.

'Alma saw Irene here on the Sunday that Bert was killed,' said Emma. 'That's why she killed her.'

'Poor Alma,' said Verity. 'I was sorry about that.'

She sounded it too. Emma wondered if Verity knew about Alma's supposed affair with Bert. Did she dare ask? But Verity answered the question herself. 'Sheena once hinted that Alma had been Bert's mistress. "Someone close to you" is what she said. But I never believed it. I even thought it might have been Pamela. But never Alma. She was on my side. She looked after me and I looked after her. I got Bert to give her extra money every month. In her account. Not Dave's. A woman should always have her running away money, that's what my mum used to say.'

Those must have been the payments that had made Sheena Billington think the worst, thought Emma. Had Verity had her own running away money? Had she ever considered leaving Bert? She thought of Verity saying that she wanted Alma in Lytham so she had someone on her side. Alma had been on Verity's side to the end.

'Irene says that she poisoned Bert,' said Emma. 'She just walked into the house on September the nineteenth and put rat poison in his whisky. She knew he always had a glass after lunch.'

'Yes, he did,' said Verity with a sigh. 'He did like a spot of malt.'

'As I think I said earlier,' said Emma, 'I suspect that Bert had been ingesting small amounts of poison for some time prior to his death. It's hard to see how Irene could have done that while she was working in Whitby.'

Verity looked at Emma with her pale, shrewd eyes. 'I suppose we'll never know.'

No, thought Emma, they would never know. She had finally seen the post-mortem. It was annoyingly inconclusive but Emma thought that Bert had built up a tolerance for the poison which was why he hadn't vomited when he had been given the final, fatal dose. Emma had no doubt that Irene had administered this last dose. It was the previous slow poisoning that she was considering now. Emma remembered Meg saying that Verity hadn't seemed surprised when Irene appeared in the doorway. 'So now you know,' she'd apparently said. She thought of Verity picking roses on the day that Bert died. Barbara used to be called the rose girl.

'You're a very clever girl, Emma,' said Verity. 'But you can't expect to know all the answers. Only God knows the secrets of the heart.'

And she smiled at Emma very fondly. Outside, Aaron was whistling as he mowed. It sounded like one of Verity's old songs.

Sam was waiting by the gate, astride her Triumph Tiger Cub. She had arrived back from Manchester last night, very annoyed at missing the denouement of the case. Emma had promised to fill her in on the details. Edgar was at home with the children. He had even offered to cook lunch.

Emma climbed onto the back of the bike. 'Where to?'

'Let's go to the beach,' said Sam.

They went to Black Rock and walked along the shingle beside the Volk's railway. The miniature trains were still running but otherwise the beach was quite deserted. It was a still, overcast day, the water as smooth and luminous as glass, the lights of the Palace Pier ghostly in the distance.

'You know they're talking about building a marina here,' said Sam. 'A huge great harbour.'

'That'll never happen,' said Emma. 'I can't imagine a marina in Brighton.'

They walked on for a while, their feet slipping in the loose stones. Sam said, 'So it was the wardrobe mistress all along. That was a turn-up for the books.'

'I suppose so,' said Emma. 'But we did think that the murder was linked to Bert's past and the King Rat pantomime in particular. It was just that we were focused on the wrong girl. Glenda instead of Barbara. Meg found out that Barbara had died in August. She was in a bad way, apparently. That must have been the final straw for Irene. She decided to get her revenge.'

'How much did Verity know?' asked Sam, picking up a pebble and skimming it expertly.

'That's the question,' said Emma. 'I think Verity wanted us to make the connection with the Liverpool pantomime and King Rat. I'm pretty sure she told Seth to post that flyer, just to point us in the right direction. She showed Meg a picture of Bert with Glenda and Barbara. That must have been for the same reason.'

'But did she know about the poisoning?' said Sam.

Emma said, slowly, 'I'm not sure. Irene has admitted killing Bert and she definitely killed Alma but I think someone had been giving Bert poison long before that.'

'My money's on the toothpaste,' said Sam.

Emma stopped and stared at her partner. 'What?'

'When I spoke to Aaron, he seemed touchingly proud that his dad still had all his own teeth. It would have been easy for Verity to put some rat poison on his toothbrush every morning.'

'That's what I think too,' said Emma. 'Irene might have given the final dose but Verity had prepared him.'

'Are you going to tell the police?'

Emma was silent for a few minutes, looking out over the still water. The horizon was hazy, impossible to know where the sky ended and the sea began.

'I don't think so,' she said at last. 'There's no real proof and, anyway, what good would it do? Bert is dead. Verity seems to be reconciled with her sons. And Irene did kill Alma. Verity was genuinely upset by that. She never believed that Alma was having an affair with Bert, by the way.'

'Was Verity working with Irene?' said Sam. 'If so, why employ us?'

'I think she hadn't counted on Aaron suspecting her,' said Emma. 'And, deep down, I think she wanted Bert to be found out. That's why she kept pointing us towards King Rat and 1949. She might have been poisoning Bert on her own behalf or she might have been in cahoots with Irene. Meg said she wasn't at all surprised when Irene suddenly appeared in her sitting room.'

She hadn't helped Meg either, when Irene attacked her, thought Emma. She didn't say this aloud.

'It wouldn't help Irene to implicate Verity too,' said Sam. 'Not when she's confessed to killing Alma and trying to kill Ted. At least, whatever happens, Irene won't go to the gallows now that capital punishment has been suspended. Even Brady and Hindley won't hang and, if anyone deserves it, they do.'

But people don't get what they deserve, thought Emma. She was against the death penalty but maybe she would feel differently if she knew what Sam knew about the Moors Murders. They were nearer the pier now. Emma could see the signs advertising that year's pantomime. *Puss in Boots*. Wasn't that *Dick Whittington* in disguise?

'Verity paid us,' she said. 'So the agency is making money at last.'

'Another successful case for Holmes and Collins,' said Sam. 'We even found the lost dog.'

'Well, he found us,' said Emma.

'Even so,' said Sam. 'I think we deserve some chips.'

'Edgar's cooking lunch,' said Emma. But she followed Sam across the beach and towards a stall where a rather terrifying fish called Mr Cod offered a bag of chips for 4d.

The DI visited Meg just as she was having breakfast. It was very embarrassing to be caught sitting up in bed in a borrowed nightdress, eating toast and jam. Visiting hours hadn't started yet so everyone in the ward stared as the dark-suited figure approached Meg's bed.

'How are you feeling, WDC Connolly?'

'Fine,' said Meg, although her head still ached slightly. 'They say I can go home today. After the doctor's seen me.'

'I'll send a car to take you home.'

Meg laughed, assuming this was a joke. The DI smiled politely. The woman in the next bed, who seemed slightly dotty, leant over to ask Meg who her fancy man was.

'He's my boss,' said Meg.

'Irene Dodson has been charged with the murders of Bert Billington and Alma Saunders,' said DI Willis. 'She's made a full confession. You did very well to apprehend her.'

'I didn't really,' said Meg. 'That was Emma.'

'Blasted Emma,' said the DI. This was strong language coming from him. 'She always manages to be in the right place at the right time.' But he smiled when he said it.

'How is Verity today?' asked Meg.

'I called in earlier and she seemed fine. Her son was with her. The youngest one. Aaron.'

'I think Aaron was the person Leonard Holt saw leaving Alma's house on the day she died,' said Meg. 'I think he'd gone to see her to ask if she'd really had an affair with Bert. I don't know what she said but maybe it's made Aaron feel friendlier towards his mum.'

The DI looked rather confused by this, as well he might.

'After all,' Meg ploughed on, 'it couldn't have been Seth because he was with Lydia Lamont.'

Now the DI just looked mortified. 'It's good to have the loose ends tied up,' he said at last. Meg was relieved when Matron appeared to tell the DI that he had to leave because 'Doctor' was starting his rounds.

'Goodbye then,' said the DI. 'And well done again. No need to come to work tomorrow.'

'Thank you,' said Meg, though she fully intended to be back at the station first thing on Monday. If there were any congratulations flying around, she didn't want to miss them.

'Bye-bye, sailor,' shouted Meg's neighbour at the DI's departing back. He didn't look round.

Two nurses cleared away Meg's breakfast and tidied the bed, pulling the sheets so tight that Meg thought they might break. They even attempted to tidy Meg, offering her a comb and an elastic band for her hair. Meg tied her hair back into an untidy ponytail. That would have to do.

The doctor, an elderly man with a monocle, didn't seem to notice Meg's appearance. He declared her fit to leave the hospital. 'Just don't get into any more fights,

Margaret.' His coterie of medical students laughed heart-
ily at that gem.

Meg hadn't believed the DI about the car but there it
was outside, a liveried panda driven by a PC she didn't
recognise.

'WDC Connolly? I'm to drive you home.'

Great, the neighbours would think that she had been
arrested. It felt very odd to sit in the back of the car. Like
royalty. Or a prisoner. And, as they approached Meg's
house, the street seemed to be very full of people. Of
course, it was Sunday. No one had anything better to do.
The Irish families were walking back from mass. The
others were preparing to go to the pub.

The panda car drew up outside the Connollys' house.
The driver even opened Meg's door for her.

'There you go, ma'am.'

Ma'am. Was this some kind of practical joke? Meg wasn't
wearing uniform, her mum had brought her a change of
clothes yesterday. Maybe the neighbours would think
she'd spent the night in the cells? But, as she got out of
the car, she was amazed to hear a thin ripple of applause
from the families standing at their front gates.

Meg's mother came to the door.

'Welcome home,' she said, as if Meg had been away for
years.

'Why are they clapping?' said Meg, when she got close
enough to whisper.

'Because you're a heroine,' said Mary. 'You caught that

woman. The one who killed your man, the theatre chap. DI Willis told me all about it last night. He says you might get an award.'

'I didn't do anything really,' said Meg. 'I was just there.' But, as the applause continued, she raised her hand to acknowledge it, feeling like Princess Margaret at the Proms.

THIRTY-FOUR

Sunday afternoon, thought Verity Malone, was a sinister time of day. The streets were empty. Everyone was inside their houses. Who knew what was going on in all those sitting rooms, kitchens and bedrooms? Betty Friedan was right. The home was a dangerous place. Especially for women.

It was dangerous, too, because your guard was down. Usually Verity managed not to think about the past but, today, after a surprisingly delicious lunch prepared by Aaron, she had allowed herself a single glass of port. It had opened the floodgates. Other Sundays. Changeover day, struggling with her bandbox on freezing trains. Walking along the beach at Lytham, holding Aaron's hand whilst trying to stop Seth and Barry running into the sea. Gossiping with Alma in numerous dressing rooms, drinking coffee with powdered milk or whisky out of toothmugs. Going back to a darkened theatre to meet Max. Listening to her father preaching in the front room of the house in Bow. The upstairs rooms, so cold you could see your breath, sharing a bed with her sister, the sound of her father's footsteps on the stairs.

That was the trouble with memory. It always took you all the way back, whether you wanted it to or not. Verity thought she'd erased Bow, the way she'd eradicated every trace of her cockney accent. Of her five siblings, only one was still alive, her youngest sister Patience – her mother really liked those 'virtue' names – now living in Ireland. There was no one else left who remembered the terraced house with its smell of fear and drains. Their father, Frank Malone, had originally been from Ireland but, somewhere along the way, he had ditched his native Catholicism and founded his own, far more brutal, form of Christianity, the rules of which were known only to him. They had all lived in fear of Frank and his best friend, God. Frank used to call upon God to witness how wicked his family were and none of them were in any doubt that God would be on Frank's side. After all, they were both men, weren't they?

Then, as Verity got older and her charms became apparent even to their neighbours who rarely thought beyond the next meal, Frank started to look at her in a different way. 'Verity could be a real help to us,' he used to say and something about his glance, sly and appraising, made Verity long for the days when she had only been afraid of a good hiding. Frank made Verity apply for a job as a dancer for a touring company. He even took her to the audition himself and advised her what to wear. The thought, even now, made her stomach turn. 'She's a good girl,' he told the dance captain. 'She'll do what she's told.'

And she did do what she was told. She became a dancer and then a singer and, eventually, she had enough money to buy her mum a nice little house in Streatham. Frank was dead by then. He'd died suddenly while eating jellied eels. Verity had thought that rather fitting for a man who prided himself on his taste for esoteric East End food. She'd brought him the eels specially and knew that he'd never share them with anyone else. You could always count on Frank Malone to think of himself first. And last. Well, the first shall be last and the last shall be first.

When she'd met Bert, she hadn't at first seen the resemblance to Dad. It was Mum who'd said, almost admiringly, 'He's such a forceful man, just like Frank.' By then, Verity was engaged to Bert. She'd left it late to get married. She'd been thirty, almost on the shelf, and just so *tired* of it all; the men making passes and then being angry when they were rebuffed, the older pros offering help in return for unspecified, but nonetheless sordid, favours. She wanted what Bert offered: security, money, a family of her own. And, to be fair to Bert (she always tried to be fair, whatever anyone said), he had provided those things. She hadn't expected him to be faithful and he wasn't. That didn't bother her much. Until Glenda. That poor silly girl. If only Verity could have spoken to her. 'You can't let a man matter that much,' she would have said to her. 'You have your child and your friends. That should be enough.' But, perhaps unsurprisingly, Glenda did not come to Verity for advice.

Alma had been her great support. She'd been there in the early days, when sometimes they'd had to barricade themselves into the dressing room to avoid the attentions of men who'd called themselves admirers but were actually hell-bent on nothing short of rape. Alma had come up to Lytham in those cold early days of marriage when Verity had been missing London and audiences and even, to her surprise, her family. But then, after Glenda, Alma had deserted her. Was it because Bert had made a pass? Possibly. Verity still didn't believe that Alma would have had an affair with Bert. 'I would never have done that to your mum,' Alma had told Aaron on the day that she died, 'Verity had suffered enough.' But maybe Alma had thought it safer to be out of Bert's orbit for a while. Verity could understand that.

Verity looked out over the striped lawn, so recently mown by Aaron, and saw a small figure approaching. Eric. Thank goodness he didn't have that dreadful Lola with him. Verity had been terrified of dogs ever since a costermonger's mastiff had bitten her. 'You mustn't show them you're scared,' Frank had said. 'Look them in the eye, stare them down.' But Verity had learnt that there were better ways of confronting your enemies than looking them in the eye.

Verity gestured to Eric to open the French windows. He

was carrying a bouquet of rather bedraggled carnations which he now offered to her.

'Thank you,' said Verity. 'That's very kind.'

'They should have been roses,' said Eric. 'I know you like roses.'

Verity nodded towards the silver bowl. 'I've already got some.'

'You're not really allowed to cut flowers from the communal garden,' said Eric.

'I know,' said Verity, 'but I like to live dangerously.'

'I saw you cutting flowers that Sunday,' said Eric, 'the day Bert died. I saw Irene too. But I didn't say anything to the police.'

Irene had written to Verity to tell her that Barbara was dead. 'He killed her,' she wrote, 'as surely as if he'd held a gun to her head. He used her, like he used Glenda, and then he threw her away. She'd sunk so low, my poor beautiful girl, that death was a merciful release.' Those words had triggered something in Verity. She'd started to give Bert small doses of rat poison, in his food and drink, even on his toothpaste. She'd watched, almost with satisfaction, as he started to complain of stomach pains and headaches. This is what it's like, she'd thought, when you get your just deserts. Frank had got his in the end. Now Bert was tasting retribution. There was a good bit in Proverbs: *They must eat the bitter fruit of living their own way, choking on their own schemes.* When Irene had arrived that day, the angel of death in her brown coat, Verity had simply left the poison on the table next to Bert's whisky. She'd known what Irene was going to do but had lacked the courage to administer the *coup de grâce* herself. Or maybe it was because, at the end, she didn't want to think of herself as a woman who had murdered her husband. Until death us do part and all that.

If only Alma hadn't been there. Alma was unpacking the groceries in the kitchen when Irene passed on her way to the sitting room. Alma must have recognised Irene – they'd often run into her on the circuit – but she hadn't said anything to Verity. She wouldn't have said anything to anyone, Verity knew, but Irene had thought otherwise. After you've killed one person, the second murder is easy.

Eric was still looking at the rose bowl.

'Do you remember her?' he said. 'Babs? The rose girl?'

'I remember,' said Verity. There had been a song to accompany the flower throwing. *Roses we bring tra la la, anthems we sing tra la la.* Once again, she needed Alma to remember the words. There was another verse about *flowers so true, something something so blue.* But flowers could lie too.

Verity had employed Emma and Sam to unearth the truth about Bert. She'd wanted him to be remembered as King Rat. That was why she'd asked Seth – sweet, susceptible Seth – to send the flyer, just in case the police hadn't got the message. She hadn't thought that they'd follow the thread back to Irene but, after she'd killed Alma,

Verity no longer cared if Irene was arrested. She'd known that Irene would come back. She would come back to kill Verity, the only other person to know what she'd done. Verity had been expecting to die but Meg had saved her. She was a game girl, Meg. The future belonged to women like her.

'I'll never say anything,' said Eric. 'There aren't many of us left from the old days. We have to stick together.'

'We're a dying breed,' said Verity.

'You can trust me,' said Eric.

'I know I can,' said Verity.

But, if life had taught her anything, it was that you couldn't trust anyone. Especially a man. Verity held the flowers to her face and smiled at Eric through their deceitful petals.

Monday, 13 December

Puss in Boots was a very tedious pantomime, thought Max, as he passed yet another sign on the Palace Pier. The only good part is the Ogre and even then you're overshadowed by an ingenue in a cat mask and thigh boots. He stopped to see who was in this production. Puss was played by a woman called Debbie Buswell who wore a costume with disturbingly human contours. Max was amused to see that Dame Victoria Sponge was played by Denton McGrew, with whom he'd performed on this very pier, almost fifteen years ago. He looked at the foot of the poster. 'A Bert Billington Production'. Bert might be gone but his company lived on, presumably managed by his sons. Impresarios, like pantomime dames, never die.

Max thought about Bert's middle son, Seth. Lydia and Seth were, apparently, madly in love. They wanted to get married which meant that either Lydia or Max had to provide evidence of adultery. This was why Max was in Brighton, the traditional setting for such legal niceties. Of course, Max could have refused. Lydia was the one who was unfaithful, he could have told that to the court. But then he thought of his children reading the story in the papers and, less nobly, of himself cast in that age-old role, that of cuckolded husband. So Max had booked a room at a seafront hotel – not the Grand – under the name Mr and Mrs Smith. Later on, he was meeting an old flame called Gloria, who knew the score and thought it all 'rather a hoot'. The maid, a generous tip improving her memory, would be able to say that she saw Max Mephisto enjoying breakfast in bed with a lady who definitely wasn't his wife.

It wasn't a bad way to pass an evening, thought Max, but he was looking forward to the morning's assignation more. He continued on his way, past the penny arcade and the boarded-up stalls. The pier was almost empty, the merry-go-round horses encased in tarpaulin. Schools hadn't broken up yet and the season hadn't started in earnest. But there was still a Christmas tree at the front of the theatre, rather battered by the sea winds, and fairy lights along the wrought-iron arches. Max thought of the time he'd performed here in *Aladdin*. It had been a rather low point in his life but he'd picked himself up and carried on, as he no doubt would again. He was surprised, actually, how buoyant he felt. He was buying a flat in

London, his favourite place in the world, and Wilbur had offered him a part in a film he was making next year. It was actually a rather interesting role and Max found himself looking forward to it. Perhaps he could act after all? Wilbur certainly thought so. And the previews for *The Prince of Darkness* had been surprisingly good. 'Max Mephisto and Seth Billington make the perfect deadly duo.' The divorce scandal wouldn't hurt the box office receipts either.

Max passed Astarte's gypsy caravan. Should he go in and ask Emma's friend to read his palm? But he thought he knew what the future held. Lydia would divorce him and marry Seth in an exclusive ceremony attended only by hundreds of their closest friends. Max would live in London and Lydia and the children would stay in Somerset. He'd see Rocco and Elena whenever he could and, when they were older, he'd take them on holiday to Italy. He'd continue to make films but he'd only choose scripts that really interested him. He'd help Ruby with the baby. He'd see Edgar and Emma regularly. He was starting to see the value of old friends. There were still some unknowns, of course. That was what made life so interesting.

Max walked on to the end of the pier where a woman in a biker jacket and woolly hat was waiting for him.

ACKNOWLEDGEMENTS

Rottingdean is a real place and the beautiful Sussex village does contain St Margaret's Church, Dean Court Road and the house once owned by Rudyard Kipling. Tudor Close is real too, although all the characters and events in this book are entirely fictitious. In the 1930s and 40s, Tudor Close was an exclusive hotel, beloved of Hollywood stars. The buildings were converted into private homes in the 1950s. There was even once a board game called Murder at Tudor Close. For this and other fascinating historical detail, I am indebted to my friend and neighbour, local historian Mike Laslett. Thanks also to Robert Griffith-Jones for the Balsdean story.

Whitby and its Abbey are also real although I have taken some liberties with the graveyard and the hotel.

The Midnight Hour was written in lockdown and I'm eternally grateful for the support of my publishers, Quercus Books, and especially my wonderful editor, Jane Wood. Thanks also to my fantastic agent, Rebecca Carter, and all at Janklow and Nesbit. Thanks to everyone at Quercus who worked so hard to produce, market, publicise and sell this book under very difficult conditions, especially Florence Hare, David Murphy, Ella Patel, Hannah Robinson and Hannah Winter. Thanks to Ghost Design for the beautiful cover and to Liz Hatherell for her meticulous copy-editing. Thanks to Naomi Gibbs and everyone at my American publishers, HMH, and to Kirby Kim at Janklow US.

The Brighton Mysteries were inspired by my grandfather, Dennis Lawes, an actor and comedian. It's therefore a special pleasure to dedicate this book to his youngest daughter, my aunt Corinne Slee. Love and thanks always to my husband Andrew and to our children, Alex and Juliet.

Finally, thanks to the bookshops and libraries who worked so hard to keep us reading during lockdown. And thank you to everyone who has bought, borrowed or recommended my books. I appreciate you more than I can say.

Elly Griffiths

2021